ONE SNOWY DAY

SHARI LOW

Boldwood

First published in Great Britain in 2025 by Boldwood Books Ltd.

Copyright © Shari Low, 2025

Cover Design by Alice Moore Design

Cover Images: Shutterstock

The moral right of Shari Low to be identified as the author of this work has been asserted in accordance with the Copyright, Designs and Patents Act 1988.

All rights reserved. No part of this book may be reproduced in any form or by any electronic or mechanical means, including information storage and retrieval systems, without written permission from the author, except for the use of brief quotations in a book review. This book is a work of fiction and, except in the case of historical fact, any resemblance to actual persons, living or dead, is purely coincidental.

Every effort has been made to obtain the necessary permissions with reference to copyright material, both illustrative and quoted. We apologise for any omissions in this respect and will be pleased to make the appropriate acknowledgements in any future edition.

A CIP catalogue record for this book is available from the British Library.

Paperback ISBN 978-1-83518-490-5

Large Print ISBN 978-1-83518-491-2

Hardback ISBN 978-1-83518-489-9

Ebook ISBN 978-1-83518-492-9

Kindle ISBN 978-1-83518-493-6

Audio CD ISBN 978-1-83518-484-4

MP3 CD ISBN 978-1-83518-485-1

Digital audio download ISBN 978-1-83518-488-2

This book is printed on certified sustainable paper. Boldwood Books is dedicated to putting sustainability at the heart of our business. For more information please visit https://www.boldwoodbooks.com/about-us/sustainability/

Boldwood Books Ltd, 23 Bowerdean Street, London, SW6 3TN

www.boldwoodbooks.com

ON THIS SNOWY DAY WE MEET...

Jessie McLean, 65 – Married to Stan for over four decades, hair salon owner, and mother to Georgie and Grant, who both followed her into the hairdressing profession. It's her sixty-fifth birthday, the first day of her retired life, and her last day in Scotland, before jetting off to a life in the sun.

Stan McLean, 68 – Recently retired electrician, now looking forward to spending the rest of his days on a golf course in Tenerife.

Val Murray – Sixty-something. Says she forgot her age during the menopause and refuses to look it up. Jessie's long-time pal. Widow. Chief of the neighbourhood watch. Sees and hears all things in her little village of Weirbridge.

Cathy McLean, 77 – Jessie's cousin, mum to Helena, gran to Eve, and aunt to Georgie and Grant. Also a former salon owner but now retired. Lives in a bubble of bliss since reuniting with her first love, Richie.

Georgie Dern, 38 – Jessie's daughter. Recently divorced from Flynn, and empty nested when her daughter Kayleigh left home. A hairdresser who is taking over Jessie's salon, Copper Curls, now that her mum is retiring.

Grant McLean, 34 – Jessie's son. A celebrity hairdresser with his own bustling salon in London, lives in Kensington with his partner of ten years, the much-loved TV presenter Gabriel Halton.

Kayleigh Dern, 18 – Georgie's daughter, who left a huge hole in her mum's heart the previous summer when she went off to study law at the University of Edinburgh.

Alyssa Canavan, 27 – Owner of The Once Upon A Time Café in Weirbridge, single, adores her life, her business and the role that her café plays in the community.

Ginny Canavan, 24 – Alyssa's sister, a jobbing actress and admirer of blokes with impressive abdominal muscle definition.

Dorinda Canavan, 51– Alyssa and Ginny's self-obsessed mother. Former wild child. Was absent on the day that the gods gave out empathy and maternal tendencies.

Hugo Canavan, 69 – Alyssa and Ginny's grandfather, who – together with his late wife, Effie – played a huge part in raising them. A former carpenter, he is Alyssa's very favourite man, employee and confidante.

Lachlan Morden, 34 – Glasgow born but now London-based, owns a small construction company, single and absolutely no desire to mingle. Son of the late Martyn Morden, an eminent Glasgow businessman and property mogul and his first wife, Felicity.

Jason Morden, 36 – Lachlan's brother, a property developer who inherited his father's drive and ambition, but none of his diplomacy, charm or moral integrity.

Tanya Michaels, 34 – Lachlan's former fiancée, a forever-broken piece of his heart and a reminder of his best and worst moments.

Margaux Mackay, 34 – Lachlan's lifelong friend, eternal optimist and wildly bendy thanks to her career as a yoga instructor.

Ollie Chiles, 33 – world-famous, Glasgow-born TV star, recently opened a community drama and music academy to support the talents of kids from under-privileged areas.

Moira Chiles, 58 – Former pub singer and cruise ship crooner, now a coach at the aforementioned academy. Recently moved to the village of Weirbridge.

1ST DECEMBER

8 A.M. – 10 A.M.

1

JESSIE McLEAN

Jessie McLean tucked her boobs into her comfiest bra, pulled on her white towelling dressing gown over her pyjama bottoms, slipped her feet into her marshmallow-soft pink slippers and padded downstairs, leaving Stan to snore alone. It was that or put a pillow over his face until the noise stopped, but that option came with a risk to her husband's life that she wasn't prepared to take. The poor soul couldn't help it if he sounded like the revving engine of a sit-on lawnmower every time he closed his eyes.

Down in the kitchen, she poured a glass of water from the tap, added a slice of lemon from a Tupperware box in the fridge and then flicked on the coffee machine so that a cup would be brewed by the time her first hydration of the day was done. Drinking more water had been one of the resolutions she'd made on her sixty-fourth birthday one year ago today – along with taking up meditation and doing 10,000 steps a day. Achieving one out of three wasn't bad. Actually, it was one out of seven, but cutting out caffeine, shunning alcohol, giving up chocolate and religiously following a skincare regime that would give her flawless pores had all been non-starters on her last birthday, when she'd consumed a bottle of Prosecco, two Irish coffees and a slab of chocolate sponge during dinner with her pals, before falling asleep with her make-up on. Maybe sixty-fifth time was a charm and today would be better.

A soundtrack of 'Happy Birthday To... Me' began to play in her mind.

Six and a half decades. How had that happened?

Usually, her birthday coincided with the opening of the first flap on an advent calendar, a slightly tacky tree and a truck-load of twinkly lights going up, the festive to-do list being started, a dance around the kitchen to Last Christmas, and the bookings at her hairdressing salon coming in thick and fast, with people preparing for work nights out and family parties. But not today. Today was the first day of her retirement. Her last full day in this house. Her final day in the village she loved. And tonight she was throwing a party that would be her big farewell to her working life, her family, her friends and a whole world of love and purpose.

Today was the day she'd been secretly dreading for months now.

Before she could ponder the way-too-rapid passage of time, her mobile phone, on the charger next to the toaster, burst into life. She'd stopped charging it on her bedside table when she'd heard that radio waves or some such thing could give you brain fog. She'd had enough of that in the menopause and was only just starting to remember whether she left her socks in the washing basket or the freezer.

At this time of the morning, on this day, she knew it would either be her daughter, Georgie, or her son, Grant.

'Happy birthday, Mum!' Georgie's voice boomed so loudly, Jessie had to take the phone away from her ear. 'I'd sing to you, but as you know, I couldn't carry a tune in a bucket.'

'Thank you, love, and much as I think you're wonderful in every way, you're right about the singing voice.'

'So, what's the plan for today then?' Georgie asked breezily.

Anyone listening in would be fooled, but Jessie wasn't. Her daughter was thirty-eight years old, and Jessie could read every single tone and underlying sentiment in her voice. Today, Georgie's words were being delivered by fake cheeriness, barely concealed sadness, top notes of stress and an undercurrent of dread. And Jessie was about to volley back with the fake cheeriness too.

'Well, this morning I'm having coffee and cake with Aunt Cathy and Val at Once Upon A Time...' That was the café on the Weirbridge Main Street, directly across from Copper Curls, the hair salon Jessie had owned since the eighties, named after her own mane of hair. Back in the day, copper had been her natural colour, but now it was assisted by a monthly touch-up to hold back the grey invasion. 'After that, we'll come over to the salon so you can beautify us for my party tonight.'

'Not that you need beautifying, but I'll make you gorgeous as ever. How are you feeling about leaving? I'm going to miss you so much, Mum.'

Jessie swallowed hard. 'Don't mention it, love, unless you want to make me a blubbering wreck at this time of the morning.'

'Okay. Right. I'm changing the subject.' There was a distinct wobble in Georgie's voice too. They'd worked together in the salon since Georgie was in high school and earning extra pocket money by washing hair and sweeping floors on Saturdays. Jessie hadn't pushed her, but she'd been delighted when Georgie had chosen to join her full time when she was sixteen, and since then they'd spent twenty-two years side by side. Their new reality was going to take a bit of getting used to for both of them. Georgie cleared her throat and came back with, 'I did Val's roots on your day off last week, so I'm up to speed with her life...' Val was one of Jessie's oldest friends, another lifelong resident of Weirbridge, a bustling little village about twenty minute's drive from Glasgow. 'But how's Aunt Cathy doing?'

Technically speaking, Cathy wasn't actually an aunt to Jessie's children, but they'd always called her that. She was Georgie and Grant's second cousin once removed – or was it first cousin, twice removed? She could never remember. Jessie and Cathy had met back in 1978, when eighteen-year-old Jessie had got a job as a junior stylist, floor brusher, tea maker and all-round dogsbody in Cathy's salon in the west end of Glasgow. Five years later, she'd left with all her hairdressing qualifications, and a fiancé called Stan McLean, a handsome big devil and a younger cousin of Cathy's husband, Duncan. Stan had come in for his monthly free haircut and Cathy had played Cupid and fixed them up on a date. Poor Duncan had passed away years ago, and now, in her seventies, Cathy had remarried last year to Richie, the high school sweetheart that she'd found again after decades apart.

It was impossible to think of Cathy's new chapter in life and not smile. 'She's still floating on a cloud of love's young dreams.'

'I'll have one of whatever she's having,' Georgie quipped, laughing. 'Anyway, Mum, I need to go and so do you. Can't believe it's your last day here...'

'Let's not go there,' Jessie cut her off. 'Let's just focus on the good stuff today, and think about everything else tomorrow.'

'Deal.' The barely concealed sadness was back, and they didn't need to discuss it to know they both felt the same – they weren't ready to say goodbye.

Why hadn't she given herself more time here? Why had she agreed with Stan that they could leave tomorrow, move lock, stock and barrel to Tenerife, to the wee holiday home they'd bought just outside Los Cristianos thirty years ago? She already knew the answer – because it had always been his dream. For all these years, they'd rented it out most months to help pay it off, but now they were selling up their Weirbridge home and moving there full-time, with a plan to only come back to Scotland for short trips or special occasions. It had seemed like a great idea about ten years ago, when Stan had first raised the prospect of retiring to the sun.

No, that wasn't true. Even then, she'd bristled at the thought of leaving her life here, but she'd gone along with it because she didn't think he'd actually ever do anything about it. This was the man who'd left every detail and organisational task to her for the last forty years. She had a three-page to-do list before every family holiday and would show up at the airport exhausted and frazzled, in charge of luggage, children, transport, tickets, snacks and every other detail of their lives, while he waltzed in with a holdall containing nothing much more than seven pairs of pants, his swimming trunks and two interchangeable golf kits. He woke up every Christmas morning, in contented assurance that the Festive Fairies would have taken care of every little thing that made the day special. When anyone in the family had a birthday, he had a practised 'of course I know what's in the gift you're about to unwrap' face, even though Jessie had given up telling him what she'd bought for everyone sometime back in the nineties, because he was happy to leave it all up to her.

So it was a perfectly reasonable state of denial to assume that his plans to spend their retirement in Tenerife would be a pipe dream that she could put off indefinitely by just not getting around to making it a reality. But no. In an uncharacteristic burst of activity, the bugger had gone and planned out the whole thing. Leaving tomorrow morning on a 10 a.m. flight. The For Sale sign was going up outside their house at some point today, and the estate agent was going to handle the viewings after they were gone. They'd taken his advice to leave the place furnished while they were in the process of selling it, and they would pop back for a few days after the sale had been agreed and dispose of everything then. She'd suggested keeping the house here, so they could come back for long holidays, but Stan had rightly pointed out that it was a hassle and an expense they didn't need, and they could always stay with Georgie when they were here, especially as their daughter had two spare rooms now. Jessie knew he was right and that's why their cases, with all their personal stuff, were sitting packed in the hall, ready to go.

'Okay, sweetheart, I'll see you later. Love you.'

'Love you too, Mum,' Georgie replied. 'I'll see you later and we'll make sure you have the best day.'

The best day. The last day.

Jessie inhaled, exhaled, then poured some freshly brewed coffee into her favourite mug. Cuppa in hand, she stood at the sink, looking out over the garden of her semi-detached home. The lawn was still white with the overnight frost and over the fence that separated their grass from her neighbour, she could see that Linda next door had forgotten to switch off the Christmas lights she'd put up mid-November, so the darkness was illuminated by thousands of fairy lights, and a six-foot flashing reindeer that had fallen off the roof and was now lying, wounded, next to a set of goalposts on the grass.

Focus on the positives, she told herself. Tomorrow she'd be in the sunshine, and that could only be a good thing. Working in Copper Curls this last couple of months since the clocks went back, meant going into the salon in the dark, and leaving in the dark. She was pretty sure there wasn't an ounce of vitamin D left in her body. Winter was only beautiful when it snowed, and there had been no sign of...

Jessie's chin dropped, as a flurry of thick white snowflakes dropped down the window, as if someone in the heavens agreed with her. Snow. It had come out of nowhere, but it was the kind of thick curtain of flakes that would lie if it kept coming down like this. She hadn't even thought to check the weather forecast, but it felt like Scotland was giving her something extra special to remember it by.

'Good morning, gorgeous.' Stan's voice made her jump, but her heart rate was immediately soothed when he came up behind her and wrapped his arms around her, careful not to spill the coffee in her hands. He kissed her neck, then rested his chin on her shoulder. 'I ordered the snow for your birthday.'

'Diamonds would probably have been easier to wrap,' she joked, making him smile, before he gently turned her around and kissed her on the lips this time.

'Happy birthday, Jessie. Our last one freezing our bits off in this weather. This time tomorrow, we'll be on our way and I can't bloody wait.' He couldn't hide the excitement in his voice or the glee on his face and it made her heart swell to see him so happy.

Like every couple, they'd had their ups and their downs over the last forty-odd years, but his happiness mattered to her. Yes, he could be infuriating. A bit thoughtless. Getting him off the golf course would take a bomb threat and a United Nations task force. Over the years, their pool of joint interests had got smaller, as they'd both become set in their ways. And well, all that bendy stuff was about as regular as a full moon these days. But he'd worked hard all his days as a self-employed electrician, and he deserved all the time off that he'd had since he hung up his tool belt last year. Besides, he probably found many of her ways irritating too, but he never criticised, never complained, and if they had a disagreement, he just took himself off to the golf club and came back a couple of hours later like nothing had happened. That low-key, accepting guy was just who he was now, and sure, sometimes a bit of excitement would be great, or even just for him to show an interest in the things she enjoyed, but she knew better than to even think about trying to change him. For better or worse, until... yada-yada and all that. If she wanted to have a bit of fun, a good gossip or a weekend theatre break, that's what her pals and her adult children were for. She just hoped that they'd all make frequent visits to see her after she moved. That thought made the coffee in her stomach swirl, so she shook it away and refused to think about it right now.

From behind his back, Stan produced a small, gift-wrapped box that she immediately guessed was a piece of jewellery. 'I knew it was pointless getting you flowers or chocolates today, and I thought this birthday deserved something special, so here you go, love...'

As he handed it over, Jessie felt a wave of gratitude. Maybe she hadn't been wrong about the diamonds being easy to wrap. Not that they ever bought each other gifts like that. They'd always had enough to live a comfortable life, with a few extra luxuries – Stan's golf club fees, a dinner out at the weekends and a couple of trips to the Tenerife house every year – but they'd never been ones for expensive gifts or flash brands. Although, if there was ever going to be a time to make a big gesture, it would be today.

'Love, you shouldn't have...' she said before she'd even opened it. It took her a moment to untie the ribbon and unwrap the gold foil paper.

'Georgie helped me with the wrapping. And the present too,' he admitted, telling her something she'd already assumed. Last year, he'd got her a Dyson vacuum cleaner (which, in fairness, she had said she wanted), and the year before that had been an air fryer, so he didn't have a track record of elaborately wrapped tokens of romantic sentimentality.

As she flipped up the lid on the box, she saw that she was wrong about the diamonds, but right about the sentimental stuff. Nestled on the blue velvet pad was a silver chain bracelet, with five little charms dropping from the centre. A pair of scissors. A heart. And three coloured gems.

As she gently touched the deep-hued jewels, Stan said, 'That's our lot's...'

'Birthstones,' she interjected, before he got there. She'd spotted the significance right away – the charms represented Georgie, their son, Grant, and their granddaughter, Kayleigh.

'The scissors are for your salon. And the heart is for us. Not that I'm taking credit, because, like I said, Georgie helped me.'

Jessie curled her arms around him. 'It's perfect, Stan. I love it.'

So here she was. One more day of her life here in Weirbridge. Her birthday. Her retirement from the salon she'd founded and worked in for decades. Her party. Her goodbyes to the people she loved.

Today was the day that Jessie's life was about to change forever.

And tomorrow she'd start a whole new chapter, just her and the man who'd been by her side through it all. It should be the perfect happy ending.

So why did she feel like she didn't want to turn the page?

2

GEORGIE DERN

Georgie hung up the phone and groaned as her head flopped back onto the pillow. It took way too much energy to sound cheery when, inside, she felt anything but.

Of course, she'd been supportive when her mum had announced that her dad wanted to move lock, stock and bloody barrel to Tenerife, because she hadn't thought for a single fricking second that her mum would actually do it. Jessie McLean was a woman who loved her life and her environment, one of those people who would live a perfectly happy and contented existence forever tied to the village she'd been born in. Not that her mum wasn't ambitious, because her salon proved otherwise, but she was someone who adored her community, thrived on social contact and cherished her wide and varied circle of pals. What the hell was she going to do in Tenerife, where the neighbours on one side were London stockbrokers who visited the island twice a year, and the other side was an Airbnb that typically hosted hen and stag parties? Georgie had always enjoyed going there for holidays, but she'd lost count of the number of nights she'd been woken up at 1 a.m. with a crowd of women next door belting out 'Girls Just Wanna Have Fun', or a shower of blokes trying to extinguish a raging inferno because someone with a dangerously high blood alcohol level thought it would be a great idea to pee on the fire pit.

And yes, she should be thrilled that she was about to take full responsibility and sole charge of the Copper Curls salon, but that sentiment was being overruled by too many negatives to count – the most overwhelming one being that she didn't want her parents to go, and couldn't bear the thought of not seeing her mum every day. It wasn't some weird co-dependency, it was just the simple truth that her mother was her second favourite person on earth, topped only by her daughter, Kayleigh. Having Jessie McLean around just made her world a better place.

'You look deep in thought there,' Flynn said, as he came back to bed, carrying two coffees.

Georgie supressed another groan. Bugger. How had that happened? Flynn had brought Kayleigh back from university yesterday, stayed for dinner and well… If she was in a better mood, she'd probably make a joke about being the pudding.

Instead, she took the coffee and shooed him away, whispering, 'You have to go. I don't want Kayleigh to know that you stayed here last night. It's too confusing and I don't want to get her hopes up.'

There was an amicable divorce, and then there was this. Flynn Dern, her husband of almost eighteen years, then her ex-husband of two years, thanks to his mid-life crisis and a decision to go off to Asia for a year to find himself. As evident by his presence, he'd found himself back in Scotland twelve months later, living in a one-bedroom flat in Stirling, and having adopted a regular habit of dropping in to visit her. Infuriatingly, he was uncannily good at showing up when Georgie was happy and in the mood for some passion to celebrate, or sad and in the mood for some passion to cheer her up, or stressed and in the mood for some passion to take her mind off her troubles. She wasn't quite sure what category last night fell into, but it was a toss-up between the last two.

He ignored her request to leave, sliding back under the duvet and taking a sip of the froth on the top of his cappuccino. His hair was wet, so he must have jumped into the shower before she'd woken up and called her mum. Mother of God, it was like he'd never left.

'Would that be so bad? I mean, Kayleigh getting her hopes up?'

Georgie's eyes widened. 'Yes! Of course it would. I only let you stay because she'd already crashed out and I know she won't wake until noon.'

He tried to get cute, displaying an admirable ability to nuzzle her neck without spilling his coffee. 'That's the only reason?'

'That and the fact that I have normal needs, and I haven't got time to shave my legs so that I can have sex with anyone else.'

If he was pissed off by that, she didn't wait around to find out. She'd loved this man and had wholeheartedly expected to stay with him forever, but then came the cataclysmic hurt and shock when he blew up their marriage. Somewhere along the line, like childbirth or chickenpox scars, the memory of that pain had subsided, and while there was still love, now she was fairly sure – when they weren't naked – that it was of the nostalgic, loyal, companionable variety. In fact, much as it had been devastating at the time, and for a long time afterwards, now that there had been healing, space and a million grovelling apologies on his side, she could admit to herself that she was grateful in some ways that he'd called it quits. He'd seen the issues in their marriage before her, realised that they were coasting, going through the motions, that they'd outgrown each other. Although, hell would freeze over before she uttered that sentiment aloud and gave him any form of defence or justification for breaking their family apart.

He pushed himself up on one elbow. 'Look, Georgie, I'm just putting this out there...'

If telepathy was a thing, he'd shut up right now, because she sensed what was coming and every cell in her body was willing him not to say it. Unfortunately, her silent communication was an epic fail, because he kept going.

'...I want to try again. I want to move back in, and put our family back together.'

'The family that you left for a long-term jolly to Thailand.'

'It was a transcendental meditation retreat, and yes, I know what I did, but it wasn't like I went off and shagged my secretary.'

'You don't have a secretary.'

'I know but... God, you're infuriating.' He rolled his eyes, and the corners of his mouth turned up in that really adorable way that used to make her heart flip. In fact, if she didn't count Daniel Craig in his Bond years, he was the only man who'd ever actually made her heart flip. And yes, there was something tempting about having that kind of attraction, companionship and hairy-legged sex on tap back in her life again. Maybe if she allowed herself to remove all the walls of defence that she'd put up when he'd done a runner, then she could consider what reuniting would feel like. But she couldn't think about that right now. Not today. Not when she was on the verge of a mini-midlife crisis of her own.

'Wouldn't it just be easier if you did the normal middle-age-male-divorcé thing and went searching for twenty-five-year-olds on Tinder?'

He ran his fingers through his Hugh-Grant-in-the-Notting-Hill-era waves. 'I don't want anyone else. Why would I be interested in someone else, when I know the right person for me is you? I just needed to go through the break to realise that. Anyway, think about it. Please. And much as I want to stay right here, I have to get moving or I'll be late for work and the world of solar panels will crumble.' He pulled the duvet back and reached down for his jeans, pulling them on as Georgie realised she couldn't sit still and climbed out of her side of the bed.

'I'm just going to go grab a shower. Don't make any noise and let yourself out.'

Before she made it to the door of her en suite, the one that she'd redecorated to remove all traces of him when he'd left, he added, 'Kayleigh reminded me that it's Jessie's birthday and retirement party tonight. And that she's leaving tomorrow.'

'It sure is.' It ached even to say that out loud. 'You know, she invited you to the party.'

The fact that her mum had ferociously supported her when Flynn deserted them, yet still remained amicable was a credit to her cool head and emotional intelligence. 'He's Kayleigh's dad, love,' her mum had said back then. 'And the lass is upset enough without us fuelling the flames and making the rift wider. There's a lot we could say now, but if things get better, we can't un-say them.'

Of course, she was right. And now, with the benefit of time and mended fences, Georgie was relieved that she didn't have to worry about a stand-off between her staunchest defender and the man who made a stupid mistake that he now, apparently, regretted.

'I know, but I have a work thing. Give her my love though.'

'I will. You have a good day. And thanks for not noticing that I've got legs like an Alpaca.'

'I didn't say that I hadn't noticed...' He joked, and ouch, there were the corners of his lips up again.

She locked the door behind her just to make sure she wasn't tempted to go back out there and delay his departure, but this time she knew it would definitely be down to option 3 on the 'excuses for having sex with the ex-husband' list – taking her mind off a stressful situation.

Instead, she stood under a cold shower for several minutes, until her mind was blank, her lips were turning blue, and she was confident that her libido had gone back into hibernation.

When she eventually switched the water off, she used a thick, fluffy towel to dry her body and wrapped a turban around the wild mass of copper curls that came directly from her mother's side of the gene pool. Back in the bedroom, she pulled on the pink fleecy dressing gown Kayleigh had bought her last Christmas, then slipped her feet into her white Ugg slippers. She picked up her cold coffee from the bedside table, took the mug downstairs, slotted it under the Nespresso machine she'd bought after being swayed by a George Clooney advert, and made herself a fresh cup. It had just finished pouring when Kayleigh wandered into the kitchen behind her.

Surprised, Georgie hugged her girl. 'Ah, it's so good to have you here again. I've missed your face in the mornings.' The last four months of empty nesting since her daughter had gone off to the University of Edinburgh to study law had been excruciating. Lonely. Challenging. Nobody warns a parent that when the kids leave, for the first time since two blue lines appeared on a pregnancy stick, you begin to reassess and analyse what you really want out of life. Georgie had definitely asked herself the questions... and she still didn't know the correct answers.

Kayleigh indulged her sentimental moment. 'I've missed you too, Mum.'

Georgie gave her one more squeeze before reluctantly letting her go. 'I didn't expect you to wake this early.'

Kayleigh shrugged. 'Dad made too much noise when he was sneaking out. Are you two still pretending that you're not sleeping together?' There was no missing the amusement in her daughter's voice.

The amusement was all Georgie's now as she feigned innocence. 'I've no idea what you're talking about.'

Kayleigh had her head in the fridge, going for the teenage breakfast trifecta of a bottle of water, a smoothie and last night's leftover pizza. 'You know he wants to get back together, Mum.'

It was way too early for this conversation, but now that it was here...

'I do. How do you feel about that?'

Kayleigh delivered her second shrug of the morning. 'It's up to you. Please don't fall for that clichéd thing and do it for me though. I honestly am fine with how things are now.'

Georgie nodded sagely. 'I don't know how you ended up this cool, but I'm taking the credit.'

'Good genes and absorbing the wisdom in Taylor Swift songs.' Kayleigh made her way to the door, food stash in hands. 'Be nice to see you happy again though, Mum.'

Had it been that obvious that she was unhappy? Cue a fresh wave of maternal worry that despite her best efforts, maybe she hadn't maintained an emotionally stable environment throughout her divorce and the subsequent years. Had she scarred her kid for life? She let the shutters drop on that one before it took hold, and she climbed onto one of the gorgeous silver mesh bar stools at her kitchen island, thinking as always that she really needed to buy new ones that were beautiful, but didn't leave your arse looking like you'd been sitting on a cheese grater.

She pulled her phone out of her dressing gown pocket and saw there was a text from Grant. It must have come in while she was in the shower.

> Sis! On my way. Be there about 11 a.m. Any news on the job offer yet?

The job offer. Personal hairdresser for world-famous Scottish actor, Ollie Chiles, on the set of an American TV show. The only benefit of fretting over her parents leaving was that it had temporarily distracted her from stressing about this potential opportunity to land the kind of role that defined a career. One that had come out of the blue a few days ago and completely rocked her world. One that she hadn't even known that she wanted until it became a possibility. One that would definitely put an end to any prospect of rekindling her marriage. One that would throw her mum's plans for Georgie to take over the salon into complete chaos. She couldn't possibly entertain it.

Could she?

She'd been told that confirmation of the official offer would come by phone call or email, but she'd heard nothing. Maybe it wouldn't even come to fruition. Yep, that would be the best outcome. Move along. Nothing to see here. Nothing lost. No impossible choice to be made.

Until she had all the details, there had been no point even considering it, so she'd chosen denial instead. But now that Grant had brought it up, it was right back, front and centre in her mind, and a huge wave of mixed emotions – anxiety, regret, anticipation, fear, and yes, undeniable excitement – came with it.

She tried to flip back to denial. Don't look. Don't do it. Don't think about it.

Apparently, her hands were ignoring her brain.

With shaking fingers, she checked her calls. None missed. She flicked to her emails. Nothing much more than discount codes for online shopping and a reminder that she was due a smear test.

Other missed texts? Just one from her Aunt Cathy saying her sister, Aunt Loretta, had been on the throat lozenges and hot tea with honey, and she reckoned her voice was going to hold up for the singing at Jessie's shindig tonight. It also said that her daughter, Helena, a hotshot lawyer and the scariest member of their family, and Cathy's lovely granddaughter, Eve, were going to make it to the party too. Georgie knew Kayleigh would be thrilled about that. Despite Helena's sharp, brusque manner, Kayleigh adored her, and she'd been the biggest inspiration in her decision to study law.

But other than that?

Nothing else. Nada. No word.

Clearly this was the universe taking the choice out of her hands and that could only be a good thing.

Today was the first day running the show at Copper Curls and Georgie just had to be content with that.

Because if the role of her wildest dreams had come through, then she would have to choose between taking it or continuing Jessie's legacy in the salon her mum had built from scratch. How could she pick a new life, on the other side of the world, knowing that it would break her mother's heart? No. She could never leave. And that was fine, so time to forget the whole crazy pipe dream and get on with real life.

And she was just about to do that when her phone began to ring...

3

ALYSSA CANAVAN

This was Alyssa's favourite time of day. She'd come down from her flat upstairs to The Once Upon A Time Café on the ground floor hours ago, but it wasn't yet open, so back in the café kitchen, it was just her, with the radio on in the background. Michael Bublé was crooning that it was beginning to look a lot like Christmas – and given the sudden downpour of snow outside, he wasn't wrong. There was fresh coffee on the table, and the gorgeous aroma of cinnamon rolls coming from the oven as she rolled out the dough for the fresh baked croissants that would go in next. Her gaze flitted to the old clock on the wall, made by her grandad, Hugo. A former engineer, he'd built it for their gran, Effie, a couple of years before she passed, when he still had fingers that were nimble enough to put the tiny parts of the mechanism together, and the patience to make it work. Now he'd say life was too short and have a wee dance to an old Beatles tune instead. That was why both the customers and Alyssa loved that he worked in the café now, but given that he was past retirement age, he only came in from 10 a.m. to 2 p.m., and even then, he had free rein to take any day off if he felt like going fishing.

Her other member of staff, however...

'Don't panic, I'm here! Everyone as you were,' came the usual morning command as her younger sister, Ginny, breezed in the door, beanie hat pulled down over her chestnut hair, ear pods in, trainers on, and phone in hand, despite Alyssa telling her on a daily basis that, according to social media, phone snatching was rife and she should leave the handset in her bag at all times.

'Considering the closest we get to a crime wave in Weirbridge is the occasional theft of a pot plant, I think I'll be fine,' Ginny would inevitably argue, so Alyssa had now officially given up.

Alyssa wiped some flour from her nose with her forearm, giving Ginny a window for a small act of theft of her own. She picked up Alyssa's coffee mug and took a sip, then sighed as if it was the only thing standing between life and a slow death from hypothermia. 'Oh, I needed that. It's about minus ten out there. There are bits of me I can no longer feel.'

Working with a sibling could be fraught, irritating and frustrating and there were moments when spending the day with Ginny was all of those things, but Alyssa wouldn't swap it for anything. Except perhaps an employee that actually showed up on time. Although, Ginny's excuses were so elaborate, sometimes Alyssa hoped her sister was late just so she could be amused by the creativity of her defence. In the last month, there had been a hostage situation on the bus, a romantic interlude with Channing Tatum and a last-minute audition for a role on *Coronation Street*. None of which was true, but it was all a testimony to Ginny's acting skills, which had been developed by many years of studying drama at the Royal Conservatoire of Scotland.

'Sorry I'm late. Penguins in the high street caused a traffic jam. It's a whole cold-weather wildlife situation out there.'

'So, actually, you slept in and hit the snooze button four times before you could escape your mattress?' Alyssa suggested, one eyebrow raised in amusement as she stopped kneading the dough and poured her sister a fresh mug, before reclaiming her own.

'Five. Caden stayed over and I spent the morning staring at his abs while he was sleeping. I accept that's both irresistible and a bit creepy, but he doesn't have to know.'

Caden was Ginny's boyfriend of six months, a fellow actor who was currently playing Judas on a national touring production of *Jesus Christ Superstar*, so he didn't make it back to Glasgow too often. And yes, having seen the show several times, Alyssa could concur that he did in fact have a fine set of abdominal muscles. Not that she paid much attention. Since her own last relationship – Matt, 32, something in finance, devoid of fine abs – had broken down because he wanted a girlfriend who '*was free to live life and be in the moment with him on weekends*', men and romance were far, far down her priority list. Right now, growing her business, keeping Ginny in gainful employment between acting gigs, and giving her grandad a reason to get out of bed in the morning were all far more important to Alyssa than finding out a bloke's favourite colour on a first date.

'Okay, the cinnamon buns, flapjacks, bread rolls and Danish pastries are all in the oven, the cakes are prepped and ready to go, and I'm doing the croissants and the gingerbread slices right now, so if you can get to work on the soups that would be just dandy. Scotch broth, minestrone and chicken noodle – they're forecasting snow and freezing temperatures will last all day, so we're going retro and wholesome in the hope that anyone actually leaves the house.'

When she'd first opened the café four years ago, she'd tried to push the soup envelope with stilton and broccoli, or creamy shrimp and crab bisque, but the reality was that her regulars liked traditional comfort food best, especially in this weather, so Alyssa had given up the fancy stuff and stuck to what she knew her customers came for. This place was her dream, and she hadn't built it up to be a solid, profitable venture just to drive everyone away by going for 'all that posh stuff', as her grandad called it. She knew her market in this village. Retired folks, parents with toddlers, yoga mums from the community centre and home workers looking for a change of scenery during the day. After school, it was time for the older kids, usually accompanied by frazzled parents who needed a reasonably priced dinner for the family while the offspring did their homework on the pretty checkered tablecloths out in the café. And, of course, at all times of the day, came the readers looking for their next book.

The local library had fallen foul of a round of council budget cuts a few years back, so when the owner of the last remaining bookshop in the village had retired and sold the outlet to a kebab shop just as Alyssa was taking over the café, she had taken out an extra loan and bought the bookshop's beautiful old white oak shelves and a large chunk of their stock. Books now lined both of the side walls of the dining area and gave a little something extra to her customers. Alyssa didn't mind if someone curled up on one of the sofas for a couple of hours to read, just as long as they bought a cuppa or a cake.

'There must be a union I can join to complain about this unreasonable treatment,' Ginny objected. 'Making me show up here and actually work, instead of allowing me to drink coffee and socialise all morning must contravene my human rights. And remember I can only work for a couple of hours today because I've got my final interview this afternoon at the theatre academy.' Ginny had applied to be an acting coach at the Moira Chiles Academy of Music and Drama, a non-profit facility in Glasgow that provided free coaching for kids from underprivileged areas. It had been founded by the actor, Ollie Chiles, and named after his mother and it was the café's claim to fame that Moira Chiles now lived in this very village and popped in for ginger slices and apple turnovers on a regular basis. A job at the Academy wasn't the starring role in a new TV show that Ginny dreamed of, but it was the next best thing, and Alyssa knew her sister would be brilliant at it.

'I remember, don't worry. Grandad is coming in today to cover for you. You'll definitely be back to help with Jessie's party tonight, won't you? I prepared the sausage rolls, the satay sticks, the mini steak pies and the chicken tempura last night, so they just need to be heated later, but I still have a million sandwiches and wraps to make today.'

'Like I said, there should be a law against these kinds of demands,' Ginny said, with a dramatic hand to the forehead.

'You're right. I am sorry. At your interview, be sure to ask if you can just drink coffee and mingle all day if that's now your essential employment condition,' Alyssa teased her.

'I'm having it written into the job description. Oh and I brought in the mail. The postman was early this morning and got me to sign for this big brown one – said it was a special delivery.'

For the first time, Alyssa noticed that there was an envelope sticking out of Ginny's cross-body satchel. Ginny pulled it out and placed it down on the huge stainless-steel work bench, then went off to put her jacket and bag in the staff cupboard and wash up, ready to get to work, already singing along to the Lady Gaga track that was now playing on the radio. Alyssa could make a mean strawberry tart, but she was the first to concede that Ginny was the one with all the theatrical talent.

Hands still deep in dough, she squinted to read the name of the sender that was stamped on the official-looking brown envelope. Huntington Farrell.

Huntington Farrell. She repeated it in her mind, until the recognition clicked. It was a legal firm based in Glasgow's city centre. Alyssa was familiar with the name because it was the company that had originally arranged the paperwork for the lease on the café. Bugger. She just hoped that they weren't putting the rent up. The coffee machine was on its last legs, and she had been putting as much as she could spare into the emergency fund for when it finally went to the overpriced barista heaven in the sky.

Her gaze went to the clock again. Half an hour until opening time. She should really just finish up what she was doing, then go get everything switched on and set up in the café. It was Monday, so there was usually a morning rush of coffee orders for the mums going to the postnatal Kegel classes at the church hall. Explaining that one to Ginny had been both hilariously informative and an effective method of contraception. Although, in this weather there was every chance that this week's class might be cancelled.

However, Alyssa's natural anxiety had set off a twisting sensation of dread in her stomach that was only going to be stopped when she opened the envelope, reassured herself that it contained nothing life-changing or problematic, then got on with her day. Removing her fingers from the sticky mound of dough, she gave her hands a quick wash, dried them with a paper towel, then picked up the envelope. It felt light, so hopefully that was a good sign. She ran her finger under the seal, then pulled out a single piece of A4 paper and a stapled sheath that she recognised as being a copy of her lease. Strange.

Her attention returned to the letter. The lawyer's name was at the top again, with hers on the left-hand side, above the address of the café.

Dear Miss Canavan,

She skimmed the page, picking out the relevant lines in the text.

On the instructions of our clients, the estate of Mr Martyn Morden, we hereby notify you that, as per the terms of your lease, we are communicating a termination notice of sixty days hence.

Alyssa's brow furrowed. Hang on, what? She didn't understand. She must have read that wrong. The twisting feeling of dread was now spreading rapidly and bringing with it a wave of nausea that was making her sweat.

She went back to the start. Read it again. It still said the same thing.

The estate of Mr Martyn Morden. Termination notice. Sixty days. Even if this were true, it couldn't be correct. She had a six-month notice period on both sides, so it had to be some kind of error.

We refer you to the attached lease, page 8, clause 3.4. 'In the event of the death of either party, the standard six-month notice period shall be reduced to sixty days…'

Again, what?

She read it a third time, some of the salient details finally sinking in. From what she could gather from the formal terminology, the owner of this building, Mr Morden, had died and his estate was kicking her out of her home and her café in sixty days, thereby, in effect, she was categorically screwed.

'Are you okay? Bad news? If it's an STD, you can get antibiotics…' Ginny continued tying the strings of her apron as she spoke, but when Alyssa didn't reply, she must have realised something was serious, because when she spoke again, there was concern in her voice. Not that Alyssa could hear it over the thunder that was roaring in her head. 'Lyss, what is it? What does it say?'

There was a delayed reaction, before Alyssa's motor skills kicked back in and she slowly raised her head.

How to answer that question? Today should have been just another lovely day in the life that Alyssa Canavan had worked so hard to build.

But, instead, it was going to be the day that changed everything.

4

LACHLAN MORDEN

The plane hit the tarmac at Glasgow airport with a thud so strong that the bloke in the rugby top next to Lachlan gripped his arm, then flushed to the colour of his scarlet sweatshirt before clearing his throat and acting like it had never happened.

Lachlan went along with the pretence, continuing to stare out of the window at the thick flakes of snow that were falling on the runway, and beyond the perimeter fence, all the way to the white peaks of the hills in the distance.

The view reminded him of a previous time he'd landed here. Three years ago. He and Tanya had been on their way home from a winter ski break in Verbier and when they'd touched down in Glasgow, they'd been stunned to see a white-out that was just as stunning as the one they'd left in Switzerland.

Three years and a whole lifetime ago. Back then, the engagement ring he'd given Tanya a few days before, in front of a whole crew of cheering pals, was sparkling on her finger. Under her navy sweatshirt, her tiny bump was gently growing. And both of them had cheesy, grins that probably made them fairly insufferable to everyone around them. If that couple could have seen what was in front of them, they'd never have believed it.

'Ladies and gentlemen, welcome to a rather chilly, snowy Glasgow. The

temperature outside is minus two degrees and the heavy snowfall is expected to continue throughout the day. Please remain seated, with your seatbelts fastened, until we come to a standstill at our allocated gate...'

'Coming home or just visiting?' It took Lachlan a moment to realise that the question was coming from the bloke in the red sweatshirt and was directed at him. And it took him another moment to settle on the correct answer.

'Both. I'm from here, but I live in London now, so just up for a meeting. You?' Reciprocating the question felt like the right thing to do, even though he really didn't care and would much rather just keep to himself right now. He had too many other things to think about.

'Just coming back from my stag week in Vegas. Had to fly via London though, so feels like my arse has been on a plane seat for days.'

Lachlan was in too deep not to ask the obvious question. 'Congratulations. When are you getting married?'

'Christmas Eve. But the missus insisted we had the stag do early in case my mates shaved off my eyebrows. Said I'd need a few weeks to grow them back.'

'Smart lady.'

'Aye, but worrying for nothing. Eyebrows are still there,' he pointed at the bushy slugs above his peepers. 'The legs are a different story right enough.'

Two of his buddies in the row behind them must have overheard that little exchange because they let out a loud, goading cheer, while a hand came from behind to scrub the head of the groom.

Another memory. His own stag party. Not quite Vegas, but a brilliant night out in Edinburgh with twenty or so friends and Tanya's brothers. His own brother, Jason, hadn't been able to make it, but Lachlan hadn't missed him. Tanya and his mates were his family. The one he'd chosen for himself.

He gazed out of the window again, to the soundtrack of beeps from a dozen nearby phones as they all connected to the networks now that they'd landed.

He checked his phone screen, assuming there would be nothing there, but he was wrong. Margaux. His friend since they were tossing a football back and forward over the fence that separated their homes growing up.

She'd offered to pick him up, but he knew he wanted a car for the day, so he'd declined and suggested meeting up later.

> Still on for lunch? Let me know when and where and I'll free up a space in my hectic diary. Xx

He texted back.

> Hey. Just landed. Lunch sounds good. Will let you know as soon as meeting is done. Lx

At least that would be something to make this day worthwhile, because there was no other part of it that he wasn't dreading.

The seatbelt sign clicked off as the plane came to a standstill and there was the usual scrum of people jumping up and jostling to get their luggage out of the overhead bins. Lachlan reached down for the small backpack he'd stored under the seat in front of him. He wasn't going to be here for long. He hadn't even brought a full change of clothes, just a sweater to pull on after the meeting so that he could get rid of the shirt and tie. This was going to be one day, in and out. Home on the last flight tonight.

Although checking the weather ahead of time might have been an idea because in this suit, he was going to freeze his bollocks off out there today. Forward planning was usually his thing, pretty essential in his work. He was a builder, who predominately worked on bespoke new homes and extensions. He'd started life as a joiner on his father's building sites, and Martyn Morden had been a perfectionist who'd demanded top quality work, especially from his son. Lachlan had always risen to the challenge, and had maintained those standards when he had branched out on his own, setting up his own construction firm when he was barely in his twenties. More than a decade later, and now based in London, the manual work was still what he loved most, but he ran a small but mighty team of subcontractors that included electricians, plumbers and labourers. He co-ordinated every job, but only after he'd worked with the client to make sure he knew exactly what they wanted, and that they both understood the end goal. Today his only end goal was to avoid frostbite, then get back on a plane and get the hell out of here as soon as possible.

'Good luck with the wedding. Hope it all goes well,' he told the groom.

'Thanks, pal,' his travel companion with the intact eyebrows replied with a wink, and Lachlan thought this was the thing he missed most about Glasgow. You could share one conversation with someone and instantly you were elevated to 'pal' status.

Among a sea of puffa jackets reminding him of his poor planning skills, Lachlan made his way off the aircraft and along the long peninsula to the main terminal building. He must have flown in and out of this airport a hundred times in his life, so he switched to autopilot: head down, just keep walking. He'd already booked the car hire online, so he made his way straight to their desk on the ground floor, veering round the huge, sparkly silver Christmas tree that stood in the centre of the terminal hall. If there was a desk that provided festive spirits, he should probably be first in the queue because celebrating special occasions seemed pointless now. Christmas Day in London would be just another day of consciously avoiding other people's happiness so that he wouldn't be forced to think about losing his own. Denial was a much better place to be.

There were a couple of people ahead of him at the car hire booth, so he scrolled his phone, looking for any kind of distraction while he waited. Shit. Every single sports blog was carrying a story about his main client, a premier league football player called Dax Price, reporting that he'd been caught falling out of a casino at 3 a.m. on Saturday morning, just hours before he'd played the worst game of his life in front of fifty thousand raging fans twelve hours later.

He was still reading about Dax's antics, when another text popped in. Jason. His older brother.

> Just checking you're going to make it today?

His first reaction was to ignore it, but he knew his brother too well – if Jason didn't get a reply, he'd be straight on the phone demanding to know what was going on and he'd hound Lachlan until he got an answer.

His thumb handled the situation, typing, 'I'll be there.'

As soon as he sent it, he saw that the previous text to his brother said exactly the same thing. 'I'll be there'. That one had been sent a few weeks ago, when he'd been notified of the details of his father's funeral, a man that Lachlan had loved, despite his fair share of flaws.

His dad had been ruthless in business. A workaholic. Someone who had loved his sons in his own way, but had very much prioritised his work and ambition over his presence as a father. Their mum had been the glue that had held the family together, and after she died, five years ago now, his dad had remarried and been persuaded by his thirty-five-year-old second wife, Demi, to spend his semi-retirement in Monaco, swayed by the sunshine and the tax-free life. When Lachlan had received the phone call to tell him that his dad had quite literally dropped dead on the golf course, he'd offered to go to Monaco immediately, but his stepmother had insisted that she didn't want 'a whole big mourning drama at the house'. Instead, Demi had asked that the brothers just show up for the funeral – a small, impersonal affair with only the people Dad had met in Monaco. Jason had texted him with the details and Lachlan had replied that he'd be there, even though it felt so wrong. He couldn't help thinking that his dad should have been buried in Glasgow, in the city he loved, but the choice hadn't been his. Just as the choice to attend this meeting today hadn't been his either.

The people in front of him at the car hire booth went off, car keys in hand and pushing two trolleys with a dozen pieces of luggage between them. He hoped they'd reserved a transit van because there was no way that lot was fitting in a Ford Focus.

Lachlan placed his driving licence down on the counter and smiled at the middle-aged bloke behind it. 'Hi. I've got a car booked. Lachlan Morden.'

'Good morning and welcome to sunny Glasgow. We're all out of snow-ploughs, I'm afraid.'

Lachlan smiled. 'That's okay. I went for a standard saloon. Prefer things a bit more low-key.'

'Right, let's see what we've got then.' He began tapping on the screen in front of him. 'Okay, well I have good news and bad news…'

And there it was, starting already. He'd hoped to at least get to his meeting before everything went to crap.

'The bad news is that we're all out of standard saloons. With the weather and my superior customer service skills, many people who'd booked smaller cars have upgraded to mid-size vehicles this morning.'

Lachlan had sudden visions of trying to fold his six-foot frame into a Fiat 500. That had happened to him once before, when he and Tanya were on holiday in Italy and he'd lost the feeling in his legs somewhere between Florence and Pisa.

'But the good news is that because it's most definitely our fault, and I can see you're a member of our loyalty program, I can offer you a free upgrade this morning.'

Maybe today wasn't going to be all bad after all. Not that Lachlan particularly cared about cars. He just needed something to get him from A to B without his knees being up somewhere around his ears.

'Now, we have had a particularly busy weekend, so I only have a couple of options prepped and ready to go.' He glanced at the screen again. 'So the choice is a Mercedes two-seater convertible – we don't get a lot of demand for them in Glasgow in December and probably not the best traction in this weather.'

Lachlan didn't disagree. Plus, sports cars weren't really his thing. He drove a Ford Ranger pick-up in London, big for the city, but essential for his work.

'And the other one?' he asked.

'A Range Rover Discovery,' the advisor announced with a pleased-as-punch grin.

Lachlan felt he should act appropriately grateful, given that the gent looked so chuffed. Besides, with the snow outside, a four-wheel drive could definitely be a better option.

'Okay, I'll take that, thank you. But can you add on the top level of insurance because I don't fancy wrecking that in this weather and being left with the bill.'

'Wise choice. If I could just have your credit card...'

Lachlan handed it over, then whisked through the formalities, before saying a thankful goodbye as he left with the car's location map and key. Outside, he was slammed by the bitter cold, squinting against the torrent of snow hitting his face as he crossed the road, before cutting through the main car park, then back outside to the car hire company's designated area.

There, he saw the couple who had been ahead of him in the queue playing some kind of luggage Jenga as they tried to fit a dozen suitcases into a Dacia Duster.

He pressed the button on the key fob and watched as the lights of a black Range Rover Discovery flashed ahead of him, guiding him in. He threw his backpack into the back seat, then brushed the snow from his shoulders and hair before climbing into the driver's seat. He started the engine, switched on the heating, and familiarised himself with the location of the windscreen wipers.

Okay, time to go. He plugged his phone into the car's media system and called up his maps, then punched in the address of his first destination. Huntington Farrell, the legal firm that had represented his father's affairs for decades.

The letter summoning him here today made it quite clear that his presence was required this morning. Apparently, his father had left explicit instructions that his will was to be read old-style, in the presence of his family. Lachlan had wanted to reply saying that he didn't care. Not even a bit. But there was something inside him, some last shred of loyalty to man who had given him half of his DNA.

He flicked the Range Rover into drive and gently pressed his foot on the accelerator, hearing the snow crunch under the tyres as he began to move off.

A year ago, he'd left Glasgow and made a promise to himself that he wouldn't return.

He had a feeling deep in his gut that today was the day he would find out that breaking that vow was a mistake.

10 A.M. – NOON

10 A.M.–NOON

5

JESSIE

Jessie watched as her pal, Val Murray, crossed the threshold of the café and shook her head like a golden retriever, shedding little flakes of snow off her red furry hat onto the black rubber mat underneath her feet, before bursting into a chorus of 'Happy Birthday'. Thankfully, they were the only people daft enough to venture out in this weather, so the café was empty of other patrons.

'Happy birthday dear, Jessie... Happy birthday to yoooooooooooo.' As she threw her arms wide, Val held the last note for so long, Jessie could only admire her lung power. Song over, Val gave herself another shake, then made her way to the only occupied table in the room and greeted Jessie with a hug.

'Happy birthday, ma love. There's only one woman that I would leave the house for on a day like this, Jessie McLean, and you'd better be rewarding me with cake for breakfast.'

Jessie pointed to the Victoria sponge in front of her, elaborately iced with 'Happy 65th Birthday Jessie!'

'Ready and waiting, lovely. Although, a tinfoil jacket and a ski mask would probably come in a bit handier today. Our Cathy came in looking like a double duvet in her new coat. She's just nipped to the loo.'

Val shrugged off her familiar bright red ski jacket. 'I always know it's nearly Christmas when that jacket comes out,' Jessie told her fondly, already knowing what the reply would be. Val reminded them every year that she'd bought it for a ski trip to the Highlands thirty years ago.

'Glenshee, 1995, and still going strong. Never made it to the slopes, because I twisted my ankle at Stirling services when I ran in for a cup of tea and a hot pie. And then my Don put his back out carrying me back to the bus.' As always, there was a softness in Val's voice when she mentioned her late husband, who'd had Alzheimer's disease and passed away a few years before. She changed the subject as she draped her jacket over a chair at the next table. 'Anyway, I was just thinking that the last time it snowed like this was last year, when I hit a pothole outside your house and had to seek refuge in your kitchen.'

Jessie pursed her lips. 'The council still haven't fixed it. Bloody thing is the size of a paddling pool now. Took out two transit vans last week. It's keeping Kwik Fit in business.'

Val plonked down on a chair, her gaze flitting round the room. 'Ooh, it's gorgeous in here today,' she said, taking in the twinkling green tree, bedecked in white and gold balls and ornaments, as Jessie nodded.

'I was just saying the same thing to Alyssa. The lass put all the Christmas decorations and lights up early for my party tonight. It's lovely, so it is, and it's going to be beautiful when everything is lit up tonight.' Jessie tried really hard to stop her voice from quivering. The café was like a pretty winter wonderland today. Candles on all the wall shelves, white tinsel draped along the tops of the bookcases and the display cabinets that held today's cakes. On the tables, there was an assortment of little reindeer and snowmen and penguins. And in the background, Bing Crosby was crooning his very apt tribute to today's weather.

Val's gaze met hers, and her pal's perfectly pencilled eyebrows narrowed. 'Oh no...'

'What?' Jessie wasn't sure where this was going.

'Yer chin is wobbling. Don't deny it. Are you okay, love?'

Jessie knew she could admit anything to Val and it would never be judged or repeated, but she wasn't going to spoil her last day here by crumbling into a heap and confessing that she was stressed up to her elf earrings about leaving tomorrow, dreading saying goodbye to everyone, anxious about a life with only her husband for company, and panicking now that the reality of this moment was here. So instead she played it down with, 'Och, I'm just going to miss our cuppas.'

Thankfully, the arrival of Alyssa saved her from further scrutiny.

'Good morning, Val. Usual?' Alyssa welcomed Val like an old friend, which, Jessie knew, wasn't too far from the truth. Val and Jessie had both lived in the village of Weirbridge their whole lives, and there was barely a person, scandal, story or piece of gossip that didn't reach one of them. Alyssa was village-born too, and when she'd opened the Once Upon A Time Café on Main Street, almost directly across the road from Jessie's hair salon, the women had quickly made it their regular coffee spot.

Val pulled off her hat, to reveal a blonde bob that barely quivered, thanks to enough Elnett hairspray to give a Highland cow a ten-inch high beehive hairdo. 'Yes, please, love. And if you could throw in a blowtorch to warm up ma feet, that would be grand. There are parts that even a Victoria sponge can't reach.'

As Alyssa got busy making Val a beverage to defrost her toes, Jessie's cousin-by-marriage, Cathy, bustled back from the loo, her hair a helmet of perfection now that she'd also discarded her hat and given her curls a quick fluff up with the hand drier. 'Morning, Val. Did I hear singing?'

'Aye, I think it was Mariah Carey. She popped her head in the door on the way to Aldi.' As Cathy took a seat, Val leant over to kiss her on the cheek. 'Do the posh folk know you're here, Cathy? They might not let you back in.'

Cathy picked up the mug of steaming tea she'd ordered before she went to the loo. 'I got a special visa. As long as I'm back by sundown, they'll forgive me for mingling with riff-raff.'

Jessie chuckled at the banter between her relative and her pal. Both of them could dish it out and take it in equal measure, so this was their idea of a friendly exchange. Especially as they both knew that none of the teasing was actually grounded in reality. Yes, Cathy had lived most of her seventy-seven years in the upmarket West End of Glasgow, and now lived in a lovely retirement flat there, but she was born and bred near the shipyards and had worked her bunions off for most of her life in her hairdressing salon in Partick.

Val got to work, slicing up the cake in the centre of the table. 'Well, I hope you've got skis to get you back there because that big handsome weather bloke on the telly was saying we're in for a belter of a snow day today. Anyway, Jessie, how's the first day of retirement going? I'm surprised you're not doing a Joan Collins, luxuriating in your bed until lunchtime, wrapped in white fake fur, with thirty-year-old oiled-up bodybuilders feeding you grapes. Actually, I don't know that Joan Collins does that, but I like to imagine it that way.'

'I'm not having oiled-up bodybuilders anywhere near my bed, thank you.' Jessie countered. 'I'd need to boil wash my sheets and it would take the pattern right off my duvet cover.' A duvet cover that, like all her other bedding and linens, would be discarded or donated as soon as their house here was sold. They only used cotton sheets in Tenerife because it was too warm, even in winter. Her earlier resolve not to think about it crumbled as the reality slammed into her chest again. And the very thought made Jessie want to cry.

'Jessie, are you welling up or has someone let a cat in here and triggered your allergies?' Cathy asked her, genuinely concerned about either possibility. Her pals knew she wasn't a crier, except when she watched *Long Lost Family* or *Call The Midwife*, which inevitably got her in such a state she could lose a full set of false lashes by the end of the episode.

Jessie answered by letting a big fat tear drop down her face. So much for her earlier resolve not to give in to sadness today.

Cathy was the first to put her hand on hers. 'Oh Jessie, what is it?'

Jessie shrugged, trying to clear the lump in her throat so that she could speak again. 'It's just... today. I know I should be delighted about my birthday and retirement, but all I can think about is that it's my last day here. I'm heartbroken to be saying goodbye to people, but then, at the same time, I'm worried about the party tonight. What if no one comes because of the snow and I *don't* get to say goodbye? That would be even worse. And every time I look at the salon...'

All three of them turned to stare out of the window at Copper Curls across the road. On a clear day, she could see in the windows from here, but given the snow that was still coming down thick and fast, she could just make out the outline of the building and the sign above the shutters. The salon on the Weirbridge Main Street had been her dream when she was growing up here, and then her reality for most of her adult life. Back in the eighties, when Stan had agreed to settle here in her home village, it had coincided with a vacancy for a trained hairdresser in that salon. Jessie had jumped at the chance to have a ten-minute walk to work every day. A few years later, she'd taken out a loan and bought it from the previous owner who'd married a Balinese yoga instructor and gone off to explore her chakras. When Grant and Georgie had come along, she'd worked right up until their births both times, and been back on the scissors a month later.

Looking back, she must have been crazy, but they'd made it work somehow. Sometimes on a Saturday, when money was still tight or she didn't have a babysitter, the children would come to work with her and play all day in the staffroom, reading comics, chatting to customers, or watching TV on the tiny portable that only worked if you gave it a thud on the side. Now they were grown adults and both of them had joined the business at one time or another. Only Georgie had stuck with it, though. When Grant was a teenager, he had gone off to a trendy, upmarket salon in Glasgow's city centre, and his undeniable talents and starry ambitions had eventually taken him down south. Now he lived in London, where he had his own swanky salon in Kensington, with a roster of celebrity clients and occasional guest spots on morning TV shows.

She cleared her throat, then repeated what she'd just said, this time mustering enough strength to finish the sentence and express how she felt.

'Every time I look at the salon, I think how much I'm going to miss it. How much I'll miss my life here. How much I'll miss popping down to London to see Grant. How much I'll miss... Ah, there's our Georgie there now.'

Jessie saw Georgie trudging up the road in a padded coat and wellies, before stopping outside Copper Curls.

Val must have noticed Jessie's wobbly chin had returned, because she squeezed her hand. 'But you can always come back whenever you want. My spare room has had more people in it than a Premier Inn and it's empty right now that Sandra is back on her feet.'

Sandra was Val's latest lodger. A woman who'd been involved with an abusive piece of scum called Larry McLenn, a former politician who'd lost everything when it was discovered that he'd taken bribes and blown them on a cocaine habit. He'd later spent time in jail for causing an accident by driving while drunk and on drugs. His ex-wife, Alice, was a friend of Val's, and the two women had stepped in when they'd discovered that Sandra was suffering at his hands. They'd helped her escape him, found her a job, and Sandra had been in Val's spare room for over a year while she saved up the deposit for her own place. That's the kind of woman Val Murray was. And Jessie was going to miss every bit of her.

'I know, and I love you for offering but it won't be the same as having a home here. What am I thinking, starting all over again at my age? And, aye, I know I'm sounding pathetic. I've been acting all positive in front of Stan and the family, but how do I know this isn't a huge bloody mistake?'

'Sometimes you just need to take a leap of faith, and it all works out, Jessie.' That came from Cathy, and they both knew that she had solid evidence that it was never too late to start over. Only a couple of years ago, she'd sold up her family home and moved to the retirement flat and it had been a wonderful surprise to them all when she'd bumped into her first love, Richie, and he'd swept her off her feet. Not literally. Apparently, he slipped a disc back in his younger years, so he avoided any form of lifting. Bad back aside, they were like a couple of teenagers again, and Jessie had never seen her happier.

'You could be right, Cathy. The thing is, Stan and I have been together for all our lives, and we had our own way of doing things. Our own roles. I had the kids, and work, and that made life busy and interesting. And he always liked the fact that I was independent and didn't rely on him to entertain me.' On the edge of the tight ball of anxiety that had been lodged in her chest for days and weeks, there was a tiny thread of relief that she was saying this out loud. Admitting her fears. Not that it would change anything. The bags were packed, the plans were made, and the tickets were bought – but at least, right in this minute, she wasn't having to pretend to be ecstatic.

'My Don was the same,' Val agreed. 'Strong silent type. He always said that I made sure there was never a dull moment, and he made sure I took time to stop for breath. He wasn't exactly the Dalai Lama, but he could be a wise man sometimes.'

The wistful expression that flitted across Val's face caused a twinge in Jessie's heart. Losing Don three years back had been almost unbearable for her pal, but Val Murray was bloody bulletproof, and somehow, she'd found the strength to keep getting up in the mornings. Val's stoicism made Jessie flush with guilt. There was her pal, who would give anything and go anywhere if she had her Don back for a single day, and here Jessie was moaning about spending her retirement in Tenerife with the man she'd been married to for decades. She really had to suck it up, count her blessings and just get on with it.

The three of them were distracted by the ding of the bell above the front door, as a new arrival entered the café, brushing the snow from sleeves of her jacket. Even with the woman's hood up, Jessie knew exactly who it was.

There was only one person in this village whose very existence haunted Jessie McLean. Only one person that Jessie would be happy never to clap eyes on again. And right now she was staring at her.

'Hello, Dorinda. Long time no see.'

Maybe there was something to be said for moving thousands of miles away from here after all.

6
GEORGIE

Georgie pushed up the heavy steel shutter that covered the window of Copper Curls, and then did the same with the shutter in front of the door. Her hands were so cold, she struggled to get the key in the lock, and then, inside, took three attempts to switch off the alarm, because her frozen fingers wouldn't obey her. It was her own fault for leaving the house without gloves, but she'd been in such a fluster when the phone rang right before she left. Her heart had almost stopped with the anticipation of whether it was going to be the call from the TV company delivering a life-altering dilemma, but it was only Flynn, saying he'd left his wallet on the bedside table and he'd pop back over for it after work.

Kayleigh's comment about them sneaking around floated back into her mind, along with the acknowledgment that it was slightly ridiculous that her eighteen-year-old daughter was taking a more mature, pragmatic view of this situation than the fully-fledged adults in the equation. A decision on how her future relationship with her ex would look was going to have to be made, but not today. Today, there were way too many other things on her mind.

If felt strange coming into the salon on a Monday, because that was usually the weekday that they closed, except when she was asked to make an exception for special clients or special occasions. Today, both of those things were true. This was her mum's birthday and her first day of retirement, so a pamper here was going to be a lovely treat for her (with her pals, of course) and a fitting way for her mum to say goodbye to the salon – by getting spoiled and beautified, after decades of doing that for everyone else.

Although, for her own wellbeing in this moment, Georgie tried not to think about her mum actually leaving Scotland tomorrow morning. She had no idea how she was going to deal with the party tonight either. How could you celebrate two of the people you loved most in the world buggering off to another country? And who threw a party on a Monday night? Georgie and Grant had both suggested that they plan a big, lavish soirée on the previous Saturday, but Jessie had refused, saying she wanted somewhere she could 'open the top button of her skirt after too many sausage rolls'. Besides, most of the people coming were retired, so the night of the week didn't matter to them.

Georgie walked the length of the salon to dump her bag in the staffroom at the back, pressed the booster button on the heating thermostat that lived in there, then wandered back through to the main salon. Despite her inner turmoil and churning stomach, she couldn't help but think how gorgeous Copper Curls looked. Her mum had invested so much in this place, and she was meticulous about keeping it both modern and pristine. Just last year, she'd blown a chunk of her profits on a complete renovation. There were new copper tiles on the floor, the walls had been panelled and finished in a luxurious cream, and the shelves in front of each seat had been replaced with bespoke marble counters, and copper-edged mirrors above them carried on the metallic theme. White leather chairs and a dramatic but modern globe chandelier completed the look. At the back of the room, outside the staffroom door, the old backwash basins had been replaced with gleaming new sinks on top of an oatmeal marble pedestal. The end result was chic, stylish and would do them for another decade – which was Jessie's intention. Her mum and dad still owned the building, but the running of this place was all hers now, and it had been such an incredibly generous gift.

'I just wanted to make sure I leave you something that won't need another penny spent on it for a few years to come,' her mum had assured her, and Georgie had been thrilled with the thought that this was where she'd spend the rest of her career. Delighted. Over the moon. Now, replaying that conversation in her mind took the stomach churn to spin-cycle levels. The potential career-changing opportunity that had come her way last week had been a bolt from the blue, but even so, how could she even consider leaving here after her mum had done that for her? How ungrateful could she be? She was so busy with the self-flagellation that it took her a moment to notice her phone was ringing again. She pulled it out of her pocket. Unknown number.

This time, she refused to get her knickers in a twist because it was probably Flynn calling from his work to say that he'd also left his pants, his socks, or his razor, or someone trying to sell her double glazing.

'Hello?' She didn't even try to hide her weariness.

'Hi, can I speak to Georgie Dern please?' She couldn't pinpoint the accent. Probably one of those AI scams she was always seeing warnings about on TikTok.

'Speaking.'

'Good morning. At least I think it's morning over there. This is Bonnie Katowski, and I'm one of the assistant producers on *The Clansman*. Ollie Chiles has passed on your details and a request that we bring you on board.'

'Sorry, what?' Oh God. Oh God. This was what it must feel like when a radio station called to say you'd won a cash prize or a tumble drier.

Bonnie Katowski repeated the important part. 'Ollie. Chiles.'

Georgie had heard correctly the first time, but just wanted to make sure. Earlier she'd wondered if the damned universe was playing games with her and now she knew it definitely was. She plumped down on the nearest chair, ironically, the same one that Ollie Chiles – actor and a bit of a superstar – had sat in on his last visit. Yes, that was correct. The man who had achieved worldwide fame as the star of *The Clansman*, a show about sixteenth-century rebellious Scots, had first found his way into this non-celebrity neck of the woods when his mother, Moira, had moved into the village six months before.

He'd dropped Moira off for her weekly shampoo and blow-dry with Jessie, and when he'd come early to pick her up, asked if Georgie, who was sitting at reception, having a quick break and reading the latest edition of *Vogue*, could fit him in for a quick trim. Georgie had almost fainted when she'd realised who was standing in front of her. There had been an emotional chain reaction that had gone something like: shock, disbelief, momentary thrill, panic, fear, knee-jerk reaction.

'I'm sorry, but no. I've got my Aunt Cathy for a violet toner in ten minutes and if I'm not ready for her, she could run riot and wreck the place.'

'Really?' he'd asked, with a grin that she'd only ever seen on the telly.

Georgie had winced as she shook her head. 'No, but it was the best I could come up with at short notice. I'm actually just terrified that I'll see your photo on TMZ this weekend and there'll be snarky comments under it asking who gave you a dodgy haircut. I'm good, but I'm not used to that level of public scrutiny, and I don't think my nerves could take it.'

He'd taken a pause to consider her objections, and she'd thought about how he might be the most attractive man she'd ever clapped eyes on. Not that he was available. Moira gave them a running commentary every week about his girlfriend, Stevie, who, in another non-celebrity twist, was a radiographer up at Glasgow Central Hospital.

'Okay, well, how about if I handle your Aunt Cathy…'

'You're a brave man.'

'And if my hair turns out dodgy and anyone comments, I'll tell them that I let Ben Affleck cut it for a dare.'

Georgie had jumped to her feet. 'Done.'

And that's how a Hollywood TV star, and a thoroughly nice guy, had become her regular client and ended up in this very chair every fortnight for a trim and sometimes a few highlights too.

It had all been perfectly lovely and surprisingly easy until last week, when he'd opened a conversation with, 'You know, I don't want you to get too big-headed…'

'Too late,' Georgie had told him over the sound of the clippers. 'I'm already insufferable now that I'm having regular brushes with fame. But carry on.'

That had made him chuckle. They'd got entirely comfortable with each other over the last few months, and he loved the fact that here he was just another customer. Although, they did pull the blinds down and keep his appointments strictly confidential so that he didn't get mobbed by the lunchtime bingo crowd coming from the church hall.

He had looked at her reflection in the mirror. 'I wish I could take you with me.'

'Where?'

'My work. On to the set. I'm just about to leave to leave this tropical paradise...' The torrential rain outside had been almost horizontal. '...to go film the new series of *The Clansman*, and my regular guy has been poached for the next *Mission Impossible*...'

'They did ask me, but I wasn't available,' Georgie had gone along with the joke.

'Georgie, I'm serious. Would you be interested?'

'In what?' She couldn't quite get her head around what he was saying.

'In coming to America to work on set as my hairdresser. I know it's a big ask. It would mean at least six months away from your family, and it could be even longer if we get the green light on future seasons. Would you consider it?'

She had almost taken his left ear off with the clippers. Thankfully, Jessie had been over at the dryers discussing the price of cocktails in Tenerife with Moira, and out of earshot. 'I don't know. I mean, yes! But no...!' There was a sudden realisation of what that would mean. She'd have to leave Copper Curls. Just when her mother was handing it over to her. Jessie's life's work. Her legacy. One that Georgie should be dedicated to preserving. But... oh wow, it sounded incredible. She'd groaned, and circled back to, 'I don't know.'

The lovely Ollie hadn't appeared fazed by her conflicting responses. 'Look, I don't want to pressure you, but how about I get production to contact you with all the details and an official offer. If you're interested, great. If not, no worries.'

No worries. So of course, she'd worried about it ever since.

The only person she'd told about all this was her brother, Grant, who'd asked her five times a day ever since if she'd heard anything, and who wasn't even here to be her emotional support crutch.

Now the call had come.

'Sorry, yes. Ollie did mention that you might call.' This wasn't happening. Flynn had spiked her coffee or she was high on some crazy hormonal orgasmic afterglow, and she was imagining this whole thing.

'Great. I'm actually calling from LA – it's 2 a.m. here – but I wanted to catch you early in your day. Okay, so the bottom line is that we start filming in Colorado in one week – December eighth. Not great timing, just before Christmas, but we need the snow.'

This woman clearly hadn't seen Glasgow today.

'We'll also be shooting in LA and Croatia over the course of the season. I'll get all the details in an email to you, including the compensation package, living arrangements and the terms of the contract. I do have to tell you that it's a six-month contract and we don't usually hear whether we'll be commissioned for another series until this one airs, but we're on season ten right now, so, all being well, the run will continue. We're so excited to have you on board. Ollie speaks so highly of you. Do you have any questions?'

Georgie had at least a thousand, but they all appeared to have deserted her for now. Except...

'Can I think about it?'

There was a brief silence at the other end of the line. Bonnie Katowski was obviously used to a more enthusiastic reaction.

'Yes, of course,' she spluttered when she recovered. 'As I said, I'll put it all in writing. Ollie gave me your email address, so I'll fire that over to you now. We are in a time crunch though, so we would need your answer in the next twenty-four hours. Would that work for you?'

Would that work? Absolutely not. It took her twenty-four hours to decide whether to have chips or a baked potato for dinner. Life-changing decisions required at least a month and a half of angst.

'Yes, of course. Thank you for calling.'

She disconnected the call, then stared at her phone for several seconds, before making her way to the reception area at the front of the shop and slumping onto the stool behind the desk.

This was it. The kind of job that could change her life. At least for a while. And her pragmatic head told her that was one of the problems. Six months. And no guarantee of another season.

Finding someone she trusted to come in and run the salon on that basis would be just about impossible. More importantly, her mum would never allow it. When Aunt Cathy had retired, one of her long-term stylists had taken over the business, but that was a plan that had been in the making for years before it happened. Here, it had always been just Jessie, Georgie and junior stylists who stayed with them until they invariably went off to trendy salons in Glasgow or Edinburgh. No, Mum wouldn't trust the salon she'd treasured for forty years to a stranger. Georgie knew she'd cancel her plans to move to Tenerife and stay here to take care of her third child. It was the way it had always been. Grant. Georgie. And Copper Curls. The three much-loved offspring of Jessie McLean.

And then... Oh God, Georgie's mind began to spiral. What if her mum or her dad were one of those statistics that you read about, where someone retires and then drops dead almost immediately, despite being in apparently good health. Then Georgie would have deprived them of their last weeks or months together and the surviving parent would never forgive her.

Although, yes, she was fully aware that she was now catastrophising this whole situation and her mother would live until she was a hundred, but still...

If Georgie wanted to take this job, she knew her mum would move heaven and earth to make this happen for her, even if it was at Mum's own expense. And that was the very reason Georgie couldn't do it.

'Did someone say there was a party happening around here tonight?' Ten minutes late, Grant McLean entered the building, a bottle of champagne in each hand.

Georgie's first and only reaction was to groan and put her head on the reception desk.

'There is. But first I need you to hold my hand while I turn down the opportunity of a lifetime.'

7
ALYSSA

'Mum, what are you doing here? I didn't expect to see you this morning.' Alyssa's mum, the very glamorous Dorinda Canavan, popped into the café maybe once a week, and even then, it was usually only because she wanted a quick cuppa or some free cakes to take to whatever client she was trying to woo. Working as an estate agent gave her lots of flexibility, especially now that she was a freelance agent for a national franchise, with no office to report to every day.

'I took the day off because I was doing showings all weekend, and I was on my way to the nail salon for a touch-up when I saw your grandad trudging here, so I gave him a lift. Ridiculous a man of his age being out in this weather.'

Just at that, her grandad, Hugo, came through the doorway, after kicking his boots against the step to get rid of the snow.

Alyssa shook her head in her grandad's direction. 'Grandad, I told you I'd come and pick you up. Why were you walking?'

Hugo shrugged off his anorak. 'Because my coat is warm, my legs still work perfectly well, and maybe a man just wants to enjoy a bit of snow. That used to be the biggest excitement of the year when I was a boy.'

There wasn't really any arguing with that. Her grandad had every right to live his life however he pleased and if that meant taking a walk in the snow, that was up to him.

'Good morning, ladies! How are we all doing on this fine day?' Hugo greeted Jessie, Val and Cathy, and got a rousing chorus of 'Good morning, Hugo' in return, before Val added, 'I was just saying to Jessie earlier... I remember when we would all make sleds out of scraps of linoleum and head up the Weirbridge hill when it snowed like this...'

This was exactly why Grandad loved working here. He was sixty-nine, a few years older than Jessie and Val, but all the born-and-bred villagers knew each other and enjoyed their memories. If Alyssa had a pound for every time she heard a sentence that began, 'Do you remember when we used to...' she'd be able to buy out her frigging landlord and own this building.

The thought made her wince on the inside. She couldn't close the café. Not just because she had poured her heart and soul into building her business, but because as well as it being her favourite place and a much-loved, invaluable hub for the community, it was a lifeline for her grandad too. What would he do without all this chat every day?

Apparently, her mother didn't feel the same about her father's employment status, because as she followed Alyssa back behind the counter at the far end of the room, she hissed. 'As I've said too many times to count, I don't know why you humour him by having him work here.'

Alyssa felt the hairs on the back of her neck bristle. 'I don't "have" him work here, Mum. I'm grateful that he works here, and he enjoys it because he doesn't want to be at home all day. He loves it here. And I love that I get to spend time with him.'

No matter how many times Alyssa had told her mother that, it still hadn't sunk in, probably because Dorinda would never understand the relationship between her daughters and her father. Grandad had been the only male presence in their lives, because their dad hadn't been around. Even now that she was an adult, Alyssa didn't know the full details, only what she'd gleaned from overhearing stories and the crumbs of information that Dorinda would let slip when she'd had a champagne or two on special occasions. The bottom line was that village life hadn't been enough for Dorinda, so she'd gone off seeking adventures with a travelling salesman that she'd met at the golf club, but that hadn't worked out and she'd returned after a few years, when Alyssa and Ginny were toddlers. She'd brought the guy – Alyssa and Ginny's dad – back with her, but he hadn't lasted and he'd taken off, never to be seen since. There had been countless other men after that. Alyssa didn't even want to think about the gossip that must have caused, but she hadn't realised it when she was a kid, because these things were never discussed. As far as she was concerned, she'd had a perfectly happy childhood, with their gran, Effie, and grandad taking care of them while their mum worked, or socialised, or nipped off to Marbella for a week with a new man. Her grandparents had never judged or complained, and the girls had just assumed all families worked that way. And besides, Grandad was brilliant at helping with their homework and Gran was a great cook, so it was a win-win. Gran had been proud as punch when the café had opened. If she hadn't passed from pneumonia a couple of years ago, Alyssa knew she'd be here now too, baking up a storm in the kitchen.

But there wasn't time to linger on that right now, because Dorinda had zeroed in on her daughter's face. 'Are you coming down with something? You're far too pale and your eyes are bloodshot.'

Another zinger of support from her darling mother. On any other day, Alyssa would just shrug it off and it wouldn't even make a dent in her mood, but not today. Not when her head was still scrambled from the letter she'd opened this morning, saying they wanted to take away her café and her home.

The first thing she'd done was let Ginny read it. Her sister's initial, jaw-dropping gasp of 'Fuckers!' had just about summed it up.

Next, she'd called the lawyer's office. No answer. She'd called again every five minutes until 9 a.m. when someone had finally picked up the phone.

'Good morning, you've reached Huntington Farrell. How may I direct your call?' Just the sound of the woman's superior, officious voice had made Alyssa's teeth clench.

'Can I speak to...' She'd scrambled for the letter and then checked the signature at the bottom. 'Jeremy Sprite.'

A pause.

'I'm afraid Mr Sprite is in a client meeting all morning. Can I ask what it's regarding and have him return your call when he's available?'

'Yes, my name is Alyssa Canavan. I received a letter from him this morning about the lease on my property.'

'And the property address is...?'

Alyssa had rhymed it off, then added her phone number, before going on, 'It's just that I think the letter must be a mistake. Or maybe not, because there was a clause in my lease that would indicate it isn't.' She knew she was rambling, and the woman at the other end of the phone would have no idea what she was talking about, but she didn't seem to be able to stop speaking. It was probably for the best that the woman cut her off.

'Miss Canavan, I'll have Mr Sprite phone you when he's free. Thank you for your call.' And with a click, the line had gone dead.

Over at the range, Ginny had been listening the whole time, while stirring a huge vat of minestrone soup into a frenzy. 'So what do we do now?'

Alyssa wished she had a more productive answer other than, 'Nothing. We wait. Look, don't mention it to anyone, especially Grandad. I don't want to worry him.'

Now that her grandad had come in happy and positive as ever, that sentiment was even firmer. She wasn't going to mention it to her mother either, not when she was already on the offensive. The last thing Alyssa needed right now was her mother's input on her disaster. She hadn't wanted Alyssa to open a café in the village in the first place, extolling the virtues of going out into the 'big bloody world out there' and 'exploring life outside this mind-numbing bubble of boredom', so this definitely had the potential to ding the bell at the top of her mum's 'Told You So' scale.

Alyssa instinctively picked up a cloth and began to clean the already pristine counter. She had taken so long to answer her mother's question, she'd almost forgotten what it was. Something about her being pale and ill.

'No, Mum, I'm fine.'

She didn't add the more authentic 'distraught, shocked, terrified, worried and feeling sick to my stomach'. 'Fine' would do for now.

'Well, maybe try a bit of fake tan in the mornings. I've got a coconut one that I just spritz on my face after my shower and it works wonders. I'll give you the name of it and you can pick one up in the chemist. Make you look a bit less peaky.'

Before Alyssa could answer, Ginny came shooting out of the kitchen behind them. Saved by the sister. 'Team, we have a problem. A huge big fricking problem.'

Noooooo! Alyssa clenched her jaw, and pursed her lips as she made warning eyes at her sister. Yes, they had a huge fricking problem, but hadn't they agreed not to share it yet?

'What's that, dear?' their mother asked, before turning back to Alyssa. 'Don't do that frowny thing, Alyssa, you'll give yourself wrinkles.'

Alyssa wondered how long she'd have to bang her own head off the temperamental, clapped-out coffee machine before she induced a coma.

'The buses are off!' Ginny blurted. 'And I've got my final interview in town in an hour.' Ginny's big break – a role as an acting coach at the drama and music school Ollie Chiles had founded for underprivileged kids. She had her heart set on it and had already been for a preliminary audition that focused on her acting and singing talents, but this was the last stage in the process, a meeting with a panel of people who ran it.

True to form, their mum didn't even attempt to conceal her disinterest in Ginny's panic. 'Ah well, I'm sure they'll understand. This weather is terrible today. You can just rearrange it.'

'No, I can't, Mum! If I fall down at the first sign of a challenge, what does that say about me? This job is teaching drama in a theatre school – there are going to be loads of obstacles to overcome. If there are three or four people after this job and I'm the only one that can't get there, they'll shred my application.'

Alyssa watched as their mother finally showed a pique of interest, but quickly realised it came from a place of self-interest.

'Is this the one at the academy that Ollie Chiles set up?' Mum asked, but didn't wait for an answer before going on. 'By the way, I showed his mother a perfect house before she moved here, but she chose to go with a flat down by the river. Terrible choice. Anyway, you should definitely go then, darling, and if you're speaking to him, you could drop in that the manor house over in Burnbank has just come up for sale and he'd be perfect for it.' Burnbank was the next village, just a mile or so down the road. 'Give him my details and I'll set up a viewing for him. It would be a great long-term investment property and it's just five minutes from his mother, too.'

Alyssa was torn between relief that Ginny wasn't spilling her secrets, and the urge to point out that not everyone felt that being in close proximity to their mother was a good thing. She kept her mouth closed.

'Great! So will you give me a lift there?' Ginny asked, her body sagging with relief and gratitude. But only for a second.

'Oh no, Ginny, I can't. I mean, first your grandad, and now you – I'm not a taxi service. Besides, those roads out there are treacherous. Can't you do it, Alyssa?'

'Mum, I have a café to run, and Jessie's party to prep for tonight... Ginny, you can borrow my van and drive there if that helps?'

Ginny clearly reached the obvious conclusion that nothing was going to change their mum's mind, because she was now looking at Alyssa with pleading eyes. 'I can't! I've never driven in the snow and it'll lead to certain death if I try. I can barely manoeuvre that van around the village on a sunny day. Please drive me there, Alyssa. I swear I'll give you my first-born child. Or... or... my boyfriend! Yes, you can have Caden. And his spectacular abs.'

Alyssa opened her mouth to object, but as she did, another idea dropped in. Something her mother said about investment properties. This café had to be a decent investment for the owner of the building, because she knew he'd owned it forever. That probably meant there was no mortgage on it and her rent money was pretty much pure profit. Maybe his estate, or his family, or whoever had inherited this building didn't realise that she intended to stay here for the long term, and perhaps if they knew that they might understand that it could bring them a guaranteed ongoing return. Maybe she just had to give them all the information. And perhaps she could kill two birds with one stone. Besides, she couldn't sit around and wait for someone to call her back. Not when she could go and see the lawyer and ask him to put her in touch with the relevant people so that they could talk. Negotiate. Contrary to popular opinion, she truly believed that most people were fundamentally decent and had good hearts. If her landlord's family heard her story, hopefully she could persuade them to change their minds, or at least to extend the notice period so that she had time to come up with some other plan.

'Okay, Mum, if I take Ginny into town, could you stick around for a couple of hours and help Grandad?'

Cue horror and immediate objection. 'But I'm getting my nails done.'

'Mum, please. You can see how important this is. I doubt anyone will be coming out today anyway.'

Alyssa hadn't realised that Jessie was passing them on the way to the loos, until she spoke. 'I can hold the fort for you, love. I was only going to get my hair done anyway. And it's the least I can do with you giving up your night tonight to let us have the party here.'

Alyssa was about to gratefully decline Jessie's very kind, but too generous offer – she couldn't let one of her favourite people give up her plans on her birthday and very last day in the village – when her mother must have suffered an out-of-body experience, because she suddenly changed her tune and blurted, 'No, it's fine. Of course, I'll do it. You two nip off and I'll just move my appointment to later.'

For the first time since she'd opened the letter, Alyssa felt a surge of hope. Her mother was being uncharacteristically nice. All she needed now was for her former landlord's family to be decent people with good hearts.

Surely that wasn't too much to ask?

8

LACHLAN

Lachlan parked in a space about fifty yards down from Huntington Farrell on West Regent Street in Glasgow's city centre. At least, he hoped it was an official space. It was impossible to tell with the six inches of snow that was now lying on top of the road markings. After leaving the airport, he'd taken a slight detour, much to the displeasure of his satnav, and nipped off the motorway at the Braehead shopping centre. There, he'd dashed into an outdoor clothing store, so he was now the proud owner of a North Face jacket so thick it could lag an igloo.

He checked his watch. Twenty minutes until the meeting, and he was just going to wait in the car, because he had no desire to arrive early and risk exposure to his family. He immediately corrected himself. Not family. His brother. That was it. Jason was the last person on this earth he wanted to spend time with. His stepmother didn't count, because he barely knew her. Demi had been – oh the cliché – his dad's executive assistant and had consoled his dad when Mum had died. Barely a year later, they were saying their 'I do's' under a flower arch in the Bahamas, then moving lock, stock and barrel to Monaco, where they'd had four years of married life before his dad passed.

Despite the obvious gold-digging, thirty-year-age-gap, stereotype of it all, Lachlan was happy for them, because watching his dad drown in grief and solitude after Mum had died would have been awful. Lachlan now knew exactly how that felt. Losing Tanya... well, that had been the kind of heartbreak that he wouldn't want anyone to suffer. For a year afterwards, every song, every place, every flashback had been like a nail gun being fired into his gut, until the only thing to do was to leave, escape the memories and start again.

And now he was back and he'd rather be anywhere else than here.

To distract his mind, he put a call into his friend and client, Dax Price, to give him an update on the job he was starting for him later this week. Dax had been Lachlan's catalyst for the London move in the first place. He'd been playing football for a Glasgow team, and Lachlan had transformed the star striker's home in the suburb of Bothwell into the house of dreams for a talented kid who'd grown up with nothing and gone on to be one of the top professional footballers in the country. The kicker was, though, that as soon as the house was finished, Dax had been transferred to a London team. The timing had worked for Lachlan, however – a new start in a place with no memories. So he'd packed up, moved down south, worked with Dax to find the perfect crumbling investment in Essex, then got to work creating a second dream home for his client. A six-car garage. A swimming pool. An extension that included a high-tech fitness room and – a new one on Lachlan – a spa that was purely for his barber and skincare specialist to take care of his appearance.

Lachlan had also taken on other clients, building his company and his reputation, but now he was due to start work on converting the basement of Dax's mansion into a games room and bar. Should be pretty interesting, given that the player was all over social media today. 'Hey Dax, just a reminder that we'll be there Wednesday morning to start on the demo. If that doesn't suit, give me a shout.'

He checked his watch again. Five minutes. Okay, time to go.

He grabbed his backpack, tossed it in the boot, locked the car and did a runner to the swanky glass office building that housed Huntington Farrell. It was exactly the type of office he expected of a high-flying corporate firm. The marble floors, the glass chandeliers, the water flowing over the glistening granite on the whole expanse of one wall – if he were a client, he'd definitely be contemplating how much they were overcharging him so they could maintain this place.

'Good morning. I have an appointment with Jeremy Sprite,' he told the receptionist. 'My name is Lachlan Morden.'

She checked something on her computer screen, then issued him with a pass on a lanyard. 'Mr Sprite is expecting you. The lifts are just there to your right, and he's on the third floor. His assistant will meet you there.'

Last chance to run, but what was the point? He'd only have to do it again. So instead of fleeing, he followed the instructions and nodded gratefully to the smiling assistant who was there to greet him when the lift doors opened on the third floor.

'This way, Mr Morden. They're all waiting for you in the boardroom.'

He almost smiled at the passive-aggressive dig under the breezy welcome. Yes, he was last. He'd planned it that way. In, out, shortest time possible.

He managed to keep his heart rate under control, and his demeanour calm as she opened the door and he passed her into the boardroom. Jeremy Sprite, his father's lawyer for many years, was at the head of the table, with his brother and Demi next to each other on the faraway side, in front of floor-to-ceiling windows overlooking the stunning winter view of the city.

His internal dialogue kicked into damage-limitation mode. *Act cool. Calm. You've got this.*

Demi started to rise, so he automatically went round to their side of the table and kissed her on each cheek, as any dutiful stepson would do, despite the obvious fact that they were almost the same age and if they'd gone to the same high school, they could have been classmates. Next, he shook Jason's hand, ignoring his brother's predictably knuckle-crunching squeeze, but clocking the slight wariness, or maybe apprehension, in his eyes as he said, 'Glad you made it.'

In his impeccably cut suit and red tie, Jason looked exactly what he was – a successful property developer who was all about business. When Lachlan had seen him at the funeral, the focus had been on their father's passing, and they'd managed to keep their distance and avoid contact during the service. Lachlan had wondered how he'd feel today, facing him in a room, and now he knew. Jason's general air of entitlement. His raised chin of superiority. His smug face. Lachlan had never hated him more. And judging by Jason's refusal to meet his eye, the feeling was mutual.

Lachlan shook Jeremy Sprite's hand, then sat down opposite them, on a camel leather chair with a chrome frame that probably cost more than his couch at home.

The lawyer got straight to it, taking the lead. 'Thank you all for coming today and I want to reassure you that this won't take long. Your father took the unusual step of insisting that you all be present today for the reading of the will, and the reason that he did so will become apparent as we continue.'

Lachlan noticed that a pulse was throbbing on the side of Jason's face – his lifelong tell that he was focused and ready for battle. Lachlan had no idea what there could be to fight about, but he didn't much care. He'd be naïve if he didn't think there was a significant inheritance coming. Their father had been driven. Relentless. Focused. Like Lachlan, his dad had also started his working life in as an apprentice joiner on a building site. His street-smarts and ambition needed no further evidence than the reality that he'd ended his working life with considerable wealth, a substantial property portfolio and a reputation for being a savvy businessman who trusted his gut and reaped the rewards.

'I have had the privilege of being your father's lawyer for almost thirty years and what I'm about to read is your father's wishes for the dispersal of his estate.'

He then went on to spout a whole lot of legal jargon, before getting to the point of it all.

'As you know, Martyn liquidated substantial assets before purchasing the house in Monaco, and that home is hereby bequeathed in entirety to his wife, Demi.'

Demi sniffed and dabbed her eyes with a hanky and Lachlan could be wrong, but he was pretty sure Jason rolled his eyes.

'In a similar vein, and in accordance with Scottish law, Demi is hereby awarded fifty per cent of his moveable estate, approximately £250,000 pounds sterling.'

So his dad had half a million in the bank when he died.

'That's all he had? Half a million?' That astonished outburst came from Jason, and the pulse on his cheek was beginning to look like a gobstopper that could explode at any minute.

'Your father did anticipate that you would question that amount, but he wanted you to know that he has taken considerable and deliberate steps to spend his wealth over the last few years. I believe that after the death of your mother, he made the decision to – as he put it – enjoy every day like it was his last.'

Lachlan smiled – he'd heard his dad say that on every occasion they'd met up since Mum died, so that wasn't a surprise.

'He does also have a substantial overseas property portfolio, with a current value of over a million pounds, which has also been bequeathed to you, Demi.'

Another big sniff and more cheek dabbing, but this time there was a good chance it was tears of joy. Demi was now set up for life. And if that was the cost of giving Dad his last few years of happiness, then good on her.

'No way! Fuck that,' Jason spat.

Jeremy shut down the objection. 'I understand your surprise, but I can assure you that was your father's wish. But please let me continue. I now turn to your father's assets in the UK. Technically speaking, under law, the offspring is entitled to fifty per cent of the moveable estate, which in this case is the cash reserves only, and it would be split equally between you both,' he said, addressing both Jason and Lachlan now.

'So all we get is 125 grand each?' Jason's voice was two octaves higher than usual, but Lachlan stayed silent. It was Dad's money, his lifetime earnings. As far as he was concerned, his dad had every right to leave it to whoever he damn well pleased.

'That's not quite all,' the lawyer continued, an unmistakable reprimand in his tone. 'As you may know, your parents owned a large dwelling on the edge of the village of Burnbank, which passed solely to your father after your mother's death...'

Burnbank. That was where they'd grown up until they were six or seven, when Dad had moved them all into the Georgian terrace in the Park Circus area of the city. Lachlan had lived there until he'd started work and moved into a flat with some mates, while eighteen-year-old Jason had borrowed fifty-grand off their dad to do his first property deal. Dad had sold the Park Circus home when he'd moved to Monaco, but Lachlan wasn't even aware that he'd still owned the Burnbank house.

'And he also owned a commercial property in the village of Weirbridge. If I remember correctly, your father bought it for your mother's fortieth birthday – a sentimental gesture as it was where they'd met.'

Twinges of familiarity dropped in now that this story was unfolding. His parents had both been fifteen when they'd met, and yes, it was in the café where a young Felicity McSlay had worked after school. When Jason and Lachlan were kids, she'd occasionally take them back there in the summer holidays, and she told them that story every time. How his dad had walked in, she'd served him a can of Irn-Bru and a bacon roll, and it had been love at first sight. Lachlan was pretty sure she was romanticising the tale, but the smile on her face every time she told it made him believe it.

Jeremy Sprite was still speaking. 'Your father has instructed that both properties be sold upon his death. He didn't want there to be any disagreements as to the path forward. Proceeds from the house have been bequeathed to Demi, and – I must stress that this is a crucial point – as long as there is no contest to the will, the revenue from the sale of the café is to be divided equally between his sons.'

'How much are they worth?' Jason cut right to the chase, but Jeremy didn't flinch. 'We've had them both surveyed and the manor house is worth approximately £1.2 million in its current condition, and the commercial property, which consists of the café and the apartment above it, is worth roughly £360K. The tenants have already moved out of the home, and a sixty-day termination of lease has been served on the commercial property.'

'Christ, this is all going to take months,' Jason groaned, making his feelings clear. 'I want it sold way quicker than that.' Lachlan didn't understand the issue. Jason's greed aside, this was a gift – more than they were legally due – so why did he have such a stick up his ass about it? Especially when his brother's property development company could probably buy everything Lachlan owned and not even notice the dent in its bank account.

Jeremy hadn't finished. 'This brings me to the reason for this meeting. Jason and Lachlan, your father wanted to be assured that today would not cause prolonged issues between you all, so this offer stands only if it is accepted today. I have the documents here for your signature' – he slid an A4 sheet of paper towards each of them – 'with the disclaimer being that if you decide to contest his will, and pursue assets granted to your stepmother, you will forfeit the proceeds from the Scottish properties and retain only the cash sum as decreed by Scottish law. If you accept his terms, then the proceeds of the property will be transferred to you on conclusion of the sale.'

Lachlan had to supress an urge to laugh. Clever old Dad. He would have known that Jason would come for blood and make life miserable for Demi, so he'd put a safeguard in place. Lachlan knew he should perhaps feel slighted too, but he stuck to his earlier position – it was his dad's money to do with as he pleased. He didn't even have to think about it. He reached forward, took one of the pens that were in the centre of the table. 'Sounds fine to me.'

'Lachlan, don't...' Jason blurted, but Lachlan ignored him and signed on the dotted line before sliding the document back to the lawyer.

'Your father said you would do this,' Jeremy said, with a faint smile and maybe a touch of affection.

'He was usually right,' Lachlan replied. 'Are we done here?'

'We are.'

Lachlan stood up. 'Great. Demi, I wish you the best, and thank you for the happiness you gave my father. Jason, have a nice life. I wish you both well.'

And with that, he turned and left the room, jumping into the lift just as the doors were about to close on two women who'd entered before him.

Down in the lobby, he pulled off his tie as he left the lift, but had only gone a few steps when a panting Jason emerged from a door with a 'stairs' sign on it.

'Lachlan! Look, signing that was a mistake. We need to challenge it. Find a way to sell the café quicker and contest the rest of it. Get more. Can we go somewhere and talk?'

'Jason, like I said, I wish you well.' That might be a lie. 'But I've got nothing to say to you.' That definitely wasn't. 'I'll see you around.' Again, not true, but with that, Lachlan turned and began to cross the wide expanse of the reception area, stopping at the desk to hand in his security pass. Out of the corner of his eye, he saw Jason shake his head, then turn back and summon the lift. He must be going back up to argue his case. Good luck to him. Lachlan wasn't interested.

Both receptionists were busy, so he waited, thinking that the woman in front of him, brown hair pulled back in a ponytail, wearing a bright red duffel coat and jeans, was a stark contrast to the formal business wear all around him.

'Yes, I'd like to see Mr Sprite please. My name is Alyssa Canavan,' he heard her say.

'Do you have an appointment?'

'No, but it's really important.'

There was something about the urgency in her voice and the panic on her face that made him adjust his attitude. As the other receptionist came off the phone and accepted his lanyard, it was a reminder that no matter how much he'd hated the last couple of hours, there was always someone out there having an even worse day.

Now he just had to get out of this building, away from Glasgow and far from his memories, and then it would be over.

NOON – 2 P.M.

9

JESSIE

With the girls gone, and not another customer in the café, Hugo had given in to pressure and joined them at the table for a cuppa.

'Since it's your special day, Jessie – how could I refuse? Although, you're missing out with the whole birthday, retirement and going away party in one night – you should have spread it around and milked each one separately.'

'I like your thought process there, Hugo. Might have been a good idea, since I don't think anyone will be daft enough to come out in this weather tonight. It might just be the four of us and your Alyssa, all snowed in here, at this rate.'

In her peripheral vision, Jessie saw that evoke an expression of horror from Dorinda, who was sitting on a stool behind the counter, filing her nails. Jessie reckoned Alyssa's mother was probably pretending she was anywhere else but here. Might be the first time she agreed with any sentiment from Dorinda Canavan. The woman's very presence was making Jessie grind her teeth, and what were the chances that today of all days she'd be subjected to the sight of her?

'How's your Stan spending his last day here then, Jessie?' Hugo asked, still warming his hands on his mug.

Glad of the distraction, Jessie gave the same answer she could have given on almost any day since he'd retired. 'He's up at the golf club, hitting a few balls.'

'In this weather?' Val asked, surprised.

Jessie nodded. 'Aye. They've got one of those simulators.'

Cathy's head swivelled like it was on stick. 'I saw an advert for one of those on telly last night. A doctor was saying they could work wonders for your muscles. I think you can get them on prescription. Although, I don't suppose they use them for the personal bits at the golf club.'

Jessie and Val's eyes locked in a battle of restraint, before Val cracked and muttered, 'I'll take this one', then turned to Cathy.

'Cathy, love, what are you talking about?'

'Those things you were on about,' she replied, perplexed. 'Stimulators.'

As the others let out a hoot of hilarity, Jessie shook her head woefully. 'Dear Lord, Cathy, you need to get those hearing aids fixed.'

Jessie took one last sip of what was left of her tea and put the mug on top of a plate that was now empty, bar a few cake crumbs. Much as she was enjoying passing the time of day with Hugo, being in the same space as Dorinda was grating on her and she didn't trust herself to be civil to her for much longer.

'Well, Hugo, it's been a slice of heaven, but we're off across the road to get beautified.'

Hugo let out a whistle as he shook his head, a twinkle in his eye as he got up from his chair. 'Replying to that would be a political correctness nightmare these days, so I'll just say you all already look lovely.'

'Smart man,' Cathy said, kicking off a round of goodbye hugs.

Jessie was next. 'You'll be here for my party tonight, won't you, Hugo? Only, there's going to be a karaoke machine and I've heard you've got a fine pair of lungs on you.' It was the ultimate Glasgow compliment to someone's vocal talents.

'Aye, I wouldn't miss it, but trust me, no one needs to hear my singing. My dance moves, on the other hand…' He let that one lie, as Val giggled.

'Right then, Michael Flatley, we'll prepare to be impressed.'

Hugo was still chuckling as he lifted their empty plates and made his way to the kitchen with them.

'See you later, Dorinda,' Jessie shouted over to the woman sitting behind the counter, taking no part in the conversation. The words were friendly, but anyone who knew her well would detect the undertone of disdain, so, of course, Val immediately reacted with the levitation of her right eyebrow, a solemn act that was only used in times of deep suspicion or imminent fury. 'Don't you raise that eyebrow at me, Val Murray,' Jessie murmured, out of earshot of everyone else. 'You know fine well that Dorinda Canavan has never been my favourite person.'

Val remained silent, as Jessie knew she would. There were two unassailable facts about Val, garnered from decades of being her pal. The first was that there wasn't a single event, scandal or piece of gossip in this village that didn't make its way to her at some point. The second was that when it came to her pals, she was the equivalent of a human vault – nothing came past those Avon Hot Pink lips.

'Goodbye, ladies,' Dorinda said, and Jessie immediately clocked the fake smile and the reciprocal passive-aggressive undercurrent. 'Have a lovely time tonight, Jessie. Looking forward to it.'

Of course, Jessie had invited her. The party tonight came with an open invitation to everyone in the village, and given that it was in Alyssa's café, and Hugo and Ginny would both be there, Jessie couldn't exactly tell Dorinda she wouldn't be welcome, no matter how she felt about her. She'd hoped that, given their unspoken dislike for each other, Dorinda would do the decent thing and not show up, but now she saw that wasn't the case. That woman was bold as brass.

The three friends gathered their things and pulled on their coats, all of them having to give Cathy a wide berth, because she'd doubled in size now that she'd donned her enormous puffa coat.

'Jesus, Cathy, if you fancy going out at Halloween as a Space Hopper, you've already got the outfit,' Val quipped as they headed for the door.

Outside, Jessie's gaze went from one end of Main Street to the other, taking in the glistening white clouds that had settled over the community centre, the church, the rows of shops both sides of the tree-lined streets. Many of her friends had moved away over the years, especially in her younger days, when they were all going off to college, or getting married to people from other areas, but Jessie had never wanted to follow that path. Not for a second had she regretted staying in Weirbridge, and it still hadn't quite sunk in that after tomorrow morning, she'd no longer wake up in Weirbridge, in her own bed, in her own house, under her own duvet, and then wander up to the café for a cuppa. In her imagination, before the Tenerife retirement had been floated, that's how this next chapter of her life had always looked, and she hadn't yet found the will to change that mental image, no matter how much Stan tried to help her visualise sun, sea and their new life abroad together.

When they'd first talked about it, he'd reminded her of all the good times they'd shared in the Tenerife house over the years. All those wonderful holidays, when they'd go to a local café for breakfast with the kids, before going off to the beach or the pool for the day. Or later, after Grant and Georgie had grown up and no longer travelled with them, they'd sit on the balcony and drink freshly squeezed orange juice, before he went off to play golf and she'd pass the time wandering around Los Cristianos, sometimes meeting up with friends who were out there at the same time. Of course, then Kayleigh had arrived, and Georgie and Flynn would travel with them, glad of the free accommodation, the sunshine and the readily available babysitter, and Jessie would encourage them because she loved every second with her granddaughter.

But tomorrow would be different. It was just her and Stan. That was it. No one else. And much as she loved him, she couldn't seem to convince herself that was enough.

The bell above the door dinged as they entered Copper Curls, and Jessie instinctively smiled, as she did every morning when she came in here. The renovation last year had been worth every penny, and it helped her sleep at night to know that she was leaving Georgie with a business that they'd built together, and one that was thriving.

She'd only gone two steps in the door, when Grant popped his head up from under the reception desk and threw his arms out.

'Mother!'

Jessie jumped, then immediately melted as he slammed into her for a hug. 'You're back! Och, son, I've missed you. Don't try the hug with your Aunt Cathy though. Look at her – you'll bounce off and do yourself an injury.'

Ah, her boy. And yes, she still thought of him as 'her boy', despite the fact that he was in his thirties. She adored the bones of him, and was endlessly proud that, like Georgie, he'd grown up to be a decent human with a good heart. Although, that was where the similarities between them ended because he and Georgie were like chalk and cheese. Georgie was such a home bird, but this one? He'd always known exactly what he wanted. He'd worked in Copper Curls on Saturdays when he was still at school, but as soon as he'd left full-time education, he'd donned a leather jacket and a pair of trendy cargos and waltzed his rainbow-coloured locks straight into the trendiest salon in Glasgow. He'd saved up for a couple of months to book a style and blow dry with the owner so that he would have forty-five minutes of undivided attention. He'd told the owner about his experience, showed him photos of the edgy styles he'd inflicted on his mates, offered to work for free for a month and assured him he wouldn't regret giving him a chance.

He'd been right about that. Grant had worked his socks off there for years, going to college on day release until he was fully qualified, then building up his own client base until he was one of the most sought after and well-known stylists in the city. It hadn't been a surprise when he'd taken off to London, ten years ago, and opened a salon in Kensington that had become a roaring success. Although, much as she could burst with pride, she'd missed him every day since.

'I was worried you wouldn't get here with the snow,' Jessie told him.

'Mother, I'd have skied here if I had to. I wouldn't miss it. Gabriel sends his love and told me to let you know he's taking you to the Ritz on your next trip to London. He's got a full shooting schedule this week or you know he'd have been here.'

Gabriel. Grant's partner and one of the much-loved presenters of *The Morning Lift*, a live wellness and positivity show that was on every morning at 10 a.m. They'd met when Grant had done a guest spot about the potential comeback of the mullet, and it had been an instant case of opposites attracting. Gabriel was a very professional, dashing TV personality from the Home Counties, while Grant was the cool, trendsetting hair entrepreneur, who'd never lost his Glaswegian, working-class accent or his love of a leather jacket. Despite their differences, or maybe because of them, they'd shacked up and lived happily ever after. Jessie adored him, although, the whole 'live TV' schedule did get in the way of their socialising.

As she let Grant go, Jessie's cheeks were beaming so brightly they could heat the salon. 'I'll text him and tell him I'll take him up on the Ritz and that we'll miss him tonight.'

'He'll love that,' Grant said, before hugging Val and then stretching his arms to reach round Cathy.

'Where's your sister?' Jessie glanced around for Georgie, just as she made an appearance through the door from the staffroom.

'Sorry, Mum, I was just in the loo. Loving the coat, Aunt Cathy.'

'I'm glad someone around here has taste,' Cathy said, with a pointed glare at Jessie before she giggled and cuddled her niece.

Despite the joviality, Jessie could see the tightness of Georgie's smile, and the shadow of sadness in her eyes. Her girl looked tired. Weary. But then, Jessie knew this week was going to be an adjustment for her daughter too. They'd worked together every day for over twenty years, since Georgie came straight out of school.

Stan said time and time again that this was going to be great for Georgie, and she'd be delighted to have her independence and financial security, but looking at her now, Jessie wasn't so sure.

While Grant poured champagne for them and regaled Cathy and Val with tales of sitting next to Lewis Capaldi on the flight up here, she slipped her arm around Georgie's waist and whispered, 'Are you okay, ma love?'

'I'm fine, Mum.'

Jessie almost believed her. Almost. Something was definitely bothering her daughter and it could only be that Jessie was leaving. Unless it was that bloody Flynn. She was well aware that her son-in-law knew he'd royally messed up and would give anything for Georgie to take him back. Much as she'd always had a soft spot for the son-in-law she'd known since he was a teenager, Jessie had no intention of intervening or giving her opinion. It had always been her stance that where marriages, relationships and tender hearts were involved, sometimes it was best to keep her mouth shut and let things play out.

Georgie got out of the scrutiny by getting to work. 'Right, Aunt Cathy, you're with me – let's get you up to the basins and get you started with your rinse.'

Grant followed suit. 'And Val, you hit the jackpot. Fresh from my glittering, critically acclaimed salon in London, where I coiffure the heads of some of the nation's biggest names, I'm going to grab a roller tray and get started on your bouffant.' He then added with mock weariness, 'I've no idea how my life came to this,' incurring a nudge in the ribs from Val.

'Mum, I'll be back for you as soon as I've got Aunt Cathy's colour on. You just put your feet up...' Georgie wheeled a footstool over from the nearest station, and propped it under Jessie's moon boots. 'And enjoy your champagne. Here's those Lindt balls that you love...' With a flourish, she produced a bowl of Jessie's favourite chocolates from behind the desk, and put them on her lap. 'And I'll put a bit of Boyzone on the music system for you.'

Jessie gave a grateful, contented sigh. 'This is what I always imagined heaven was like.'

As the others all went off to the basin area at the back of the salon, Jessie unwrapped a Lindt truffle and popped it in her mouth, before closing her eyes and resting her head on the freshly painted cream wall. This was what retirement should be. The bliss of relaxing with her pals. Of being around the people she loved. Of doing a bit of... what was it the young ones called it? Self care. Yep, that was it. And maybe it was the champagne going straight to her head, but somehow, the voice that she'd been ignoring for weeks and months seemed to have mustered the courage to demand that it be heard.

I don't want to go.

And then the acknowledgement made it bolder, and it repeated even louder this time...

I don't want to go.

She felt two tears squeeze out of her closed lids and hastily wiped them away.

I don't want to go.

But how could she not? Everything was arranged, packed, sorted. The For Sale sign was probably being erected outside her house as she sat there. If that bloody snow let up, then her whole world was gathering tonight for a birthday-slash-retirement-slash-going away party. And all of that didn't even come close to the most important factor of all – Stan had his heart set on this. He'd been planning this for years, counting down the days, and she couldn't just pull the rug out from under his golf shoes – not after forty-odd years of marriage. They'd had a partnership that had ebbed and flowed, like all relationships, but they'd stuck it out because at the core of their bond they had love, they had friendship, and they had loyalty.

The voice in her head popped back in, and now it was getting way too argumentative.

Is that right, Jessie? Did you really have all those things?

Now that it was emboldened, Jessie knew that no amount of Lindt chocolate was going to quieten the internal monologue, because it wasn't wrong. Love and friendship? Yes. But loyalty?

The sight of Dorinda Canavan's smug face this morning replayed in her mind. Maybe she needed to face the truth on that loyalty thing. Maybe now that it was crunch time, her stance of keeping her mouth shut and letting things play out wasn't the best way to deal with life after all.

'You look deep in thought there, doll,' Val interrupted her, and when Jessie opened her eyes, she watched her pal, wet hair in an elaborate pink turban, plonk herself down on the chair next to her, pick up a magazine from the table beside her and begin flicking through it.

'I was.'

Now or never. Say it, don't say it. Pick that scab or leave it alone? The voice was yelling, *Do it.*

'You know Val, in all the years, we've never discussed this. But I think the time has come.'

Val didn't even look up from her magazine as her computer-grade brain rewound to possible explanations for the demand. 'No, I didn't nick the puffball skirt off your washing line in 1982, and yes, the Bay City Rollers were the best band of our lifetime. Although they could only worship at the temple of the god that is Tom Jones.'

Jessie was at a loss at to how to respond for a second. Val's mind truly did work in mysterious ways. As the pause stretched, Val finally lifted her gaze.

'Sorry. Did I miss the topic there?'

Jessie tried to smile, but her facial muscles weren't responding. This was the first time she was about to say this out loud. And once it was out, there was no taking it back. It would exist. Maybe only as a conversation that would never be repeated, but it would still be there.

But right now, she didn't have a choice. Because if she was about to give up everything she loved and turn the rest of her life over to one person, then she had to know that person was deserving of it.

Jessie took a deep breath, exhaled, braced herself.

'I need you to tell me everything you know about what happened between my Stan and Dorinda Canavan.'

10

GEORGIE

Georgie's body was at the colouring station, chatting away to her Aunt Cathy while carefully sectioning her curly locks and applying a purple hue that didn't actually exist in the sphere of human or animal hair, but her mind was somewhere else altogether.

She still hadn't made the call back to the TV company to reject the job of Ollie Chiles' on-set hairdresser in Colorado and LA.

When she'd greeted him with the news of the official offer, Grant had delayed the inevitable by attempting to offer a counter-argument to immediate refusal. He'd taken her hand, nodding thoughtfully, as he'd said, 'Georgie, let's slow down and think about this.' He'd then immediately rebounded and offered a very definite, 'Okay, I've thought about it and come to the conclusion that you've lost your mind if you don't take the job.'

She'd lifted her head from the desk. 'You're not helping.'

'I am. You just can't see it. Georgie, this is the kind of offer that doesn't come along twice and you should snatch it like your life depends on it. Why don't you just close the salon for six months and go do it?'

Georgie's shoulders had sagged. 'I can't. You know better than anyone that when you close a salon you have the potential to lose all your business. It might never recover. All it would take would be for another shop to open and poach all our clients and then there would be no coming back.'

He knew that was true, so he'd switched tack.

'Okay, fine. But this salon isn't the only option. You're an exceptionally talented hairdresser. If *The Clansman* thing turns out to be short term, you could go to another salon, maybe go into the city.'

Georgie had a ready-prepared argument for that one too.

'I don't want to traipse into Glasgow every day. Besides, I'm way too neurotic and not great with authority. The minute some temperamental arse bossed me around, I'd be out of there. Or all the other staff would be ruthlessly glamorous, and I'd spend every lunchtime in the toilet researching non-surgical facelifts and scrolling the Zara website for new outfits.'

She knew her younger brother would have trouble comprehending her insecurities because he was everything that she wasn't. Assertive. Trailblazing. Bold. He was the kid that had persuaded his mother to dye his hair blue in high school, and none of the other lads had even considered challenging him about it, because he was so fricking cool.

Grant had always had big plans and ambitions, but Georgie had happily taken a different path. After she'd fallen pregnant at nineteen, she'd been so madly and mutually in love with Flynn that they'd insisted – despite Jessie's request to take their time – on waltzing up the aisle.

'Oh, and Flynn says he wants me back too. Today is the gift that just keeps on giving.'

'Urgh, he's a twat,' Grant had groaned. Unlike Jessie, her brother wasn't great at keeping his feelings to himself and he'd never quite forgiven Flynn for doing a runner.

Time had given Georgie more of a balanced perspective on that, though. They'd been twenty years old when Kayleigh was born and they'd been together since they were kids themselves. Maybe it was inevitable that almost two decades later they'd need space to figure out who they were. Maybe it wasn't too late for them to give it another go. They'd been happy for a long time and if he hadn't made that one mistake, she was certain that they'd still be together. And although Kayleigh was saying she was fine with their divorce, Georgie knew how pleased their daughter would be if they were one unit again. Maybe this was how it was supposed to play out. Perhaps they were being given this second chance because there was true meaning in them choosing each other again. She could hardly tell him that everything was going to be tickety-boo if she had any intention of buggering off to Colorado.

As for Kayleigh – how would her daughter feel about her mother globetrotting across to America? Actually, that argument didn't really hold up, because Georgie knew she'd be thrilled about the whole thing. Kayleigh had already made it clear that she'd probably only come back to the village for special occasions or to visit her mum, so the prospect of spending her university holidays abroad, on *The Clansman* set, would thrill her. Not only was it one of Kayleigh's favourite shows, but she loved travelling, so it would tick all the boxes. If Georgie broached the possibility of coming to Colorado for Christmas, Kayleigh would have her bag packed and be at the airport before Georgie finished the question.

Okay, so other than the fact that Georgie hated the thought of being thousands of miles away from her daughter, she knew Kayleigh would be on Grant's positivity bus about this opportunity. Which meant that number one on the objection list was leaving the salon and thereby breaking her mother's heart and possibly wrecking her retirement. Number two? Rejecting the chance to reunite with her former husband and potentially live a long and happy life together.

However, Grant had refused to let the new Flynn information detract him from his argument. 'Let me ask you… If it was up to you, and there were no outside complications, no other people to consider, would you want to take this job?' He'd registered her hesitation. 'Stop thinking about it and just give me your first reaction.'

'Okay, yes. I would. But life isn't that simple because the reality is that I do have other people to consider. And… Oh shit…' Her attention had been broken by a sight in her peripheral vision. Outside the window. Three well-insulated ladies in padded coats, furry hats and boots that could take them on an Arctic expedition, were leaving the Once Upon A Time Café across the road, and wading through the snow, towards them.

'They're on the way. Let me go fix myself up, or Mum's spider senses will kick in. You know she can detect problems like a fricking sniffer dog.'

With that, she'd bolted to the staffroom, brushed her hair, put on a coat of lippy, sprayed a dash of perfume, pulled her shoulders back and slapped a breezy smile on her face before making an entrance and greeting the new arrivals.

She'd got away with it, but only just. Her mum's maternal sniffer dog had identified an issue, but she'd been too distracted by the occasion to pursue it and thankfully, she was now too busy chatting to Val to bring her laser-focus back to Georgie.

'Right, Aunt Cathy, that's you for thirty minutes,' she announced, carefully wrapping a towel around Cathy's neck to catch any errant drips. 'Why don't you take a seat down next to Mum and Val, and I'll get you another champagne.'

'Will do, pet. But before I go...' The last part of the sentence was delivered in a whisper, so Georgie leaned in as close as possible, without risking a purple face.

'Do you think your mum is okay? I'm worried about her. She's doing that thing where she's acting happy, but her smile isn't reaching her eyes. The last time I saw that was at her sixtieth birthday party, right before her appendix burst.'

Georgie remembered that one way too well. Her mum had been so grateful for her surprise party, so happy to see everyone, so determined not to spoil the night, that she didn't mention the not-too-insignificant fact that her stomach felt like it was being eviscerated, until she passed out, then came round on a stretcher on the way to surgery.

'I think she's just sad about saying goodbye.'

Aunt Cathy looked worried. 'Do you think she's having second thoughts about going?'

Georgie was happy to reassure her. 'No. I mean, today must be bittersweet because it's her last day, but she's been saying for years how much she's looking forward to going and starting a new life in the sun with Dad. It'll be good for them to put themselves first for a change – they deserve this.'

If Georgie didn't already have a whole list of reasons backing up her refusal to make any move that could mess with her mother's plans, saying that aloud cemented her absolute conviction that turning *The Clansman* job down was the right thing to do. No more procrastination. As soon as they were gone, she was making the call. A sudden wave of relief made her shoulders drop from the tense position they'd held all day and she felt lighter. More positive. She'd probably hate working on a TV set anyway. All those prima donnas and the unlimited food carts – she'd come home irritated and three stone heavier.

She escorted Aunt Cathy over to the free chair next to her mum and Aunt Val, who were still deep in conversation, having sent Grant out to the bakers along the street for some festive mince pies. 'My London clients do the same thing,' he'd retorted, amused sarcasm dripping from his words. 'Can't get through a set of highlights without being sent for a steak bake and a vanilla slice.'

As Georgie approached, she wondered, though, if maybe Aunt Cathy had a point. Her mum's face was etched with sadness and her eyes were bloodshot, as if she'd been crying. Maybe leaving was hitting her harder than Georgie had realised. But, of course, Mum wouldn't admit that, because she never liked to burden anyone with her woes. She was definitely of that 'keep quiet and get on with it' generation.

Georgie decided she wasn't going to let the last hours they had together be steeped in sadness, so she had no hesitation in interrupting them. 'Right, ladies, let's get this going-away pamper session into full swing.' She nipped down to reception for the champagne bottles, then came back and topped up everyone's glass, before pulling out her phone and changing the music. 'What we need is a bit of this...' she said, grinning, as the sound of Abba's 'Dancing Queen' blared from the shop's speakers. 'And a bit of this...' She continued, taking Aunt Cathy's hand and spinning her around for a dance.

Of course, Val and her mum did the only thing they could do under the circumstances – they got their bums out of the chairs and joined them, singing at the top of their lungs. And yes, there were tears in Mum's eyes again, but this time Georgie knew that they were happy ones. Mum had always said that there was nothing in life that couldn't be fixed by a dance and a bit of Abba.

By the time Grant returned, thirty minutes after he'd left and clutching a large box from the baker's and two more bottles of bubbly from the off-licence, they'd switched from 'Dancing Queen' to the Bee Gees and Barry, Maurice and Robin were doing the Saturday Night Fever strut up the middle of the salon, while Georgie howled with laughter as she danced on the sidelines. This was more like it. This was the day her mum deserved.

Grant hit the ground running, topping the glasses up yet again, before the three of them collapsed back into their chairs, party mood activated, ready for their pampering. Grant got to work sharpening up Val's razor-edged blonde bob, while Georgie gave her mum's copper curls a quick trim, before slathering on the coconut mousse that Jessie adored.

Cathy was given the salon's iPad, and put in charge of the tunes, effortlessly switching from the Bee Gees, to the Rolling Stones, to Whitney Houston, to Robbie Williams, to Madonna. There was a slight glitch when she pressed the wrong button and they got a quick blast of Metallica, but she soon realised they didn't know the words, and saved the day with Fleetwood Mac's 'Dreams'. The five of them were belting it out, so carried away in the moment that Georgie barely heard the ding at the door announcing a new arrival. She glanced over to the entrance and saw a small blonde woman, pretty, maybe in her late twenties or early thirties – it was impossible to be accurate with all the Botox, filler and procedures available these days. Only last week she'd had a new client she would have placed at thirty-five and it turned out she was a fifty-eight-year-old grandmother who'd gone to Turkey for a facelift.

Georgie switched off the hairdryer and left the bedlam behind her as she went to the front of the shop, greeting the new arrival with an apologetic smile.

'I'm really sorry, but we're not open today – I can make you an appointment for later in the week?'

The woman shook her head. 'No... no thanks.' Georgie noticed that the stranger was eyeing her up and down, frowning. Some people could be so judgemental. They pop in here for some hair product or a gift card and have an attitude the minute they step over the threshold.

'Well, sorry – like I said, we're not open today.'

She expected that to be the end of it, but the woman didn't turn and leave. Instead, she stood her ground as she said, 'Are you Georgie?'

Ah, maybe she'd been recommended by a client and just wanted some advice. Or a job. Yes, that was it! That would explain why she seemed so edgy.

Georgie immediately felt a pang of empathy and smiled to put her at ease. 'I am. Can I help you?'

'Yes. Or at least I think so. I want to know if you're sleeping with my boyfriend.'

11
ALYSSA

The tyres of Alyssa's Citroen Berlingo van crunched in the snow as they turned into the street on the south side of the city that housed the Moira Chiles Academy of Drama and Music. She'd bought the second-hand van when she first opened the café, and it may be ten years old and have questionable suspension, but it had allowed her to offer home catering and takeaways in her local areas. She was pretty sure there was still a box of cupcakes in the back, after Ginny messed up a phone order yesterday and took a dozen cupcakes to a customer who'd requested twelve vegan vol-au-vents.

Although, if things went the way Ginny hoped at her interview today, Alyssa was about to lose her most unreliable, yet essential, extra pair of hands.

Ginny had been brushing up on her factual information for the last fifteen minutes of the journey, recounting the facts out loud so that they'd have more chance of sticking. 'The Academy was founded by the actor, Ollie Chiles – by the way, I totally would – and named after his mother, who was a singer...' Ginny had broken off. 'That's the woman that Mum was talking about this morning, isn't it? Moved to the village last year and sometimes comes into the café? A large cappuccino and a ginger slice?'

'What?' Alyssa had answered, distracted, then she'd run the conversation back in her head until she'd reached the correct answer. 'Yes. She's really nice. Gets her hair done over at Copper Curls.'

Ginny had nodded. 'I hope she's here today and part of the interview panel. Would you be upset if I offered her free ginger slices for life if she gives me the job? I'm not above a bit of bribery.'

'No, but you'll have to be quick, because apparently I won't have a café in sixty days.'

'Oh shit, sorry. Here's me rambling on about an interview and you're on the verge of losing everything...'

'Thank you for the recap,' Alyssa had said, with a sad smile, before giving herself a shake and focussing on her enthusiasm for Ginny's opportunity the rest of the way. Now, as she brought the van to a stop outside an old church building, a huge sign on the front announced they were in the right place. When she pulled on the handbrake, she turned to her sister, pushing her own woes to the side yet again. 'I'll wait here.' She leaned over and gave Ginny a hug. 'You're going to get this job because you're brilliant and talented and they'd be lucky to have you.'

'Brilliant and talented and they'd be lucky to have me,' Ginny repeated, as if memorising that too. 'Honest to God, I'd rather recite *The Gruffalo* in front of a hundred five year-old schoolkids than be interviewed by a panel. And five-year-old schoolkids are brutal.'

A primary-school reading tour was just one of the many gigs Ginny had taken on in the last few years as she'd attempted to make a living while at college, and then as a jobbing actress. Alyssa knew she'd be brilliant in the role that she was about to interview for, though. Teaching drama and music to teenagers was right in Ginny's wheelhouse – she was incredibly talented but super-cool and relatable too. Alyssa just hoped the panel saw that in her today, and that she got the job, because worrying about Ginny was just another big fat cherry of problems on the icing of the shitshow of a cake that had been delivered today.

As Ginny climbed out of the van, Alyssa shouted another, 'Good luck,' and gave a cheery thumbs up, before dropping the smile immediately when Ginny disappeared through the doors.

She let her head fall onto the steering wheel, and left it there for a while, until it stopped aching. What. A. Nightmare. Her cunning plan to speak to the lawyer had been a total waste of time too. They'd stopped at his office on the way here and she'd begged the receptionist to let her speak to Jeremy Sprite, but after a phone call, she'd been told that Mr Sprite wasn't available.

'Can you ask when he will be free?' she'd asked, not accustomed to being forceful, but feeling like she had no choice.

The receptionist had grudgingly picked up her phone again, hit a few buttons and asked the same question, although, for all Alyssa knew, she could have been talking to a dialling tone, because the second call got them no further forward. When she'd put the phone down, she'd simply said, 'Mr Sprite's secretary has advised once again that he's unavailable. She suggests that you put your request to see him in an email and he'll respond accordingly.'

Accordingly? What did that even mean.

A loud bang on the van window shocked her out of her thoughts and she jolted her head up to see an elderly man in a flat cap and thick peacoat, with his face pressed up against the window. As soon as she reacted, he pulled his head back and she watched him smile with what looked like relief. She quickly rolled down the window.

'Jeezo, lass, you gave me a fright there. I thought you were deid,' he told her, chuckling.

'Sorry, no! I mean, not sorry that I'm alive, but sorry if I scared you.'

'Och, that's okay. Sometimes we just need to test that the old ticker is still working,' he told her, clutching his heart as he wandered off down the street.

After the absolute wankery she'd just been thinking about, it was a much-needed reminder that some people could be nice. Which took her back to her earlier thought about her landlord's family. Maybe they were decent people who would listen to her. And just because she couldn't speak to the tosser of a lawyer – who might actually be a very nice man, but she wasn't prepared to give him the benefit of the doubt after he refused to see her – didn't mean that she should give up. This was just an obstacle that she had to find a way to overcome because she damn well wasn't going to lose her home and her business without a fight. Maybe there was another way to reach the people she needed to speak to. Inspired, she lifted her phone from the centre console between the driver and passenger seat and googled Martyn Morden. An obituary in *The Herald* newspaper from several weeks ago was the first thing that popped up.

> It is with deep sadness that the family of Martyn Morden, husband, father, and notable Scottish businessman, announce his passing on the 10th October 2025.

Nearly two months ago. That made her feel two things – first of all, sadness at the loss of this poor man's life, and then a depressing realisation that the events that had led to this moment had kicked off weeks ago, and she'd had absolutely no idea that her future was in jeopardy this whole time.

She skimmed through the rest of the obituary, which listed a whole load of Mr Morden's achievements in business and philanthropic endeavours. Given that it was a long list, it seemed like maybe he was a decent kind of guy after all. Hopefully those genes had been passed on to his family.

She skipped down to the bit she'd been looking for.

> Mr Morden is survived by his wife, Demi, and his sons, Jason and Lachlan.

Yasss! He had a wife. And two sons. Now she just had to know where to find them. She went back to the article.

> The funeral will be a private ceremony, but will be followed by a service of reflection on 11 November, at the Cimetière de Monaco, La Colle in Mr Morden's beloved adopted homeland of Monaco.

Alyssa groaned. Monaco. How the hell was she going to reach these people if they lived in bloody Monaco?

It was no use – the lawyer was her only way in and she was going to have to find a way to reach him. Bugger. Bugger. Bugger.

She said that many more times, only stopping when the passenger door opened and Ginny climbed in, face flushed, eyes bright as she tossed her parka into the back seat. Alyssa immediately dropped her rage and directed all the optimistic energy she could muster to her sister.

'Well, how did it go?' she asked, grinning, picking up on Ginny's positive vibes.

'Good, I think. Apparently, I was the only one who braved the weather to get there – thank you again, I owe you a body part should you ever require it. They asked me a bunch of questions, got me to talk about my experience and what I could bring to the students, then told me that they'd review all my audition tapes and previous interview. They said they'll let me know by Friday.'

'Amazing! I knew you'd be great. For what it's worth, I'm really proud of you and I think you're going to get this because you're fricking fantastic.'

Ginny responded with a cheeky grin. 'You're right. I am.'

Alyssa was laughing as she pulled her seatbelt back on. 'Okay, let's get back and put Mum out of her misery.' Alyssa knew Dorinda had only agreed to man the fort because Jessie had offered and shamed her into it.

They were just out of the street, when Ginny remembered another pertinent piece of information.

'Oh, and Moira Chiles was there. When I told her I worked in the café, she said she knew she recognised me. Hopefully that's in a good way. Anyway, she was lovely and I didn't even have to bribe her with cake.'

'We've got a dozen cupcakes in the back if you want to change your mind on that,' Alyssa joked. Yes, definitely a joke. But something in it...

She swerved to the side of the road, stopped, then reached for her phone and put the address of Huntington Farrell into the satnav again, while Ginny watched, confused.

'We're going back to the lawyer's office?'

'We sure are.'

Twenty minutes and a hastily concocted plan later, they were back in the space they'd left after they'd drawn a blank earlier. This time, Alyssa reached into the glove compartment for her Once Upon A Time Café baseball cap, then retrieved a slightly bashed box of cupcakes from the back of the van.

'Wish me luck,' she told her sister. 'If it's the same receptionist, I'll come straight back out and get you to do it instead.'

'You know that just because this happens all the time in movies, it's still highly unlikely to work in real life,' Ginny pointed out, woefully failing to reciprocate Alyssa's positive pre-interview encouragement.

'I do, but it's the only thing I can think of, so it's worth a shot.' She reached back for Ginny's parka and pulled it on, having decided that her own bright red duffel coat would probably be too easily remembered from earlier.

'You're right. And don't worry...' Maybe Ginny was going to be positive after all. 'If you get arrested, I'll have a whip-round for your bail money. But I'll need my parka back before they cart you off.'

Alyssa didn't rise to it, just pulled her hat down tight over her head, fastened her jacket, grabbed the box of cupcakes and made a run through the falling snow for the door. For the second time today, she entered the glittering foyer of the building that housed the offices of Huntington Farrell. Her gaze immediately went to the desk in front of her and she was relieved to see that it was a different receptionist to the two who'd been there earlier.

'Hello, I have a delivery for Jeremy Sprite,' she said, with as much confidence as she could muster. She just had to get upstairs to speak to the lawyer face to face, and she was sure she could convince him to help. This – false pretences and the promise of a calorie-laden sweet treat – was how she was going to do it. As Ginny had pointed out, it was a scenario that had worked in more TV shows and movies than she could count. It was a sure thing. A definite win. Her key to turning this whole crappy day around.

'If you leave it here, someone will come down for it.' The receptionist burst her bubble with a proverbial pitchfork.

Bollocks. Alyssa had to think on her soggy feet.

'My instructions are to have Mr Sprite sign for them. It's cupcakes. They're from his wife and she insisted that I deliver them personally.'

She sent up a silent plea to the gods of big fat porkies. *Please let him be married. Please let him be married. Please let him be married.*

'Hold on,' the receptionist told her, with just a touch of wariness, as she picked up the phone and went through the same procedure as the earlier visit. 'Hi. I have a delivery here for Mr Sprite and her instructions are to deliver it personally. It's from his wife.'

And again... *Please let him be married. Please let him be married. Please let him be married.*

Alyssa watched as the receptionist's eyes narrowed, and she nodded her head, listening intently. Was this when her cover was blown and the receptionist learned the Mr Sprite was either single, gay, widowed, or divorced his wife in 2016? When the phone was hung up, Alyssa realised she could no longer breathe.

'I'm sorry, but it won't be possible to deliver them personally.'

She forced her lungs to kick in, 'But I have to. Can you ask again? I know he's a busy man.'

'No, you don't understand. It's not possible because Mr Sprite has already left for the day. He's not expected back in the office until next week. I'm surprised his wife didn't know that.'

Alyssa somehow managed a weak smile. 'Yes, erm, me too,' before retreating as gracefully as a woman clutching a battered box of cupcakes could do.

Ginny went to the obvious conclusion when Alyssa climbed back in the van. 'It didn't work?'

'Nope. He's gone for the day. And the rest of the week.'

'Bollocks, I'm sorry, Lyss. But also slightly relieved that I don't have to rustle up bail money. Okay, so what's the next plan then, Lara Croft?'

Alyssa tossed twelve stale cupcakes into the back of the van. 'I don't know, but I'm going to think of something, because I'm not giving up.'

12

LACHLAN

'Well, check you out in your fancy Range Rover,' Margaux teased him, as he jumped out of the car in front of the pub they were meeting in.

He had no idea how long she'd been in the doorway, but hopefully not long, because wrestling that Range Rover into the space now that the snow was even thicker had been like guiding an oil tanker round a lazy river.

'Pity you park like a ninety-year-old man with cataracts though,' she added, just when he thought he'd got away with it.

Margaux lived in Renfrew now, in a flat on the edge of the River Clyde, next to the shopping centre he'd popped into for a jacket earlier. The pub they'd arranged to meet in was adjacent to the shopping centre, and only a two-minute walk from her home. Or rather, a three-minute trudge in this weather, but Margaux was super-fit and had refused his offer to pick her up on the way.

They found a table in the corner, out of earshot of the few other people who'd ventured out today, and both peeled off their heavy jackets. 'Thanks for dressing up for me,' he teased her, gesturing to her usual uniform of athleisure wear – today was bright pink yoga flares and a sage green sweatshirt, with sleeves that came down over her hands, apart from the two thumbs that were making a bid for escape.

'Sorry, my tiara is being cleaned. But I've got on my diamond knickers, so I did make an effort.' Grinning, she leaned over the table and put her hands on his. 'Liking the longer hair by the way. Oh, I've missed your ugly face.'

'Just haven't had time to get it cut. And I've missed yours too.' His words oozed affection.

Margaux Mackay was, and always had been, his closest friend. Her family had lived next door to his when they moved to Glasgow, and their six-year-old selves had become inseparable immediately. They'd gone through all of their young lives together, including the era in their early twenties when she'd bribed him with post-workout tequilas to be her guinea pig as she practised before her exams to become a fully-qualified yoga instructor. He'd reached levels of bendiness that he'd never been able to replicate since.

Now they spoke most days on the phone, so they were still fully invested in each other's worlds. She was the only thing about living here that he missed. Everything else was tainted.

'Can we get the tough stuff out of the way first? How are you doing? How did this morning go? Are you hating being back here?'

He thought about lying, but what was the point? She knew him so well her bullshit detector would go off like a car alarm. 'Every minute until this one.'

'Okay, I need details...'

Before she could continue, a waitress with a friendly face appeared at their table. 'Hi, are you ready to order?'

'I'll have a cheeseburger and fries, and a soda water with lime please.' Margaux followed that up with an innocent shrug in Lachlan's direction. 'What? That's just a light snack.' It had always been an in-joke that she looked like she survived on kale and beetroot, but actually ate like a trucker with an insatiable appetite and a fondness for carbs, even when, like today, she'd be teaching a class in a couple of hours.

Lachlan shot a quick glance at the menu in front of him and picked the first thing that jumped out. Steak pie. His favourite. His mother used to make steak pies from scratch, and it had always been his go-to comfort food. 'And a coffee too, please. Just black – no sugar.'

When the waitress left, Margaux picked up where she left off. 'Okay, tell me everything that happened this morning. I still can't believe your dad is gone. I always thought he was indestructible.'

'Me too. It's a weird feeling, though. We were never close, but I miss knowing he's out there somewhere. You know he was always pretty distant and tied up in his work while Mum was alive, but I think losing her gave him some sense of mortality, so he went the opposite way when he married Demi. He took off, didn't look back and finally eased up on work and enjoyed his life. I'm glad he had that time.'

'I get that. Although, thank God for your lovely mum. If you'd had two non-present parents, you could have ended up being a therapist's dream.' She paused. 'Speaking of therapist's dreams... How did it go with Jason this morning?' Her eyes went to his hands. 'No bruises on the knuckles, so I take it you didn't deck him. Proud of you.'

Margaux had obviously known Jason all his life too, but she'd never been a fan. One of Lachlan's favourite memories was of Jason hitting on Margaux when they were about eighteen, and her informing him that she somehow had the strength to resist him because 'despite the fact that, granted, you do resemble Zac Efron in a dim light, I'm only attracted to guys who aren't cocky, arrogant big shits'. Jason was so unused to rejection that he'd probably never recovered.

'Thank you. It did take discipline. Especially when...' Lachlan went on to give her a brief recap of the meeting this morning, rounding it off as the food arrived, with, 'So I signed. Done. Dusted.'

Neither of them lifted their cutlery, because she had one more question. 'And you still won't consider moving back here? There's still nothing I can do to persuade you?'

He didn't even hesitate. 'I can't, Margaux. Much as I'd love to see your daft face every day. There are just too many memories.'

She continued to physically lean in, the exact opposite of how everyone else had reacted to him after the losses he'd endured.

'I understand. I mean, I live in hope, but I do get it. You went through stuff that leaves scars, Lachie. The baby...'

The baby. Thomas. They'd found out the gender when Tanya was eighteen weeks pregnant and they'd named him straight away. Thomas Martyn Morden, after Tanya's dad and his. The instinct to do something so traditional had taken him by surprise, but it had felt right. In fact, every single thing about their lives had felt so right. They'd moved into their dream home in Hyndland, in the west end of the city, a renovation project, but one that would grow with their family. They'd planned their wedding, and it was only a few weeks away. Their babymoon was booked to St Lucia and they were both thriving at work. They weren't smug, but they were grateful. Life was perfect. And that's why it had stunned them when a wrecking ball tore through the very fabric of their existence. At twenty weeks, just a fortnight before they should have married, Tanya lost the baby. Then he lost Tanya. And none of the other stuff mattered any more.

He didn't reply, so Margaux filled the space with nothing but concern and care. 'That's a piece broken right off your heart, Lachlan.'

'It is.' He tried to muster a grateful smile for her understanding, but he wasn't sure that he'd managed it. 'I don't think I'd have got through it without you. And, you know, eventually fleeing the country.' He said that with a wry smile, because it was true. He'd gone for head in the sand and denial for a long time now. And he wasn't ready to change that yet. Maybe he never would be.

'You don't want to keep talking about this, do you?' Margaux asked, perceptive as ever.

He squeezed her hand. 'I definitely do not.'

'So shall we eat our food and move right on to unrelated nonsense and trivial matters?'

'I think that sounds like a great idea.'

And that's what they did.

They spent the next hour or so avoiding the tough stuff and stuck to swapping stories of a million stupid or funny things they'd shared over the years, and the daft things that had happened to her since he left. The woeful tale of her date with an accountant who'd brought his mother along was one that he'd never tire of listening to.

She groaned and put her head in her hands. 'God, life would have been so much simpler if we'd got together. Why did we never do that?'

Lachlan laughed. 'We've had this conversation way too many times and we both know it's because we have the sexual chemistry of a pot plant.'

'So sad, but so true,' she said wistfully. 'I kept hoping that those good looks of yours would stir up my ovaries one of these days, but they never did. It's tragic, really.'

'One of the great mysteries of our time,' he agreed, laughing.

'If you were any kind of friend, you'd set me up with one of your loaded clients. Is Dax Price single? I could totally be a WAG.'

Lachlan hated to break it to her, but, 'Last I heard, he was dating a fitness model influencer with 10 million followers.'

She lowered her eyes to take in her outfit of chaos. 'I think he may be out of my league. Anyway...' She quickly snapped out of her state of mock despair. 'What time is your flight tonight?'

'Ten o'clock.'

'So what are you going to do until then?'

He realised he didn't know the answer to that question.

They both automatically looked at the huge train station clock that had been repurposed as a decorative piece behind the bar. It was a few minutes to one o'clock. Before today, all he'd been able to think about was how much he'd been dreading the meeting this morning. He hadn't contemplated what he'd do after it. He'd booked a later flight because he wasn't sure how long the meeting would last or how it would go. Now he was wishing he had an afternoon one instead.

'I wish I could spend the rest of the day with you, but these are two of my weekly classes and I can't let them down. Also, they've all paid for a block booking. If I don't show up, I'll have to refund everyone. Welcome to the world of a freelance yoga instructor. If you want, you can go to my place and chill there, though. I'll be back around five and I could cancel the date...'

He had a flush of guilt about Margaux changing her plans for him, so he immediately came up with an excuse to avoid that. 'Thanks, but I'm not being responsible for you potentially missing out on meeting the bloke of your dreams. I'm just going to head out to the airport and see if I can get bumped up to an earlier flight. If not, I've got loads of work I need to catch up on and a couple of clients and suppliers I need to speak to, so that'll pass the time.'

'Okay, but if the flight gets delayed or cancelled with this weather, just come stay at mine. I'll get you uproariously drunk and force you to listen to what will inevitably be a pathetic tale about my latest romantic disaster. I now understand the term "axis of evil" – it's online dating, optimism and scumbags that send dick picks on social media.'

That made him laugh again. 'Good to know. I'll keep you posted if I get grounded.'

She checked her watch. 'Well, much as it's been special, I really need to go. My class is in Paisley in an hour, and I'm going to have to jump in a taxi because I don't trust myself to drive in this weather. If you're a ninety-year-old man with cataracts, I'm his ninety-five-year-old friend with no sense of distance who panics at the first hint of a skid.'

'I'll drop you off,' he offered straight away.

'Are you sure? I'd play hard to get, and pretend to object, but the thought of being chauffeured there in that big beast outside is pretty appealing.'

He took some cash from his wallet. 'I insist. Paisley is practically at the airport, so I'm going that way anyway and could do with the company. And I'm getting lunch too. Call it a pre-payment in case I need to sleep in your spare room tonight.'

'Urgh, why didn't I ever fancy you? I mean, now that you're minted and relatively good-looking, maybe I could be persuaded.'

He went with the same answer that both of them had given each other a dozen times over the years.

'Margaux, visualise me naked.'

'Eeeeeew, my eyes!' she wailed, groaning dramatically.

'Exactly. Now let's go before I need to do the same thing.'

Anyone else in the pub would think that the two people who were laughing as they walked out of the door hand in hand were a couple. The truth, Lachlan knew, was that they were so much more than that. And after everything that had happened before he'd left Glasgow, he'd settle for the kind of friendship he could rely on.

They climbed into the Range Rover and chatted the whole way. Traffic was horrendous, the roads were awful, and there were at least half a dozen accidents on the way to Paisley, so it took them much longer than they expected, arriving at the sports centre five minutes before the class was due to start.

Margaux reached over and kissed him, then quickly opened the door. 'Thank you for this, thank you for lunch, and remember to hit me up if your flight gets cancelled. You never know – if the date goes really badly, I might get drunk enough to contemplate you naked without chucking up my chips.'

'You're so romantic, I've no idea why you're single,' he dead-panned, before giving her a cheery wave as she dashed off up the stairs to the centre.

He drove off thinking how much he hadn't realised he needed this. Connection. Familiarity. Shared experiences that weren't just the shit kind. Other than Dax Price, everyone he knew in London was a new friend or acquaintance, someone he'd met since he moved there two years ago. Much as he'd been dreading coming back, there was something to be said for the good memories. They'd just been buried under the other stuff for a long time. The heartbreak of losing the baby and Tanya. The pain of seeing his future shredded and his happiness torn away from him. That said, this return to his roots wasn't something he had any intention of repeating. Maybe he'd invite Margaux down for a weekend or perhaps they could go on a trip somewhere, because much as he'd always loved his homeland, he had no desire to come back after today.

That was the thought that was on his mind, when he joined the slip road onto the motorway and continued along the M8 towards the airport. Only a couple of junctions. There were still almost eight hours to kill until his flight, but at least he'd be dry, warm, and he could let go of the dread and relax for the first time since he'd got the call to say his dad had passed. Besides, he was pretty sure that some people wouldn't make it to the airport in this weather, so he reckoned he had a decent chance of swapping to an earlier flight.

He clocked the sign for the airport slip road, then saw that it was blocked by blue flashing lights and an overturned transit van. Bugger. Nothing to do but keep going. He wasn't in a hurry anyway.

The next couple of exits were backed up with cars that hadn't been able to get off at the blocked junction, so again, he just kept on driving.

That's when he saw it. Weirbridge. Six miles ahead. He felt a pang of nostalgia. Weirbridge was the next village to Burnbank, where he'd lived as a child. It was also the second time he'd thought about it today, the first being when the lawyer had informed them that Dad had owned the commercial building there. He had so many clear, happy memories of his mum taking him and Jason back to both villages, to visit the place where she grew up and the café she'd once worked in.

If this was the last time he was going to be here, then maybe those were memories that he'd like to revisit.

A few minutes later, Lachlan didn't even have a conscious thought, before he realised the car was veering off to the left, onto the slip road that would take him all the way to places he used to know.

2 P.M. – 4 P.M.

13

JESSIE

'Everything okay there, Georgie?' Jessie asked, when her daughter returned from dealing with the customer who'd popped in and spoke to her at the reception desk at the front of the salon.

Georgie swiftly put on a smile that Jessie immediately knew was fake. Her girl was definitely struggling today, but she was making such an effort to cover it up that it was breaking Jessie's heart. 'Yes, of course. Just someone that noticed we were open and popped in on the off chance of a cut and blow dry. I've told her to come back tomorrow. Not having a stranger in here ruining the party.'

Jessie knew exactly how that felt because she'd been holding it together, refusing to ruin the party, ever since her conversation with Val when they'd first got here.

'I need you to tell me everything you know about what happened between my Stan and Dorinda Canavan.'

Val had held her gaze, and the pity that Jessie saw there almost broke her. Eventually, Val had spoken softly. 'That was a long time ago, Jessie.'

Val was right. It was a lifetime ago. So why did Jessie feel the need to dig into it today? If she were honest with herself, she knew the answer. Seeing Dorinda in the café, with that smug expression of hers, had brought it all back. Jessie was already feeling vulnerable and upset about going, and worried about living a life with only Stan for company. The combination of all those things had sparked a need to know the truth about the man she was giving up everything for.

Val had watched her carefully as she'd gone on, 'Are you sure you want to go back there? Some things are better left in the past.'

So Val did know something. Jessie had been counting on it.

Back then, they hadn't discussed it, but they weren't as close as they'd gone on to become over the years. Three decades of doing a woman's hair forged a rare bond, and the fact that they'd both stayed in the village and brought up families at the same time had made them integral parts of each other's life.

Jessie had nodded. 'I am, Val. And you're the only person I'm going to ask, so I'd appreciate the full story.'

The thing was, if Jessie were really honest with herself, she already knew. How many times had she replayed that night in her mind, then brought down the shutters on it and compartmentalised it in a box where it couldn't hurt her or her children?

Georgie must have been about ten, which would have made Grant six. Her and Stan were in their thirties, which felt like a hell of a long time ago right now. And Stan, well, she wasn't being biased when she would say that he was the best-looking man for miles. Ah, he was fine. Tall and always tanned from working on construction sites. Life had been smashing back then. They didn't have much money, but her salon had been up and running for over a decade and she was rushed off her feet in all the best ways. The evenings were busy with after-school activities, and late-night opening at the salon, and spending time with the kids so that their childhoods didn't go by in a flash that she missed altogether. Sometimes, exhaustion would feel like it was going to take the knees from her, but she didn't want to change a thing because she treasured it all and she knew how lucky she was. If there was a tiny dark spot in her sunshine of a life, it was that it was almost impossible for her and Stan to find time alone together. There was the odd Saturday night, when Cathy or her sister, Loretta, would babysit for them. On birthdays and anniversaries, they made a special effort to go out for a nice meal. But those were exceptions. A Saturday night was far more likely to be fish and chips, picked up on her way home from a long day in Copper Curls, and then cuddling up with Georgie and Grant on the sofa to watch whatever video they'd chosen from Blockbusters when Stan had been looking after them that afternoon.

They were a team. A squad. But they got an extra player when Dorinda Canavan began working as a barmaid at the golf club. At first, Jessie had barely noticed the shift. Like many men back in those days, Stan had often gone to the bar in the golf club for a pint after work on a Thursday or Friday. But then it became more than just one pint. He'd come in long after she'd fallen asleep on the couch and explain that he'd bumped into an old pal and got chatting. Or there was a member's meeting that he couldn't get out of. Or a dozen other reasons that she could barely recall now, but that seemed innocuous at the time because she trusted her husband and it never crossed her mind to doubt him.

That had changed when Val and Don Murray had thrown a party for their wedding anniversary – maybe their twentieth, Jessie wasn't sure now – and Cathy and Duncan had offered to take the kids for the night so that Jessie and Stan could go. Thrilled to bits, Jessie had made a real effort with herself. She'd got her junior stylist to do her hair, she'd taken time over her make-up, and squeezed herself into a little black dress that looked just like the one that Kate Moss had worn when she'd been plastered all over the tabloids that week. Although, Jessie highly doubted that Kate's frock cost £29.99 and got delivered on a sale-or-return basis from the Freemans catalogue.

That aside, Jessie had felt like a million dollars.

They'd arrived at the golf club in a flurry of hugs and hellos, and the drinks had flowed. Maybe that's why Stan had let his guard down. It was late in the night, when he went off to the bar for another round of drinks. Twenty minutes later, he wasn't back, and Jessie had gone to find him. She had no joy at the bar, so she'd asked Don Murray, who was coming out of the gents', if Stan was in there. No luck there either. She'd been about to go back into the hall and check if she'd missed him sitting at another table, or maybe having a dance, when she'd spotted that the fire exit next to the toilets was ajar. Before she'd even pushed it open, she knew why.

There had been a choice. Step forward or step back. Jessie had stepped forward.

She'd opened the door wider, pushing it slowly, so that it made no noise, then she'd initially breathed a sigh of relief, because there was no one in sight.

That's when she'd seen them.

They were tucked between two cars, and Dorinda Canavan, the stunning twenty-four-year-old wild child daughter of the lovely Hugo and Effie Canavan, was joined at the lips with Stan McLean.

The second choice. Step forward or step back. That time, Jessie had stepped back.

Over the years that followed, she'd thought about that decision often, but never regretted it. A few weeks later, the lovely Effie Canavan was in for her bi-monthly highlights and she'd said with a heavy heart that her Dorinda had gone off again. London this time. Or was it Manchester? Again, Jessie hadn't worried about the details. All that mattered was that Stan's pints at the golf club had gone back to being just an hour or so, a couple of nights a week, and he was more attentive to her and the kids than he'd ever been.

Maybe she should have made a different choice. God knows, Val Murray would have lambasted her Don through the streets of Weirbridge if she'd ever caught him straying – not that he ever would. But Jessie had known back then that she had too much to lose. If she and Stan split up, how would she manage? There weren't enough hours in the day already and childcare was difficult to find in the village and impossible for her to afford, especially if she and Stan were living in two different houses and paying two mortgages. Then there was the salon. How would a scandal like that affect her business and her friendships? Effie Canavan and her whole extended family were good people who would be mortified about what Dorinda had done, and they'd never show their faces in Copper Curls again. Most importantly, there were their children. Did Jessie really want to break up their family and take one of the people they loved the most away from their daily lives? And all that aside, she loved him with all of her heart.

Maybe nowadays she would make a different choice, but she still felt that the one she'd made back then was the right one. Her and Stan had gone on to have almost thirty more years together, and nothing had ever raised her suspicions again, even when Dorinda had returned to the village a few years later. Of course, by that time she had a partner and two young children, so Stan was out of luck, even if he'd been interested in rekindling their fling.

The only lasting trace of Stan and Dorinda's relationship was that, even from the moral high ground, Jessie could never again look at that cow with anything but distaste. And Dorinda was many things, but she wasn't stupid. She knew that Jessie knew. And that had left them, for almost thirty years, circling each other like two bulls, both of them always alert to the other one's malevolent presence.

And earlier, Val had confirmed that she hadn't imagined the whole thing.

'Like I said, it was a long time ago. Late nineties, I think. I know they had an affair, Jessie, and I'm so sorry to say that. But I can see from your face that you already knew, didn't you?'

Jessie had nodded. 'I knew. But go on.'

Val's hand had slipped over hers. 'If I remember rightly, it lasted a couple of months. My Don used to see them at the golf club and then he bumped into them once in Burnbank.'

'The whole village knew?'

Val had flushed a little. 'I don't think so, but it wasn't the best-kept secret. I'm so sorry, Jessie. For a long time, I felt guilty for not telling you, but I didn't want to interfere in your family. We didn't do that back then, did we? We let people keep their lives and their secrets to themselves.'

'I'm glad you didn't,' Jessie had reassured her softly. 'Because then I might have been forced to do something about it, instead of letting it blow over. Who knows, Val? We just all did what we thought was right and hoped for the best.'

'So why bring it up after all this time, Jessie? Are you going to do something about it now?'

That was when she'd noticed that over at the basins, Georgie had finished applying Cathy's colour.

Jessie had taken a deep breath, composed herself, 'I don't know. Right now, I'm going to act like nothing has happened and I'm going to enjoy this last party with you all, and then I'm going to think about this later.' Her old compartmentalisation skills had come flooding right back to her. And they were still holding her together now, two hours later, when they all had brand-new hairstyles, hoarse throats from singing and sore cheeks from laughing too hard.

'You're all goddesses,' Grant declared a few minutes later, surveying his finished work as he came back from reception with their coats.

'Oh, I've had the time of my life,' Cathy chirped, pulling on her duvet-esque fashion statement, before checking out her violet hair in the mirror.

'Dear God, Aunt Cathy, you could house a family of campers in that coat.'

Cathy pursed her lips. 'Grant McLean, I'm in my seventies and I have a secret stash of cash under my mattress. You're still in my will, but I'll be on to my lawyers tomorrow morning to change that situation if you keep that cheek up.'

'I was just thinking that's the loveliest coat I've ever seen,' Grant replied, acting innocent, before blowing it with, 'Does wonders for your cankles.'

This time, Cathy couldn't even feign disapproval because she was laughing too hard.

Georgie held Jessie's coat for her and as she slipped her arms into it, Georgie gave her a squeeze. 'I'm just going to stay behind and clear up a few things here, Mum. I'll see you at the party tonight. Do you need me to come early and give you a hand with anything?'

'Not at all, love. Alyssa has got everything ready to go at the café and I just need to put on a sparkly frock, so we'll be fine.' Jessie turned to Grant. 'What about you, son? Where are you off to now?'

'Well, I figured you had enough to deal with without me messing up your spare room the night before you desert us for pastures new, so I'm staying with my lovely sister tonight.' He bumped shoulders with Georgie. 'And I'm going to head there right now, because my niece is waiting for me and apparently we have an outfit to choose. I've no idea how I got to be the cool uncle, but I'll take it.'

Cathy checked a text on her phone. 'That's Richie outside now and he's still happy to drop you both off. Never get a taxi in this weather.'

'Right then, let's go, ladies,' Jessie ushered her pals out ahead of her, leaving Grant and Georgie behind after another flurry of hugs.

At the door, Cathy spotted her second husband, the lovely Richie, waiting in his classic old Jag, engine running for heat. It was a miracle that it had got through the snow, but maybe the old ones really were the best. Jessie couldn't help thinking how lucky Cathy had been. She'd had a lifetime of happiness with Duncan, and then after he passed, she'd had a second great love with Richie. And she deserved them both.

Cathy went on ahead, round to the passenger seat, while Jessie and Val made their way to the back door.

'Are you okay, pal?' Val asked quietly, and they both knew what she was referring to.

Jessie nodded. She considered taking Val's hand, but they were both wearing gloves the size of oven mitts. 'I am. I just have some thinking to do, but I'll be fine.'

They got to Val's house first, and before she climbed out, Jessie gave her a hug.

'I'll see you tonight, love.'

'I'll be there with bells on.'

Five minutes later, they pulled up outside Jessie's house and she saw there were the lights in the downstairs windows. Stan was home.

'Thank you both. Richie, you're a gentleman – for giving me a lift and putting up with this one,' she gestured to Cathy, who let out a hoot of laughter, before responding.

'He's the luckiest man ever and he knows it. Give Stan our love and we'll see you both later. My feet are already itching for a dance.'

'Will do and thanks again. Watch the pothole just along there – that's the one that nearly put Val in a ditch last year. Blew one of her tyres clean out.' She opened the door, and then had to clamber her way, fairly ungracefully, out of the low car. 'Bugger, I'd need a crane to get me in and out if I had one of these.'

As Cathy and Richie drove off, Jessie stood and waved until they were out of sight, grateful for the cold air to clear her head of both champagne and woes. Then she walked slowly up her path, deep in thought.

Everything that had happened all those years ago was ancient history, and she'd supressed it all because she always felt she had too much to lose.

But now, the tables had turned, because today, maybe for the first time, she realised that she had even more to lose by sticking *with* Stan.

One way or another, she had to decide what to do because she was running out of time.

Just like before, she had a choice to make.

Was she going to step forward, or step back?

14
GEORGIE

Her mum, Aunt Cathy and Val were barely out of the door, when Georgie slumped on one of the staffroom sofas and exhaled like her life depended on it. This staffroom had been her place of refuge since she was a kid, and Jessie would bring them into work if Dad was on a job and she couldn't find a babysitter. Georgie and Grant had loved it – a TV in the corner, lots of snacks in the fridge, and they could wander into the salon and chat to clients who would invariably slip them a pound for sweets.

Grant came into the staffroom and plonked down on the opposite sofa. 'And the Oscar for Best Sister Covering Up An Existential Crisis goes to…'

Georgie groaned. 'Oh don't. I'm exhausted. I feel like I've run a marathon. In the snow. While dancing to Abba's greatest hits. What. A. Fricking. Day.'

She meant every word. And the worst part was that it still wasn't over. The woman… That had been a shock she hadn't seen coming. She'd truly thought it was someone looking for a quick cut or a gift card.

'Can I help you?'

'Yes. Or at least I think so. I want to know if you're sleeping with my boyfriend.'

Georgie knew she must have resembled a fish gasping for air as she'd attempted to process the question.

'No!' That had of course been her first reaction, hissed quietly so that the Weirbridge Bee Gees over at the mirrors wouldn't hear her. Then, even though she was absolutely confident of her innocence, given that she hadn't slept with anyone but Flynn since the Spice Girls were in the charts, she'd immediately followed up with the obvious question of, 'Who is your boyfriend?'

'Flynn Dern.'

The whooshing noise had been the air leaving Georgie's sails. Just at that, Cathy had run riot with the iPad again and the salon had been flooded with the opening bars of 'Jump Around'.

'Look, I do want to talk to you, and I'll answer all your questions, but that's my mother and her pals over there and if I don't get back to them, they'll be here in seconds demanding to know what's going on. They've never heard of boundaries. Anyway, give me an hour or so. There's a café across the road there if you want somewhere warm to grab a coffee and I'll come and meet you as soon as I can get away.'

There had been a hesitation that had worried Georgie for a second, but then she saw the woman's gaze going to Jessie, Val and Cathy, all bopping up and down like they were at the Grammys, and she took a step backwards.

'Okay. I'll wait there. Please don't forget to come.'

'Trust me, there's no danger of that,' Georgie had assured her.

The woman had gone off, leaving Georgie to slap a smile on her face and spend the last hour acting carefree and jolly. Now she felt broken inside and knew for sure that hairdressing had been the right choice, because her childhood fall-back plan of becoming an undercover spy was clearly not for her.

'Well, for what it's worth, I think you did great with those three.' Grant tried to make her feel better.

'Honestly, not telling her about the job offer is torture for me. I've spent my whole life discussing everything with Mum. We've spent every day together and I'm a chronic over-sharer. I'm rubbish at keeping secrets.'

And now she had one she was keeping from Grant too. Even in her state of flux, she knew that telling him about the woman claiming to be Flynn's girlfriend would be a mistake, given his prevailing opinion that her ex-husband was a twat. Revealing this little nugget of info would only give Grant even more reasons to dislike him, and Georgie wasn't ready to do that. Maybe the woman was one of those fantasists from those Netflix documentaries. Although, if she was, she might have been better to target someone a bit more exciting than Flynn Solar Panels Dern.

'Are we going to talk more about the job offer, or do you want me to leave so you can comfort eat the rest of Mum's Lindt chocolates and square this place up?'

She appreciated that he cared about her and wanted her to live her best life, but... 'I'll pick option number two. I'm not taking the job, Grant. For all the reasons we talked about before. There's no way to make it make sense and I'm not going to be the one to risk this place after Mum spent her life protecting and cherishing it, and then passed it on to me.'

He got up, moved from his little sofa to hers, and hugged her. 'Now you're getting the Oscar for Nicest Person In A Family Drama...' He planted a huge wet kiss on her cheek, then got up. 'Sure you don't want me to stay and help clean up? I mean, I'd rather set my Prada snow boots on fire than brush a floor or scrub Cathy's toner off that sink, but I'd do it for you.'

Laughing, she shook her head. 'I wouldn't want to undermine your celebrity hairdresser status and gargantuan ego, so no, it's fine. I'll do it. Go help my daughter pick an outfit for tonight, and if it shows more than 50 per cent of her skin, I'll kill you,' she said sweetly.

He hugged her again. 'Good to know. I'll put her in a onesie.' He was almost out of the door when he stopped. 'You know, I miss you, sis. In case you were wondering.'

'I miss you too,' she replied truthfully, before resorting to their standard sibling dynamic and adding a cheeky, 'And I wasn't wondering because how could you not?'

Only when the bell at the front door confirmed his departure did she jump up from the couch, grab her coat from the row of pegs on the wall and her bag from the table. The cleaning up could wait until tomorrow. Her first client wasn't in until 10 a.m., and it was Mrs Dawson, former Weirbridge High School dinner lady, who was about ninety, short of sight, hard of hearing and took her knitting everywhere, so she wouldn't notice or care if the place wasn't up to its usual pristine standards.

The snow was still falling, but council gritters had been up Main Street, so the thick white blanket had been replaced by a grey, gritty sludge that crackled as Georgie trudged across the road to the Once Upon A Time Café. This whole impending scenario was giving her mixed feelings. On the one hand, she hoped that the woman had realised this was some kind of mistake and done a runner – but, on the other hand, if Flynn was in a fully-fledged relationship while trying to win her back, then she wanted to know about it.

When Georgie pushed open the door, her hopes of the woman bailing on the meeting were dashed. There she was. She was the only customer in the café, and she'd chosen a table in the corner, furthest away from the counter, beside the glistening tree with its garlands of twinkling lights. She'd taken her jacket and hat off now and Georgie could see she was in maybe her late twenties with a blonde pixie cut and a pretty face that was free of make-up, except for what looked like long, dark eyelash extensions and a slick of something shiny on her lips. Georgie felt the weight of her stare as she approached her.

It was a relief to see that Hugo was behind the counter. Her Aunt Cathy had mentioned that Dorinda was here today, and having that woman eavesdropping on this conversation and then spreading it around the village would be yet another nightmare. Although, hopefully, the sound of 'Do They Know It's Christmas' coming from the speakers would drown them out.

'All right, Georgie? What can I get you, pet?' Hugo greeted her, and her gaze flicked to the woman, nursing what she could see was an almost empty coffee mug.

'Coffee please, Hugo,' she said, as she pulled out a chair. 'Can I get you another one?'

The woman nodded, so Georgie passed that on.

'Make that two, please, Hugo.'

He'd just replied with a thumbs up, when, behind her, the café door opened again, and she felt her heart stop. If it was anyone she knew, this was about to become extremely awkward, because this wasn't the type of village that you could get away with not introducing someone to a friend.

'Well hello, Mrs Dawson – *yes, terrible weather. This is a complete stranger, who is currently shagging my ex-husband. Yes, the one who buggered off to Thailand and then came back with his tail between his legs.'*

Thankfully, the arrivals were just Alyssa and Ginny, who flew in the door, gave her a quick, 'Hey, Georgie!' and then disappeared into the back kitchen.

Okay, back to her coffee companion.

Georgie wasn't sure how these conversations were supposed to go, but she was a hairdresser with two decades of experience in breaking the ice and drawing out conversations from strangers, so she spoke first.

'I'm sorry for taking so long. Thanks for waiting. I guess you know my name, but I didn't catch yours.' Actually, it hadn't been offered, but Georgie was glossing over that.

'I'm Monica. Monica Turner. I work with Flynn at Alba Central Solar.'

That removed any doubt that they were talking about the same man.

'And we've been seeing each other for a year now.'

Wow. Just wow. He'd kept that one to himself. Georgie already had so many questions, but now that Monica was speaking, she didn't want to interrupt her.

'We were supposed to be moving in together before Christmas, but lately he's been dragging his heels, acting weird, and I didn't know why. I guess now I do.'

There was no malice in her tone, just defeat and sinking realisation. This poor woman. Georgie respected the courage it must have taken to come here.

'What do you need to know, Monica?' she prompted, gently.

'Everything. I sussed out that you're his ex-wife and he slept at your house last night – and I'm guessing that wasn't the first time – so I suppose I want to know what's going on.'

Hugo must have sensed the tension, because at that, he delivered the coffee and made a swift retreat.

Georgie took a deep breath, then began at the start, with a bullet-point recap of her marriage to Flynn, their separation, divorce, and then got to the more relevant stuff.

'And you're right – for the last few months he's being staying over sometimes. In my defence, I had no idea he was seeing you. He told me he wasn't interested in dating anyone else, and if I'd known that wasn't true, then it wouldn't have happened.'

The irony in this didn't escape her. Wasn't it supposed to be the wife that was getting cheated on with a girlfriend, not the girlfriend getting cheated on with the wife?

A point of curiosity niggled her, though.

'Can I ask you something? How did you discover where he stayed last night?' A vision of Monica following him, then sitting outside her house in the cold made her wince.

'I put an AirTag in his car. I realise that makes me sound crazy.'

Georgie put her hands up. 'I'm not judging. Clearly, I've done a crazy thing or two when it comes to Flynn too.'

Monica pre-empted her next question. 'And then I heard him on the phone this morning, saying he'd left his wallet. He'd told me he lived in Weirbridge when he was married, so I put two and two together and googled you. That's how I found the salon.'

'If you ever leave the solar panels game, you'd have a great future as a private investigator.'

Monica reacted with a rueful smile. 'Going by the reason I'm here, I'm probably way too gullible.'

Georgie wasn't an advocate of violence under any circumstances, but right now, she wanted to punch her ex-husband right in the face.

'Monica, I'm sorry. All I can promise is that now that I know about you, I won't be seeing him again. At least, not in that way. We share a daughter, but from now on, that's it. What you do with that news is up to you, but if you want my opinion, you seem really nice. He doesn't deserve you.'

Monica took that in, then reached for her bag, which was sitting on the chair next to her. 'Thank you. And, Georgie, please don't tell him about this. I don't want him to know I was here.'

'I won't. Good luck with...' She wasn't sure how to finish that sentence, so she went with, '...Whatever you decide.'

Hopefully that decision would involve Flynn Dern being poked by a large bargepole.

When she was gone, Georgie took a sip of her coffee, as she stared straight ahead, trying to process the conversation.

Flynn Tosser. Dern. What a cheek that man had.

And while they were very definitely divorced, and he was perfectly entitled to do what he wanted, to shag his way around Scotland if he cared to, he couldn't do it while trying to win her back. Nor could he feed her bullshit lines, like the crap he'd come out with this morning when he'd lied to her about being the only one for him. Urgh. Every thought she'd had just a couple of hours before about reuniting and playing happy families again was torched by a flame thrower of fury that made her teeth clench. What. An. Absolute. Tosser. How dare he play that poor woman? How dare he play her? How dare he mess with Kayleigh's world?

As if telepathy sent a bat signal from her thoughts, her phone burst into life and Kayleigh's picture flashed up on the screen.

Georgie settled herself, then answered with a breezy, 'Hey lovely, how's your day going? Has Uncle Grant arrived yet?'

'Yes, but he's up in your wardrobe searching for a nude heel. Don't ask.'

Despite the circumstances of her current shit show, that made Georgie smile, until Kayleigh wiped the grin right off her face.

'Dad is here too, though. He's asking when you'll be home. And, Mum, you know how Gran invited him to the party...?'

Georgie had to work hard to keep her voice steady. 'Yes, but he can't make it, sweetheart. He already told me that he's got a work thing tonight.' A work thing. Or, to be more specific, shagging a work colleague.

'Nope, apparently his plans have changed and he's going to come. He's got his best jeans on, so he's ready to party. It's, like, so embarrassing but kind of cute.'

Georgie was finding out that it was actually possible to speak while your face was on fire and your teeth were still clenched. But she wasn't going to be the one to let their daughter know what a lying arse he was. 'Smashing. You can tell Dad I'm on my way and I'll see him and his party jeans when I get there.'

She hung up, paid Hugo for the coffees and picked three large slices of Victoria sponge to go. One for her. One for Kayleigh. One for Grant.

Her former husband was about to get what he deserved. And it wasn't cake.

15

ALYSSA

'All right, girls?' their grandad had greeted them, as he'd nipped into the kitchen after them when they got back from the interview.

'Everything is good, Grandad.'

Alyssa had shot Ginny a warning glance, reminding her that this wasn't the time to tell Hugo that his job was at risk – not until she'd tried everything she could think of to fix this.

'My interview went well, so hopefully they'll let me know soon.'

'I'll keep my fingers crossed for you, love. You deserve a break and I know it'll come soon enough.'

Their grandad's unwavering belief in both of them had been a constant in their lives and Alyssa would always be grateful for it – especially because it balanced out their mum's equally unwavering disinterest in their existence. Talking of which...

'Where's Mum?'

Grandad had shrugged. 'Och, she was bored, so I said to her to go on home. Barely been a customer all day. Georgie and her friend out there are the first people we've had since the lunchtime bingo ladies got their coffees to take to the church hall. Not even this weather could stop that lot getting their daily session in.'

Alyssa had quietly seethed about her mum taking off, but she'd kept that to herself. Even if the café was deserted, you'd think Dorinda would have stayed to keep Grandad company. Maybe even let him away early? Her thoughtlessness could be infuriating, but it was nothing they weren't used to.

'Okay, well, you get off now too, Grandad. Ginny can take care of everything out there, and I'll get cracking on the sandwiches and the rest of the prep for tonight. I'll give you lift home first though.'

Thank God she was religiously organised and a big fan of overly preparing for every event. They'd got a special licence from the council to serve beer and wine tonight, and both were chilling in the fridge and ready to go. She'd been baking for this evening since Saturday, and had stayed down late last night to get everything else prepped and ready. Starting early that morning had put her ahead of the game again, and as long as her sandwich-making prowess didn't let her down, and Ginny gave her a hand later to set the buffet up in front of the counter, she'd be ready with an hour or so to spare. Enough time to nip upstairs for a quick shower and change into something nice for the party.

'I'll do that then, love, if you're sure. I want to get my path cleared of snow, because I don't fancy trying to navigate that after I've had a couple of lagers tonight. I don't want a lift though. I'm going to nip into the bakers on the way, and then I want to enjoy my walk and get my steps in.'

'But Grandad...' she'd begun to object, but he'd shut her down.

'Alyssa, I'm more than capable of walking for five minutes and I've been waiting all winter for a chance to wear these bad boys.' He picked up the snow boots he'd been wearing when he came in, before he'd changed into his favourite Fred Perry retro tennis shoes that he always wore in the café. 'But thank you, love.'

He'd hugged them both in turn, Ginny first, then Alyssa.

'Thanks for today, Grandad. I don't know what I'd do without you.'

'That goes both ways, lass, don't you worry.'

The little table bell on the counter tinkled and he'd gone off to take care of it. Alyssa had heard Georgie speaking to him as she'd settled her bill and ordered three slices of Victoria sponge.

He'd come back for his jacket, then said his goodbyes. Alyssa had waited for the sound of the front door, but when it came, she'd heard her grandad speaking again.

'Hello there, Moira. Lovely to see you.'

Ginny's eyes had widened as she silently mouthed 'Moira?', her puzzled frown had added the question mark, as she'd dashed out of the kitchen.

Alyssa had to know too, so she'd put the knife down and followed, and that's how, right now, she could see that Moira Chiles was coming straight towards the counter.

She decided to help out her sister by taking the lead. 'Hello there, Moira.' She greeted her with the same wide smile and cheery tone that made all her customers feel welcome. Moira had been coming in once a week or so for months now, sometimes with a pal that wore long floaty kaftans, and other times with her male friend, Nick. Alyssa wasn't sure of the exact nature of their relationship because neither of them wore wedding or engagement rings, but they always held hands and there was a lot of laughter. Ginny still hadn't spoken up, so Alyssa bridged the gap. 'I believe you and my sister here met this afternoon.'

Moira beamed at Ginny. 'We sure did. That's actually why I'm here. Although I would also like two ginger slices and four cheese and onion rolls to take away.'

'Coming right up,' Alyssa told her, moving to the glass display cabinets, while Moira continued the conversation with her sister.

'Ginny, you're my excuse to come in here and break my diet for the second time this week and it's only Monday.' Her chuckle made it clear that breaking the diet wasn't something she gave two hoots about.

'Really?' Alyssa heard the hope in Ginny's voice and got right on that bandwagon with her.

'Indeed. I was just on my way home and thought I'd save the Academy a phone call and put you out of your suspense at the same time. You interviewed so well today...'

Alyssa could barely stand the tension, and she was suddenly concerned that Ginny might faint, given that it was obvious she was holding her breath. But so far so good... Unless Moira's next word was a 'but'.

'And we'd love you to join our team. We think you'd fit in perfectly.'

Ginny handled the news very calmly, by screeching, clapping, running around to the front of the counter and throwing her arms around Moira.

'Am I to take it that you're accepting the position?'

'Yes, thank you. Thank you sooooo much. Eeeeeek!'

Moira got another hug and Alyssa felt a lump forming in her throat. When it came to problems, she was strong and kept it together. But when good things happened to people she loved? Pure mush and happy tears.

'Okay, I'm going to put you down now and back away, before you change your mind,' Ginny chuckled, coming back round to the staff side of the counter. 'But I'm so grateful. I can't wait to get started.'

'That was the other reason I wanted to pop in straight away. You did say you could start next week...'

Ginny gave Alyssa a sheepish glance and mouthed 'sorry'. But Alyssa was too happy for her sister to care that she'd be losing her from the café. Between her and Grandad, and maybe a couple of students back in the village for Christmas break, they'd make it work. That gave her a thought... Georgie's daughter, Kayleigh, was studying law and home right now. Kayleigh had worked in the café for a couple of years in school holidays, so maybe she'd be available and perhaps she could hook her up with some legal advice on contracts too. Alyssa filed that one away for later. Right now, she was back with her gleeful sister and her spectacular achievement.

'If that's still the case,' Moira went on, 'then we'd love to make that happen because we have a big Christmas show coming up and need all the help we can get.'

Ginny caught Alyssa's gaze, asked a silent question, and Alyssa nodded straight away.

Ginny then delivered the answer. 'Of course I can! That's perfect! I can't wait.'

'Great. HR will be in touch, and the other thing I wanted to tell you is that we've all been in the business for a long time, and we know that you wouldn't be coaching if there were more jobs out there, so one of the perks of the job is that we allow time off for auditions. Just because you're working with us to pay the bills, doesn't mean you have to give up your dreams.'

Alyssa didn't have a grain of acting or musical talent, but if she did, then she'd want to work with Moira too. She struck her as a woman who was street-savvy and had been through a lot in her life. And the fact that she had a son who couldn't walk down a street without getting mobbed by fans, yet she was so down to earth and normal, made Alyssa love her even more.

She put Moira's rolls and ginger slices into a bag and handed it over. 'On the house, Moira.'

'Thank you, but absolutely not,' she objected, pulling £20 from her purse and sliding it across the counter. 'Between you and I, I'd pay double for these ginger slices. They're the best thing I've ever tasted. Right, well, I'll leave you to it. Alyssa, I'll see you tonight. Jessie from across the road does my hair, and she's invited me to her party. And Ginny, it was a pleasure to meet you properly today. I'm looking forward to working with you. Bring one of these cakes in every Monday and we'll get on great.'

With a wink and a cheery wave, she left the café. She'd only gone two steps into the street, when Ginny screeched again and hugged Alyssa until she could barely breathe.

'I got it! I got it! And I know this isn't the moment for you to ditch work and celebrate with me, because you're more than slightly in the shit, but I just wanted to say thank you, because if you hadn't taken me there today, I might not have got this. And, true, they'd have been missing out on the best staff member they'll ever have, but I think this is going to be great for me. Oh, happy fricking days, a full-time salary doing a job I'll actually love. No offence. Tomorrow after work we're going to Primark, and I won't hear a single objection.'

Her happiness was contagious, and Alyssa was here for it. 'Done. I'm so chuffed for you, and you don't need to thank me because it was you who made this happen. And I'd love to celebrate with you right now, but I need to go get those sandwiches made and get a dozen other things ready.'

'Okay, tell me what I can do. Anything at all. This is the one time you can boss me around and I won't even roll my eyes.'

'I can't see us getting many more customers today, so if you could set everything up out here for the party tonight, I'll love you forever. Buffet table, cutlery, crockery and the glasses for the beer and wine.'

'I'm on it!' Ginny paused, then pointed at her face. 'See! Didn't even roll my eyes.'

Feeling so much lighter than she did a few minutes ago, Alyssa retreated back into the kitchen and resumed sandwich construction. The process was therapeutic to her. There was something about the wholesomeness of putting it all together, of creating something with her hands, that helped her mind too. Ten minutes passed, twenty, thirty and as the pile grew, so did her determination to fight for her business. Maybe Ginny getting this break today was their sign that their luck was turning.

She had several towers of bread on each side of her, when Ginny came back in.

'Holy shit, you should see the bloke who's just came in and sat down.'

Alyssa was focused on arranging her latest batch of chicken salad sandwiches onto the oak serving boards that she would cover and put in the fridge for later. 'Don't tell me... Ollie Chiles has just pitched up and is currently sitting in my café demanding a sprinkle doughnut.'

'Nope, but this guy might be just as good-looking. Not that I'm objectifying, because, you know, I'm millennial and we frown on that kind of thing.'

'I've noticed,' Alyssa said, not even trying to pretend she wasn't being sarcastic.

Ginny was still on a roll. 'But he's driving a fuck-off sexy big black Ranger Rover and it's parked right outside. Oh, and no wedding ring. I checked. Not my type – no visible tattoos and I don't think he would know Andrew Lloyd Webber if he met him in a lift, but he's totally your vibe. Good-looking, square jaw, athletic, long-ish hair all swept back like he belongs in an aftershave advert but looks like he'd wrestle a thief to the ground if he stole some old dear's handbag.'

Alyssa finished her display and moved on to the next one. Much as Ginny's dramatic assumptions about people amused her, this wasn't the time, and she didn't have the bandwidth for this discussion.

'Ginny, I love you, but the last thing I need right now is a man. Have you noticed that I'm up to my arse in problems, on the verge of losing my home, my business and I still have about two hundred more sandwiches to make before a storm of villagers come through that door?'

'Now that you mention it...' Ginny admitted, and Alyssa thought the situation was handled.

But no...

'However, I need to nip to the loo, and he's waiting for a black coffee that I've poured and put on the counter, and a toffee muffin, so I just need you to take it over to him and thank you and goodbye.' With that, she flew out of the door in the direction of the loo, and Alyssa knew she was beat.

With a sigh so deep, it removed all the air from her body, Alyssa wiped her hands on her apron and went out into the shop. As advised, the black coffee was there waiting, so she set up a plate with a muffin, knife and napkin and took it over to the gent who had his back to her and was staring out of the window to his right.

As soon as she approached, he turned to look at her and, damn, Ginny wasn't kidding. Attractive. Kind eyes. Would definitely wrestle a robber.

'Here you go...'

A flinch of confusion crossed his face when he saw what she'd brought him. 'I don't think the muffin is for me. I only ordered a coffee.'

Alyssa knew immediately what was going on. Bloody Ginny. She'd just manufactured a reason for them to converse. And why was he looking at her like that? Intense. Quizzical. As if he was trying to place her.

She didn't want to admit the truth, so she went with, 'Oh, no worries. Monday is toffee muffin day. You get a free one with every coffee. Sorry, my hopeless waitress should have told you that.'

She raised her voice on the 'hopeless', hoping that Ginny had returned from the loo and could hear her.

'Anyway, enjoy,' she said, before turning to leave.

'Excuse me...' he said, halting her retreat. 'Sorry if this sounds like a line, and I promise it isn't... but have we met?'

16

LACHLAN

The pretty waitress was now eyeing him like he was a pick-up merchant with a terrible line in chat. Which, granted, was definitely the impression he was giving.

'No, I don't think so.' She took another step away, leaving him staring at a toffee muffin, trying to summon up a sliver of inspiration as to why she seemed so familiar.

If he had to guess, he'd say she was maybe mid to late twenties, a few years younger than him, so they couldn't have been at school together. He'd never done any work out this way. And he hadn't been in Weirbridge since he was a teenager, so it couldn't be that either.

He shook it off, deciding that the emotion and nostalgia of today must be playing with his mind. That was the only explanation as to why he was sitting in this café right now.

After the accident had blocked the motorway exit to the airport and he'd kept driving until he'd seen the Burnbank and Weirbridge sign, it had felt like... well, like a different kind of sign. One that was coming from somewhere else, telling him to go say goodbye to the last connection to the family he once had.

He'd driven down decent-sized roads, then onto the windy lanes that he'd vaguely recognised, seeing brief glimpses of flashbacks as he went towards Burnbank. His mum's face, laughing as she drove them in her little green sports car past fields that stretched for miles. Jason kicking a football into a stream, then complaining because he didn't want to go in and get it back out. His dad, always serious, restless as Mum tried to get him to relax and enjoy their picnic. And removal vans, packing all their stuff up for their move to the Glasgow house, his mum wiping away tears as she told them how wonderful it was going to be. In hindsight, he guessed that she probably didn't want to leave, but back then, his dad called the shots, and Mum went along with whatever he wanted. In fact, that never changed, and his mum didn't seem to mind. The one thing that hadn't altered now that he was looking in the rear-view mirror of his childhood, was that he truly believed his parents had loved each other and had been happy with their roles within the family and the lives they built together. Jason had been so pissed off when their father had married again – primarily, Lachlan suspected, because he was watching most of their inheritance waltz up the aisle and out of their reach, but Lachlan had understood why it happened. Dad had Mum by his side since he was a teenager. That was a huge loss to live with and a big void to fill. Lachlan was just happy that their dad had found someone to do that, because after losing Tanya, he knew what living with emptiness felt like.

The entrance to Morden Manor, his early childhood home, had been completely covered in snow, so he'd almost missed it, skidding as he'd turned at the last minute. He remembered Jeremy Sprite saying that the tenants had already moved out, so he'd taken a chance that there would be no one there to accuse him of trespassing, and driven up the long driveway to the darkened house. He'd stopped the car for just a few seconds, locking the memory in, wishing his dad was still here so he could ask him why he'd kept it. Sentimentality, he assumed. The same reason he was sitting there on a freezing cold afternoon in the middle of winter, when he could be in a nice warm lounge at the airport, drinking a beer.

Driving back out onto the country road, he'd decided he was far too invested to turn back, so instead, he'd veered right on the road that brought him to Weirbridge – the village much more recognisable to him than the last one. They'd continued to come here on day trips during the school summer holidays every year, and they'd have ice cream and wander around the shops, then head to the café, the one that he'd somehow found himself in now. It looked completely different, though. The sign above the door had said, The Once Upon A Time Café, and now that he was inside, he could see why. Shelves of books lined the two main walls and there were little reading nooks for children in a couple of the corners. As well as the normal dining tables for eating, there were sofas and big armchairs with side tables for solo diners too. Everything about it was gorgeous. Warm. Welcoming. He knew his mum would have loved it.

Coming here had been good for the soul, he decided. Another memory to lock in place. Back in those long-ago summers, he remembered it being packed out, but today, with six inches of snow on the ground outside and a biting wind that made the eyes sting, it was just him, a steaming coffee and a toffee muffin that he didn't ask for, but suddenly couldn't resist.

He picked it up, broke a piece off and popped it in his mouth, immediately deciding it was possibly the best thing he'd tasted in a long time.

'They're great, aren't they? My sister bakes them fresh every morning.' He hadn't even heard the first waitress come back, but now she was beside him again.

'They're amazing,' he admitted, torn between not being rude and hoping that she wouldn't want to strike up a conversation. Depressing as it sounded, he just wanted to sit here with his memories as company. And no, he still couldn't work out why the other waitress had seemed so familiar to him.

Unfortunately, this lady didn't get the whole 'want to be alone' memo, because she pulled out the chair opposite him and sat down, with all the confidence of someone who felt perfectly at ease invading a stranger's space. On any other day, he'd probably enjoy the interaction, but not today. However, he had manners, so he would never object.

'I'm Ginny. And I'd really appreciate it if you let me sit here for a while, otherwise my sister – that's the grumpy but cute one who brought your muffin – will find ten jobs for me to do, all of them equally mind-numbing.'

On another person, this might be obnoxious, but she said it with such amusement that he decided to roll with it.

'I'm Lachlan. And I don't have a sister who tasks me with mind-numbing jobs, so I now feel very lucky. Thank you for that.'

'You're welcome. All part of the service. That, and the free muffins.'

'Does every customer really get those?'

'No, but I got a new job today, so I'm spreading the joy.'

Her laugh was cute, but not in a coy way. His intuition told him that she wasn't flirting with him. This was giving off the same vibes as his dynamic with Margaux – strictly friendly energy. Maybe even a bit of mischievous skiving. And he had to remind himself again that he wasn't in the bustle of London any more. People chatted here. Passed the time of day. That thought made him relax enough to ask the natural next question.

'A new job?'

'Yeeahh.' She stopped herself. 'Sorry. That made it sound like I'm off to join a rodeo. I'm actually just really excited because I'm a jobbing actress, and expected to be a really terrible waitress and live on the poverty line for the rest of my life, all for the sake of being able to waft around telling people that I'm sacrificing my personal wealth for the sake of my art. But today I got a brilliant job, coaching in a theatre school, teaching kids and teenagers to act and perform, while being paid a decent wage. So go me.'

He lifted his coffee as if in a toast. 'Go you. Congratulations.'

Much as he was beginning to enjoy this exchange, he wondered if she'd leave now that she'd got her good news out of the way.

Apparently not.

'So now that I've invaded your personal space...' The spookily accurate account of his earlier thoughts made him blush a little. '...Do tell me how you come to find yourself a stranger in a village in the middle of a snow storm. It's like the start of every Christmas romcom ever. And by the way, my sister, the grumpy one who displayed questionable customer service skills, is single.'

That did actually make him laugh out loud. So that's where all this was going. He'd been right on point with the mischief thought earlier. And something told him that given her reserved manner and blatant lack of interest, her sister wouldn't be at all pleased if she knew that... He flicked back to remember her name... If she knew that Ginny was out here trying to set her up with a random bloke.

'How do you know I'm a stranger?'

'Because I've never seen you before, and around here, everyone knows everyone and all their business. And, trust me, someone with a big expensive Range Rover like that one isn't going to go unnoticed.'

'Ah, fair point. Would it change things if I told you that it was a hire car?'

She sagged dramatically. 'Yes. I'd be swamped with disappointment and may possibly retract my pointless efforts to explore any romcom romance between you and my sister.'

'Then retract away because I've only got it for the day. But thank you for considering me. And my car.'

'Urgh, plot twist. But you don't get off that easy. There might still be some redeeming qualities. I'll need more information on the purpose of your visit here.'

He decided that the only way to handle this was to surrender. 'I live in London, but I had to come up here today for a family meeting. I'm flying back to London tonight, but I had some time to kill, so here I am.'

'In Weirbridge? Random.'

'Not really. I lived in Burnbank when I was a kid. My mum grew up there and when she was a teenager she worked here in this café.'

'Really? That's amazing. What was her name?'

'Felicity. Felicity Morden. Actually, she was fifteen when she worked here so her name would still have been McSlay. She's passed now, so I very much doubt there will be any trace of her.'

'Felicity...' He watched as Ginny began to repeat the name, and then suddenly stopped, as if paused by a remote control. Then her whole energy shifted, and she suddenly shouted, 'Alyssa. ALYSSA!' in the direction of the empty counter.

In seconds, her sister materialised from a doorway behind it, and she didn't look happy about it. In fact, she was definitely giving off harassed vibes.

'You called?'

'This is Lachlan,' Ginny was saying now. 'And his mum was called Felicity *Morden*.'

She put an unmistakable emphasis on the surname and her sister had an immediate reaction. She darted across to their table, pulled out the chair next to Ginny and sat down.

'I didn't introduce myself earlier. I'm Alyssa and I'm the owner here.'

That's when he realised his mistake. He really hadn't thought this visit through, probably because he hadn't thought for a second that he'd strike up a conversation with anyone. He was someone who kept to himself, someone who preserved his privacy, who would no sooner share with a stranger than run naked up Weirbridge Main Street in the snow. And this was why. You just never knew when you would say the wrong thing.

Two things happened simultaneously. First, he realised where he'd seen her before – at the reception of the lawyer's office this morning. She was demanding to see Jeremy Sprite. And secondly, in that moment, a horrible, sickening, oh-so-obvious-in-hindsight comment from this morning's meeting came back to him.

They'd notified the current owners of the café that their lease was being terminated. And now, way too late, he realised that he was about to face the consequences of that action.

4 P.M. – 6 P.M.

17

JESSIE

Stan was sitting at the kitchen table, with a mug of tea in front of him and a packet of caramel wafers by his side. That bugger could eat rubbish all day and he never gained weight, whereas Jessie maintained she could drive by Greggs on the bus and gain three pounds.

'Hello, love. How was your day?' He had a twinkle in his eye that came from either a lunchtime pint at the golf club, or pure happiness that tomorrow they were going off to live the dream. Jessie suspected it was a bit of both. 'Your hair is looking mighty fancy.'

Jessie gave a theatrical pat to her curls. 'Our lass has a God-given talent,' she chirped.

Stan chuckled, as he dipped his biscuit in his tea. 'I think it's a Jessie-given talent, myself. I believe my wife is not bad at all that hairdressing stuff too.'

Despite all her angst, her memories, her doubts, that comment warmed her heart. This was who Stan McLean was. He loved her, he took care of her, he lifted her up and he made her laugh. He'd provided for his family all his life, loved his children and they still adored him to this day.

'By the way, our Grant got back today. He did Val's hair while Georgie was doing mine and Cathy's and he's looking smashing. He's staying at

Georgie's, and Kayleigh is home too. It'll be lovely to have the full squad there tonight. I even invited Flynn...'

Jessie watched him purse his lips. He'd never been Flynn's biggest fan. Like most fathers, he felt her daughter was too good for her choice of husband – not that he'd told her that, until Flynn had buggered off and left them. 'Christ, I'd better have a beer if I need to act civil to that one tonight.'

'Don't worry, he can't come. A work thing, he said. But I think he's probably just avoiding you.'

'Good thing too. Georgie doesn't need that man anywhere near her.'

'Stan, he's Kayleigh's dad.' It was the argument she used every time, because as far as Jessie was concerned, that was reason enough for them to stay on good terms. The hypocrisy in his attitude grated a little, though. Hadn't she overlooked Stan's behaviour for the sake of keeping the peace and holding the family together?

'Aye, and that's why I'll keep my thoughts to myself. But don't expect me to have a civil word for that man. Tenerife isn't far enough away from him. Anyway, enough about him. I'll get you a cup of tea, love,' he offered, but Jessie shook her head.

'I think I'm going to have a wee Prosecco. It's that kind of day and there's half a bottle in the fridge left over from when Georgie came to watch *Strictly* on Saturday night. It'll go to waste if I don't drink it tonight.'

That thought gave her warm heart a cold shower. Saturday nights on the couch with Georgie, a takeaway and a bottle of wine were a frequent occurrence in the winter months. They'd leave the salon, pick up food on the way home, and then settle in for the night, grateful that they could spend all day together and still enjoy each other's company. Georgie even stayed over in her old bedroom sometimes. There wouldn't be a day that went by in Tenerife that Jessie wouldn't miss those times.

She opened the fridge. For decades, the fridge in her kitchen had been packed with vegetables, sauces, different butters, meats, cheeses, wine, beer, milk and everything else that was needed to feed a family of four, and then later, a couple who liked to have plenty in stock in case someone dropped in. All that it contained now was a carton of milk, a slab of butter, a couple of cans of beer and the half-full bottle of Prosecco. Everything else had been cleared out at the weekend, when they'd emptied the kitchen cupboards and every other cupboard in the house, and a lifetime of possessions had been given away, donated, or packed into boxes that were now stored in the garage, ready to be shipped when they sold the house.

She took out the fizz, and one of the two glasses that were on the drying rack, the only ones that they'd kept handy after the clear-out, to use before they left. She sat at the table and watched the bubbles appear in the glass as she poured it.

'Hugo Canavan was asking after you today. Said he's looking forward to seeing you tonight,' Jessie told him. The flinch was almost indiscernible, but it was there. Every time she'd mentioned the name Canavan in the last twenty-odd years there had been that tiny reaction. 'He was in the café this morning. In fact, all the Canavans were there. Alyssa and Ginny were working and then Dorinda pitched up too.'

Another flinch. More noticeable this time.

Jessie had no idea why she'd said that, but she hadn't been able to stop herself. Was she baiting him? Trying to lead up to asking him about it? After all this time, why now? What would be the purpose of that? Was she really so desperate to avoid leaving here that she would throw a bomb into her marriage just so she could stay? Bugger, she shouldn't have had that champagne at the salon. It was wrecking what little sense her frazzled nerves had left her with. Time to stop this. Time to get it straight in her head. She was leaving and that was that. End of story.

'He's a good man, Hugo.' Stan took a drink of his tea, before changing the subject. 'Are you looking forward to the party?'

'I am. I just wish...' Oh, bollocks, maybe not 'end of story'. Her mouth seemed to have adopted a mind of its own. 'Stan, how about we stay here a bit longer? Maybe just until the turn of the year? It's only a month away.'

She couldn't look at him because she didn't want to see the shock or the rejection on his face.

Instead, she was the one who was in for the shock, when he said, 'That's the thing, love. I don't know if you noticed, but the For Sale sign didn't go up today.'

'I did, but I just figured it hadn't gone up because of the snow.'

'No, it wasn't that, love.'

His triumphant expression gave her a stunning moment of realisation and her heart began to soar as she sent up a silent prayer of *oh dear God, thank you*. He'd changed his mind. He'd finally clicked on to how sad she was to be leaving, and he'd taken the problem away. That was how well Stan McLean knew her and how much he loved her.

'Oh Stan, you cancelled it? You've had second thoughts too? You know, I tried to go along with you, I really did, but, Lord, my heart was breaking. And I'm not saying I'll never do it, but just... not yet, Stan. Let me have a few more months here, let me enjoy my retirement with my pals and Georgie and Kayleigh. Maybe even take some trips to London to see Grant and Gabriel. And Christmas! We'll have another Christmas here. It's only a month away, and I mean, what were we thinking going away three weeks before Christmas anyway?'

He seemed astonished by that. 'Because we wanted to spend our first Christmas in the sun and then go on that cruise from Los Cristianos to Cyprus for New Year.'

She desperately wanted to point out that it wasn't 'we' who'd wanted that. Stan had waxed lyrical about it all and she'd gone along with it because her head was so far stuck in the sand she could barely breathe. Anyway, it didn't matter now because everything had changed and crisis had been averted.

'Why didn't you tell me that you felt that way?' he asked her, clearly surprised.

'I'm sorry, but your heart was just so set on it and I didn't want to take something away that you cared so much about. We've done this whole life together, Stan, and we've always been on the same page. I didn't want to admit that this time we weren't even in the same book.'

It was plain to see that he was affected by that because he looked crestfallen as he murmured. 'I really wish you'd told me, Jessie.'

She put her hand on his. 'Me too. I've had so many sleepless nights about it and I've woken up every morning with a gut full of worries. I could have saved myself all of that if I'd known you would reconsider.'

A silence descended, and she wondered how he could be sitting there, looking so crushed when they'd just made this wonderful breakthrough.

'The thing is, Jessie... I don't quite know how to say this.'

His tone was so solemn, that her gut full of worries came creeping back. Something was wrong. His mood and the moment weren't matching.

'The reason the sign didn't go up today had nothing to do with me changing my mind. It didn't go up because the estate agent called me after you left this morning, to say that they'd had an enquiry about renting this house for a few months, and he suggested we take it because coming up to Christmas is a tough time to sell.'

Her gut full of worries was now overflowing. 'I don't understand. What does that mean?'

'It means that the estate agent popped round with the family this afternoon and they loved it. We signed the lease there and then and they're moving in at the weekend.'

'So we're still leaving tomorrow?'

'*I* am, Jessie.' He put the emphasis on the 'I'. 'And I thought you were too. I thought this was our dream and we were about to go and live our best lives. But given everything you've just said, I think that's a decision you're going to have to make on your own.'

18

GEORGIE

As soon as Georgie opened the door of her home, she heard something that made her heart soar, despite the crapstorm of a day: noise.

She'd missed this so much. For the last six months, since Kayleigh had moved to Edinburgh, she'd come home every night to deathly silence, and it had eaten away at her soul. She'd even started going to her mother's house on a Saturday night to watch *Strictly*, just so she would be around people, and noise and conversation.

Why had she not prepared for that transition? Why was there not a public service announcement or a manual that warned that parenthood meant you raised these children, made them your whole world, gave them confidence and ambition and independence… and then all that culminated in them buggering off and leaving you on your lonesome?

But not tonight. She could hear Grant singing along to a Taylor Swift song and Kayleigh giggling uproariously, so she knew they must be dancing. And yes, she could hear Flynn's voice too, but for the purposes of this little interlude of reflection, she was going to forget that she was furious with him and just remember when this very scenario of chat and music and laughter was what she used to come home to every night.

She wasn't sure that she would ever stop missing it.

Her coat was damp from a fresh flurry of snow that had come down just as she'd come into the street, so she shrugged it off and hung it on the wooden post at the bottom of the stairs, then plonked down on the bottom step to pull her wellies off. That done, she sat for a moment, inhaled, exhaled, summoning the wisdom she would need to deal with this in a calm, mature manner, the cunning she would require to play it right, and the strength to refrain from telling him he was an utter arse.

Only when she felt she was in possession of all three did she get up and breeze into the kitchen.

'Well, hello family,' she greeted them with a cheerful smile and a hug for Kayleigh, who was standing centre stage in front of the cooker wearing a beautiful but tiny silky red vest top, navy velvet cargo trousers and a pair of Jordan trainers.

'What do you think?' Her daughter gestured to her own outfit when Georgie released her.

Georgie took in the fashion choices. 'I think you look stunning, I think you'll get pneumonia in that top, and I think your generation is genius for going the trendy trainers route. When I was your age, we wore shoes that made our feet bleed in the name of defined calves.'

Grant was leaning against the worktop over at the sink, holding two glasses of what looked like wine, one of which he handed over to her. 'I tried and failed to convert her to the joys of a nude heel. It's a tragedy.'

'You're getting old, Uncle Grant. Out of touch,' Kayleigh teased him, and Grant clutched his chest dramatically. 'Hush your mouth, I'm thirty-four! I'm only three years older than Harry frigging Styles. Right, let's go fix that hair before I change my mind about you being my favourite niece.'

'I'm your *only* niece,' Kayleigh pointed out, giggling again.

Grant stuck with the faux outrage. 'Exactly.'

As the two of them headed out of the kitchen, she caught Grant's eye and sent a telepathic thanks to him for being wonderful with her daughter, and loving her enough to be inauthentically civil to her ex-husband.

Flynn had been sitting at the kitchen table, watching them with amusement the whole time, but now, as she sat down opposite him, his gaze settled on her and a smile played on the lips she'd been sucking off his face that morning. Urgh. That thought made her shiver more than the sub-zero temperatures and six inches of snow outside.

'Hey,' he murmured, watching her.

Sexy grin on? Check. Sexy eyes on? Check. Sexy voice on? Check. Still a twat? Check. Aaaargh, she was furious, but she wasn't going to let him know that yet.

'Hey.' *Be nice*, her inner angel reminded her. Eyes on the prize. Jessie always said you found out more with honey than with... Actually, Georgie couldn't remember the other bit, but it was something less appealing than a sugary spread.

'Got my wallet.' He lifted it from the table to provide proof of this fact and she had the sudden thought that maybe the whole 'left wallet' thing was a deliberate manipulation so that he'd have to come back tonight. Or was she just overthinking everything about him now?

'Great. So Kayleigh said you've decided to come to the party tonight.'

'Yeah. I mean, your mum was good enough to invite me, so as long as your dad doesn't put bouncers on the door to stop me getting in, I thought it would be kind of cool to have a family night out again. *Our* family.'

Her dad's distrust and general disdain for him had never been vocalised to Flynn directly, but it didn't take a psychologist to spot it.

The reference to 'family' was very clearly loaded, though, so she decided to jump right in.

'You know, I was thinking about what you were saying this morning.'

'You were?' He looked suitably pleased with this information.

'I was.' Her answer was breezy, as she was still trying her best not to give away that he was about to stroll right into an ambush of his own making. She'd thought about how to play this the whole way home, and this was the best she could come up with at short notice. 'But if we're going to give it another try, then I don't want there to be anything that could come back and bite us on the arse later. No secrets. Nothing that could hurt us. So if there's anything you think I should know, then I need you to tell me now and we can talk about it, move on and forget it.'

A very slight frown of unease made two little creases appear between the sexy eyes, but he kept up the cool and easy vibe.

'Like what?'

She shrugged, acting nonchalant. 'Oh, I don't know. Maybe just things like whether we've seen other people since we split. No details. I mean just, like, ballpark. Bullet points.'

He immediately deflected, as she'd anticipated that he would. 'Why, have you?'

'No.'

'No one? Like, at all? Since we split up?'

Georgie shook her head, as if this was the most natural thing in the world. 'No. Not even a date. I was a bit busy with the salon and being with our daughter.'

Hopefully, despite the words, she'd managed to keep any hint of resentment or accusation out of that, because if he got defensive, then she'd never get the truth. 'I'm also inherently lazy and terrified of dating apps, so there's that. It's not a moral thing. If Ryan Gosling had shown up on my doorstep, then I totally would have.'

His shoulders dropped just a tad, but it was enough to show that she'd put him at ease again.

Time to go in with, 'What about you? And please be honest, because I can take it. Like I said, I just want to clear the decks so we both know there are no secrets.'

He took a swig of his beer before he answered. 'Look, I have seen a few people. Like I said, it's been three years since we split, Georgie. Two years since the divorce. I don't think that's unreasonable.'

'No, no – I don't either. This isn't a blame game here, and I promise there are no right or wrong answers.' She waited for a bolt of lightning to strike her down for the obvious lie there, but when it didn't come, she carried on. 'So when you say you've "seen" people – do you mean dates, or actual relationships?'

Headlights. Rabbit.

'Dates. Yeah, like a few dates, but that's it.'

'So no one long term, no one serious?'

Argh, this was so difficult. She wanted to blurt out that she knew about Monica, that the game was up, and she had all the facts at her disposal, but she'd promised that she wouldn't tell him about his girlfriend's visit, so that option was off the table.

'No, nothing like that. I think I always hoped on some level that we'd get back together, so I haven't been interested in anything that could get in the way of that.'

Oh, he was good. If she hadn't known he was lying through his teeth, she might be believing this. *Today's lesson is being brought to you courtesy of the word, 'gullible'.*

One last question for the prosecution. 'And you're not seeing anyone right now?'

He leaned forward, elbows on the table, 'No. Georgie, do you think I'd be sitting here if I was seeing someone?'

Yes. Yes, I absolutely would. But she said that on the inside. On the outside, she went with, 'I guess not. I mean, that would be a pretty underhand thing to do. You hear about guys like that, that play a couple of women along at the same time. Total shitbags. I had a client the other day whose ex-husband was trying to get her back while still shagging his secretary.'

His Adam's apple moved as she said that and there was a definite squirm in his chair, but she carried on in a light conversational tone, as if just relaying a story.

'I mean, what kind of guy would do that? If I found out that someone was trying to get back in my bed and have me commit my future to him while he was sleeping with someone else, well, I'd...'

She paused, watched him squirm a little more as he asked, 'You'd what?'

'Well, first, I'd probably dip his willy in disinfectant while he was asleep, but after that I think I'd be done with him because he's just not a decent guy. If he truly cared about me, he'd take care of his stuff first, before even suggesting any kind of reconciliation.' She leaned forward, warm smile still in place. 'Anyway, I'm glad that's not you.'

Another squirm.

'And I'm glad we had this conversation, because if I found out later you'd been seeing someone and lied to me, I think it would wreck any chance we had of friendship, never mind a relationship.' She let that hang, before dismissing it. 'Anyway, glad you're not.'

'No.' Was it her imagination or was he now sweating slightly and checking the location of the exits?

'But also...' she went on.

'Yes?' Definitely sweating.

'Would you mind if we didn't do the party together tonight? I just think it could be confusing for Kayleigh. I don't want her to get her hopes up that we'll get back together until we definitely know for sure that's what we want.'

He sat back in the chair. 'And you don't know yet?' His whole energy and demeanour had changed since she'd sat down, and she couldn't tell if he was relieved or perturbed by her request.

She pretended to mull his question over for a few seconds. 'I think we need to take more time. You know, I haven't told you this, but I feel I need to be completely honest with you too.' Time to go in with the cut-off switch, the one thing that she knew would send him racing to the hills. It was a complete lie, but the only thing she could think of that would unequivocally end his hopes of skipping off into the sunset together. 'I've begun to realise that I'd like more children.'

'You what?' The horror on his face was almost comical and made her warm up even more to the story.

'Yes, at least one more. Maybe two. Now that Kayleigh has moved out, I feel like there's a void that I want to fill. I'm only thirty-eight. Some women are just starting their families at my age.'

His wide eyes and raised eyebrows screamed pure panic. 'Georgie, I definitely don't want more children. No way. I feel like we've just hit a time in our lives where we have no commitments and it's just for us. We can do anything, go anywhere...'

Shag multiple women and lie to them, she added, but again, only on the inside.

'But that's the thing, I don't want that. I want to be home, with another couple of little ones running around. I'm sorry if that doesn't align with how you see your future, but it's a deal-breaker for me.'

'Then I'm so sorry, Georgie, but I guess it won't work.' To his credit, his sad face was fairly impressive.

'No, I guess it won't. Good thing we realised now, before either of us had our hearts torn out again.' This wasn't the time to point out that the only people who'd had their hearts decimated when he left last time was her and Kayleigh. He was too busy stocking up on SPF10 for his jolly to Thailand. 'Or before I fall pregnant again and then we're right back in it.'

He visibly paled at that thought. 'Absolutely. And you're right, I probably shouldn't come tonight.' His relief was almost palpable. 'Listen, I'll go.' He got up from his chair. 'I'll tell Kayleigh that I've got a…'

'Work emergency?' she suggested.

He missed the irony. 'Yeah, a work emergency.' He leaned down, kissed her cheek. 'I'll, erm, see you… soon.'

He was out of the door before she even had a chance to reply to that. Only after he'd gone did she notice, with a wry chuckle, that this time he'd remembered his wallet. The second thing she noticed was that her relief had shoved her fury to one side. Deep down, she knew that she'd never wanted him back and Monica had done her the biggest favour by removing the option. Lucky escape.

Dilemma number one of the day sorted. Now she just had to deal with the other one.

19

ALYSSA

Alyssa could hardly believe that this man was sitting here. All day, she'd been desperately trying to get hold of someone from the Morden family without success, and now someone with the same surname had come to her. And she had no idea how or why, but it couldn't be a coincidence. As soon as she'd introduced herself, she cut straight to finding out if this was the person she'd been looking for.

'The person who owned this building passed away recently – a man called Martyn Morden. Are you related to him?'

As soon as she saw his chest deflate and his slow, resigned nod, she knew the answer. 'He was my father.'

Business could wait a second because she could see the flinch of sadness on this guy's face and reminded herself that she might be about to lose her home and her business, but he'd lost his dad. And that was far more important.

'I'm really sorry for your loss. I read a bit about him, and it seems like he was a good man who cared about people. Losing him must have been a terrible thing.' She hoped that was the right thing to say. She and Ginny had never known their dad – he'd buggered off when they were about three and four – so she didn't have the best insight into the relationships between fathers and their children.

'Thank you.'

That was all he said. Not the most talkative of guys, but then, maybe it was just too painful a subject.

'The thing is...' she began, trying to find the right words. 'Well, I'm sorry to talk about business at a time like this, but Mr Morden owned this building. And I don't know if you're aware, but his lawyer has sent me a letter, telling me that my lease has been terminated and I have sixty days to leave.'

There was something in his lack of reaction that gave her a sense that this wasn't news to him, and that threw her off kilter. Ginny must have spotted it too, because she joined the conversation.

'Did you already know this? Is that why you came here? To make sure we knew we were getting tossed out?' There was an escalation in Ginny's tone, almost an accusation, and Alyssa watched as his posture changed and he shook his head.

'No!' he said urgently, before de-escalating and lowering the heat. 'I don't have anything to do with my family's business. In fact, the first I knew about my dad owning this building was this morning when his will was read. I didn't even know that it was still a café, and the only reason I came here today was because my late mum used to bring us here when we were kids, and I had an urge to see it again. If you hadn't sat down and spoken to me, I'd have drunk my coffee and left.'

Alyssa watched as Ginny considered that, then appeared to accept it. 'He's probably right. I only spoke to him because he's good-looking, and you're having a terrible day, so I was trying to create a romcom moment between you to take your mind off it. My bad.'

Alyssa wanted to put her head on the table until the embarrassment subsided, but the opportunity to speak to him was too important to avoid, especially now that she knew he didn't come with... What was it they called it on all those crime shows on the telly? Malicious intent. Yes, that was it. She chided herself. If he was telling the truth, then this poor man had come to have a moment of reflection in a place that reminded him of his late mother, and she was now drawing her vocabulary from Netflix shows about serial killers.

'But you know now.' Alyssa could hear the pleading in her own voice.

'I've spent four years making this café incredible and you can see how beautiful it is. We love it here and it's my whole life. But, more importantly than that, my customers love it too. It's one of the meeting places in the community, somewhere that everyone is welcome...'

Ginny leaned forward. 'Except that obnoxious guy – the taxi driver that used to be an MP and then got jailed for drink driving. Lives just up the road. He's not welcome.'

Not for the first time in this life, this year, or even this week, Alyssa noted that Ginny's mind worked in mysterious ways, but she just rolled right over the interruption and kept on going.

'Where everyone except him is welcome. Tonight, the whole village is coming here for a party. In future, where will they gather if you close us down? Losing this place would be a tragedy for the villagers, so I'm begging you to help me. Who do I have to speak to? What can I do to change this?'

Surely he'd see how important this was? This was about more than buying and selling buildings. More than just bricks and mortar and transactions on a balance sheet. This café meant so much more than that. For a long second, she felt confident, hopeful. But then she saw him shake his head and hesitate to speak. That told her that he didn't have the words she wanted to hear.

'I wish I could help you, I really do. But it's complicated.'

'So explain it to me. Tell me how it works. The letter said it was the "estate" that was ordering the sale. Is that not you?'

'Not just me. There are other people involved – other family members. My dad instructed that this building be sold, and even if I wanted to cancel the sale, or find a way to delay it, there's no way that they'd agree to that.'

She noticed that he wasn't revealing who the other people involved were, but she assumed it was his siblings. No, just one sibling. She remembered the Google search this morning and joined the dots. It said his father had a wife and two sons. If his mother had passed away, that must mean his dad had remarried. So the other person or people in this must include his stepmother or his brother, or both.

Down but not out, Alyssa decided. She flicked back through her memory for the arguments she'd prepared to share with the lawyer this morning.

'Surely, though, this building is an appreciating asset? Doesn't it make sense to keep it and let the investment grow? Especially when I'm paying a good rent, so you're gaining income from it every month?'

He leaned towards her, his elbows and forearms on the table, hands clasped in front of him. 'Yes. All of that. And it would be a solid case if it wasn't for the fact that I know one of the other parties wants to release the capital quickly and the only way to do that is to sell.'

'Can I speak to them? Would you set that up? I could convince them to wait, offer alternatives...' She knew she was sounding desperate now, but that's because she absolutely was. When she'd been working in the kitchen a few minutes ago, she'd run through the other options, the first one being the most obvious – maybe she could buy the building? That one had been immediately dismissed – there was no way she'd get a mortgage for anything even close to what would be needed because she had no savings and for the last four years, she'd only taken a small salary and had ploughed every other penny of profit back into the business. Her second thought had been that perhaps she could spread the word in the village and see if there was any way to raise the funds in the community to buy the building. However, there were two immediate problems with that – the first was that she didn't know how much the building was worth and the second was that sixty days wasn't enough time to organise it.

He had to help her. He had to. There was no other way. She tried to manifest it into existence, will him to say yes.

'No. I'm sorry, Alice...'

'It's Alyssa,' she corrected him, with a deathly calm that she definitely didn't feel.

'I'm sorry... *Alyssa*.' And he said it with such regret that she almost felt sorry for him. Almost.

'But I would be getting your hopes up and then wasting your time, because he'd never do it. He wants it sold now. End of story. As I said, even if I wanted to help you by holding on to the building, he would refuse. Nothing will change his mind, I promise you.'

He. So he must be talking about his brother then.

'And you won't even try to help me by asking him?'

They were going round in circles, but she couldn't stop herself, even though the expression on his face told her everything she didn't want to know. It was no surprise when he eventually said no.

She sat back in her chair, palms on the table, deflated. Devastated. She felt a hand go onto her lap and squeeze her leg, and she knew it was Ginny, who'd come to the same conclusion as her.

This was hopeless. He wouldn't even try. That told them so much about the kind of man this was.

'Mr Morden...' She refused to call him by his first name. They weren't friends. 'I think you should leave.'

She watched him sigh, then reach into his pocket and take out his wallet, open it, and she guessed what he was about to do.

'I don't want your money. I'm not that desperate,' she told him in a tone that left no room for argument.

He didn't even reply. Just stood up, lifted his jacket from the chair next to him, took a step away, then stopped, turned back.

'For what it's worth, I truly am sorry.'

'Really?' she challenged him, eyes blazing. 'Because when I'm sorry for something I've done wrong, I fix it. And I don't see you trying to do that.'

'It's not that easy.'

'With people like you, it never is. Enjoy your inheritance, Mr Morden. Last time I checked, this café was still mine. This building is still mine. And that door is still mine. So don't let it hit your arse on the way out.'

He didn't even argue. He just walked away, and he was at the door when the next words came out of her mouth, with absolutely no consultation with her brain.

'Mr Morden, you said that your mother loved this place. I wonder what she'd think of this now.'

It was a low blow, and she hated herself for saying it. Although, it was wasted on him anyway, because he simply kept on going. The next thing she heard was the ding of the bell, then she watched through the window as he jumped into his swanky big flash-bastard car and drove off.

She sat perfectly still, struggling to stay upright, to hold herself together, to make herself breathe, when she felt Ginny's head drop onto her shoulder.

'I've no idea who you are right now, but I need to tell you that you are fricking kick-ass fabulous.'

Alyssa didn't take the compliment from the sentence. 'I'm the person who just lost any hope of saving her café and her home.'

She wanted to cry. To punch the table. To put a chair through the window. Actually, not that, because she'd get charged for the damages and she was about to be homeless and unemployed.

'And I'm the person who still has two hundred sandwiches to make. Come on, Ginny. Let's get back to work. People like him don't deserve our time.'

As she walked back to the kitchen, she realised she was also the person who now had fifty-nine days to plan a new life. So maybe it was time to stop fighting a lost cause and get started on that.

20

LACHLAN

Lachlan was five miles outside Weirbridge, on the narrow winding roads that led to the motorway, and his hands were still shaking as he gripped the steering wheel.

What the fuck had just happened?

When he'd gone into the café, it had been daylight, and by the time he left, not even an hour later, the sky was dark – and he wasn't one for putting a dramatic flair on things, but that was the perfect metaphor for what happened in there.

That had been one of the worst conversations of his life. And for someone who prided himself on being great at managing expectations and problem solving, he was fully aware that he'd done a resolutely shit job. He'd been backed into a corner, and he'd had nothing to offer – not even hope.

The worst thing was that she was right in her assessment of him. Her comments had got under his skin, but there had been no way to avoid that because they were true.

'Because when I'm sorry for something I've done wrong, I fix it. And I don't see you trying to do that.'

He'd felt as small as he thought it was possible to be... at least until she'd delivered her next zinger.

'...You said that your mother loved this place. I wonder what she'd think of this now.'

Those were the words that were ringing in his ears when he'd walked out the door and they were still circling in his head now.

If this was any other battle, with any other foe, for any other rightful cause, he would have gone to war for her. That was what he did. The decent thing. How could he explain that this was the one person that he wasn't going to challenge because he'd learned long ago that when he went up against his brother, he lost? And the reason for that was that Jason was relentless and he played dirty – and Lachlan refused to get in the mud.

There had been a thousand examples over the years. Maybe it was because he was almost two years older, but when they were kids, Jason was the boy who needed to win at any cost. Who had to be the best. Have the most. Who couldn't bear to see someone get something better than him. The one who would go after what he wanted until he got it, whether it was his to take or not. Jason had hero-worshipped their dad, but he'd been twisted with jealousy over Lachlan's closeness to their mother too, convincing himself – wrongly, Lachlan was sure – that their mother preferred her younger son. Maybe that's why he had to triumph in every single battle or competition, real or imaginary.

And that didn't change when they were adults.

It was who his brother was. He was the guy who would undercut a friend in a property deal and not lose a minute's sleep over it. Who would cosy up to an asshole if he thought it would give him an advantage. Who would humiliate others to make himself feel good. When he won anything, from a pool game to a business deal, he made sure that the other person was wounded so badly they wouldn't want to come back for more. And he got away with it every time, because he did it all with such an easy charm and impressive manipulation. His father had respected Jason's success and ambition, but Lachlan always had a sense that their dad saw his first-born's flaws. Martyn Morden had been ruthless, but never cruel or underhand, and it was pretty bloody obvious that Jason could be both. His mother, however, had only tried to see the good in her son. And Lachlan's childhood need for brotherly approval had turned into teenage combativeness and then adult disgust, when his brother had burned him one too many times.

He slowed to navigate the bends of a particularly tight stretch of road. There were no street lights here, no cat's eyes either, so he had to stay on alert when headlights were approaching him from the other direction. It would be way too easy to misjudge one corner and end up in a ditch, or worse.

As he reached a straight stretch of road, he slid back into his thoughts. Returning to Scotland had been the mistake he'd feared it would be. Earlier, he'd almost relaxed, almost begun to focus on the good stuff: the friendships, the people, the happy memories, but now here he was, dragged back down into the gutter by association.

What he'd wanted to tell Alyssa was that his brother wouldn't even contemplate helping her, and that sending her into Jason's firing line would only prolong the agony and leave her ultimately crushed. Instead, he'd come off as the dick, the person who was blocking her chances of saving her business or at least delaying its demise.

He switched on the windscreen wipers as a chunk of snow fell from the branches of the trees that were creating a glistening silver arc above him.

Vision cleared, he saw the sign for the motorway and followed the directions onto the slip road, joining the heavier traffic of people making their way home after a day's work. If life had turned out differently, that would have been him. If he hadn't lost Tanya, he'd be married now, still running his construction firm in Glasgow, going home after a day at the office or on a building site to the home they shared. Instead, he was on his way to the airport, to get a flight back to a city where he had no family, to a flat where he lived alone, to a world where his work was his only sense of purpose.

Today, in that café, was the first time in longer than he could remember that he felt a sense of connection to the past. To his mum. To the person he was before his heart had been shredded. And it had meant something, but the thing was, as Alyssa had pointed out, none of this affected him. Not really. He could walk away, but she was the one who was losing everything. And he knew how that felt.

His speed had dropped to under forty miles an hour now, as the streams of vehicles in front slowed to avoid a tailback at a particularly busy junction. The airport cut-off was only a couple of miles ahead. Five minutes. And then all he had to do was drop the car off at the hire office. In half an hour, he should be in the lounge and putting this whole bugger of a day behind him.

The most frustrating thing was that he didn't see what else he could have done to solve Alyssa's situation. If it were up to him alone, the answer would be different. There would have been options. The points that Alyssa had mapped out made sense. The building was appreciating asset and had a steady rental income. He was in no rush to sell and release the equity from it because until this morning he neither knew nor cared about it. Even if he did think selling was the best move, he could have given her six months, maybe a year, to find a new location that worked for her, or tried to figure out something else that would soften the blow.

The airport slip road was right up ahead of him now and he couldn't wait to get there. The car in front of him suddenly slammed on its brakes, forcing him to do the same and putting the Range Rover into a skid that he had to frantically steer out of so that he didn't end up in the back seat of a beige Volvo. He regained control when his front bumper was just inches from the back of the Volvo and he sagged with relief. Christ, what a day.

What. A. Day.

When he'd had a bad day as a kid, his mum would tell him to go and make one good thing happen, so that it wasn't wasted. A tough day at school? Choose your favourite meal. Unrequited teenage love? Let's cuddle on the couch and watch a movie. A poor exam result? Stuff it, let's go and play football in the garden. He smiled at the memory. Somewhere in the shitshow of the last few years, he'd forgotten that. Or maybe, after Tanya was gone, there was just nothing that could turn his days around.

He blocked that train of thought, unwilling to go back there, and that left space for Alyssa's comment to come back to him yet again.

'Mr Morden, you said that your mother loved this place. I wonder what she'd think of this now.'

What would she think of it all?

A couple of dots joined in his mind. Alyssa had been having a crap day, and she was just trying to save it by making a good thing happen. His mum would have appreciated that and been right on her side.

So why wasn't he?

Taking all his excuses out of it, what wasn't he trying? Was the fact that it would be futile a good enough reason to give up?

Maybe it wasn't.

Fifty yards to the slip road.

Maybe he needed to man up and take his own advice here.

Forty yards to the slip road.

Had he become so spineless that he was going to back down, even when he saw that something wasn't fair?

Thirty yards to the slip road.

His flight wasn't due to leave for several hours, so was he just going to sit in the airport and wallow in the misery of this whole frigging day?

Twenty yards to the slip road.

What would getting into this fight cost him? The answer was nothing, because he had zero left to lose.

Ten yards to the slip road.

Fuck it.

With an impulsive but careful swerve, he pulled out of the left lane and into the centre, changing direction in more ways than one. He went on to automatic pilot yet again, heading to the Park Circus area of the city, where he'd lived in a spectacular Georgian townhouse with his family, and then later, in a nearby flat with Tanya.

When he arrived at his destination, he sat in the car and stared at the outside of the house he was about to visit, one that he hadn't come near for years. He could still change his mind. Still leave and no one would ever be aware that he was here or know that he didn't have the courage to face it. That's when Alyssa's words came back at him again, the same line he'd remembered earlier, but this time so loud that it drowned out his murmurs of deflection.

'Because when I'm sorry for something I've done wrong, I fix it. And I don't see you trying to do that.'

She was right. And he knew he would never forgive himself if he didn't try to fix this.

He closed his eyes. Took a deep breath. Then he summoned the resolve and adrenaline he needed to get out of the car and walk up the stone steps to the door of the two-storey duplex on the legendary curved crescent, just a few houses away from the home his father had once owned. Once upon a time, he'd thought that he would end up somewhere exactly like this too. How wrong he'd been.

He pressed the buzzer on the intercom that was mounted on one of the columns that stretched from the ground to meet the ornate mouldings that bordered the top of the door. Alexander 'Greek' Thomson had designed this, and many other stunning buildings in Glasgow, and his eye for detail and grandeur had been exquisite.

From the outside of the beautifully carved, solid oak door, he heard the chimes reverberate around the ground floor, followed by the faint sound of footsteps coming towards him. One lock turning. Then another.

When the woman answered the door, his first thought was that she was beautiful. Then he watched as her hand instinctively went to her rounded stomach, and stayed there, cradling her unborn child. And that image delivered a hammer blow to his chest that almost felled him. It took all his strength to stay upright, all his courage to stay, and all his oxygen to say the words.

'Hello, Tanya. Can I speak to Jason?'

Without saying anything, the woman who had once been his everything stood back and let him walk into his brother's home.

6 P.M. – 8 P.M.

21
JESSIE

'Och, Alyssa, it's beautiful. I can't thank you enough.' Jessie gazed around in wonder at the transformation of the café from this morning. Earlier, it had been a warm, cosy, Christmassy retreat from the cold – now it was like a grotto from a winter wonderland.

There were dozens of white and gold balloons, filled with whatever air they put in them to make them rise up and attach to the ceiling. In the middle of the room, there was a glistening Christmas tree. Over at the buffet table, the spread looked incredible. And the whole room was glowing, thanks to the clusters of candles that covered every shelf on the walls. They looked realistic, but they were the battery-operated ones because everyone knew Val's huge blonde bob contained so much hairspray it could go up like a flash if she went near a naked flame. Over at the makeshift bar, Hugo and Ginny were polishing glasses, and Jessie shouted her thanks to them too.

Alyssa gave her a hug. 'You're welcome, Jessie. I've loved working across the road from you and I really appreciate all the support you gave my business when it first opened, and every day since.'

That was a fond memory for Jessie. When Alyssa's café had opened its doors, Jessie had been delighted. The café had been closed for months at that point, after the previous tenant had realised that his concept of a gaming café wasn't going to work in a village where the daytime customers' average age demographic sat somewhere north of seventy.

Jessie had fair missed a local spot to pick up a bacon roll on a busy day so to ensure Alyssa's café thrived, she'd offered a 10 per cent discount on any hair treatment to every client who came in with a receipt for a purchase at the café. She'd viewed it as a good marketing ploy for Alyssa's fledgling business, but she'd found to her surprise that it was mutually beneficial when she'd also gained new customers who'd heard about the deal and couldn't resist the bargain.

Alyssa gave her another squeeze. 'You have a great night, Jessie, and if you need anything at all, just holler. I'm going to go check on the hot food and let you get ready to greet your guests. By the way, is Kayleigh going to be here tonight?'

'Yes, she is. In fact, there she is now.' She opened her arms to welcome Kayleigh and Grant, who'd just burst in the door.

'Gran, you're a total babe,' Kayleigh proclaimed, giving her the second hug of the last five minutes. Grant gave her the third, while Kayleigh greeted Alyssa. Her granddaughter had worked here in the summer every year since it opened, so the two of them were great friends.

'Can you come find me when you have a minute? I just want to pick your brain about something,' she heard Alyssa ask Kayleigh.

In normal circumstances, Jessie would be curious, but there were too many other things vying for her attention tonight, including her big honey of a son. 'You look fabulous, Mother,' he told her, making her beam. 'Where's Dad?'

Jessie nodded over to Stan, who was propping up the bar and already on his second beer. He wasn't exactly radiating happiness, and she didn't blame him, given that disaster of a conversation earlier. Even now, her stomach flipped just thinking about it. She'd got totally the wrong end of the stick and she'd made everything much worse. Not only were they still leaving for Tenerife tomorrow, but he now knew that she hadn't wanted to go in the first place. What a bloody mess.

When he'd told her that he wasn't changing his mind, and that it was her decision as to whether she went with him or not, she'd been so shocked, her voice had escaped her. But only for a moment.

'Like I said, Stan. We've done this life together. I'm not going to change that now. I'll be ready to go to the airport first thing in the morning.' She was going. They both were. And that was that. The only thing left to do had been to put on her red sparkly sequin frock, her favourite silver heels and enjoy the last night with everyone she loved. Talking of which...

'Kayleigh, where's your mum? and dad? She's not with you? I'm worried that no one else will venture out in this weather and it'll just be us lot. We'll never get through all those sandwiches.'

'Gran, don't worry. If that happens, we'll still have a great night. Mum's just coming. My dad was at the house earlier and he was going to come tonight too, but then he got an emergency work call and had to go.'

Jessie wasn't quite sure what emergency work call a solar panel salesman would have at seven o'clock on a dark, snowy, December night, but given that Grant was now standing behind Kayleigh making frantic slicing motions at his throat, she guessed it was something best addressed later.

Kayleigh and Grant went off to see Stan, just as the bell above the door dinged again. And again. And again. Her worries that no one would come floated off on a sea of gratitude, as the room began to fill. She was so busy greeting everyone as they came in that she only had time to talk for a few moments before the door would open again and the next lot would arrive.

Val arrived with her pal and next-door neighbour Nancy Jenkins, both of them bearing elaborately wrapped gifts.

'Thank you both. That's very kind, but you didn't need to do that,' Jessie chided them.

'It's just a couple of wee things to remember us by,' Val told her. 'Don't want you forgetting all about us.'

'As if I ever could. I won't open them just now, because I'll cry and I've just done my mascara.' She gave the two of them a quick cuddle before they headed into the mêlée, with Nancy's husband, Eddie, in tow. He was another one who'd gone to school right here in Weirbridge, and then left, but moved back a few years ago, when he'd met up with Nancy at a school reunion. Jessie often saw them around the village, and they were great for a chat and a laugh, especially if they were with Buddy, a gorgeous wee boy that Val and Nancy looked after a couple of days a week. His parents, Noah and Tress, were coming along tonight, with the rest of Noah's family. His mum, Gilda, had been a client of Jessie's since she'd arrived from Ghana just after the salon had opened, and Jessie adored her.

The next to arrive were her neighbours from the two houses on either side of her, all of them saying lovely things about how much they'd miss her. Her lip began to tremble with the loveliness of it all, so she distracted herself with more pragmatic matters and addressed Linda Nesbit from next door, a rough-cut diamond of a woman who didn't have her troubles to seek, because her man was way too fond of the booze. 'Linda, pet, don't forget to ask one of your boys to nip in every fortnight and cut Mrs Dawson's lawn. My Stan has done it for years, and it would be the size of a hedge if he hadn't, because she doesn't have the money to get someone in to do it.'

'Don't you worry, Jessie, it's the least we can do for all the nights you've watched the triplets over the years.' Jessie remembered when Linda brought those three beautiful wee cherubs home from the hospital. They were a handful even then, and over the years, they'd grown into lovable but cheeky wee rascals. They were twelve now, and much as she was fond of them, Jessie still couldn't tell them apart. They were going to be a challenge in a police line-up, and given that they'd been caught letting down the tyres of every car on Main Street several times this month, Jessie just hoped that wasn't in their future.

The gifts were piling up on the table behind her now, and Jessie realised she hadn't factored that in at all. She'd have to ask Georgie to store them because she was already over the weight limit for her suitcases on the flight tomorrow. Again, where was Georgie? Shouldn't she be here by now?

She was about to give her a call, when the door opened again, and in came Cathy, Richie and of course... 'Loretta!'

Cathy's younger sister was a riot of a woman, loud, hilarious, and up for anything. She'd been a fairly well-known pop star back in the seventies, but her career had transitioned through various incarnations over the decades, ultimately ending with a ten-year stint as a cabaret singer in Benidorm before she retired. Now that she was in her seventies, she only sang for fun, and Jessie had been thrilled when she'd offered to perform tonight. She'd have the whole place singing along in no time.

After their greetings, Cathy and Richie went on over to the bar, but Loretta hung behind and leaned in close. 'Jessie, I need to ask you...' she whispered in her quiet voice, which was still loud enough for half the room to hear. 'Our Cathy was telling me that Moira Chiles has moved to the village. Is that right?'

'It is, Loretta. She comes into the salon to get her hair done. I invited her tonight, and I think she's coming along if she's free.'

Loretta beamed at that news. 'You know, back when dinosaurs roamed the earth, her and I did a couple of show runs together. *Rocky Horror*, if I remember correctly. She was just a young thing then, but, och, it would be a treat to see her again, it truly would. She was sensational.'

As if Loretta had just manifested her arrival, Jessie spotted a familiar face passing the window. 'I think you're about to get your chance, Loretta, because that's her coming now.'

At that moment, Moira opened the door and came in brandishing a bottle of champagne and a gift bag with paper tissue blooming from the top of it. 'I'll miss you, Jessie,' she said, hugging her. 'My hair is going to be a shambles without you.'

'You'll just need to commute to Tenerife for a wee cut and blow-dry,' Jessie joked, before bringing the woman standing next to her into the conversation. 'Moira, I don't know if you'll remember...'

Moira's reaction to Loretta was priceless – there was a glance and a polite smile, then a quick double take and a squeal of delight. 'Loretta! Oh, my love, how long has it been?'

Loretta chuckled. 'Around about the last time a man saw me naked, so probably some time in the nineties.' That set the two of them off, and Jessie suddenly felt something damp on her cheeks. Too late, she realised it was tears. Loretta spotted them first and her eyes widened in horror, but Jessie immediately started fanning her face and reassuring her.

'I'm fine, I'm fine! It's just... a lot. I'll miss this all so much, I truly will.' Every word caught in her throat because she meant it more than she could say. This was her idea of a great life. Her pals. Her family. A room full of people – some she'd known for a year, some for a lifetime, but all of them in some way meant something to her.

Embarrassed that the night had only just started and she was bawling already, she had a quick glance around the room to see if anyone had noticed, but everyone was deep in conversation, and no one was looking her way... except Stan. Over at the bar, he was staring straight at her, concern in every line of that handsome face. She gave him a smile that said, 'Don't worry, I'm fine.'

'You need a drink!' Loretta declared wisely. 'Let me just go and grab you one and I'll be right back. Moira, let's do a wee duet later. You can be Dolly Parton and I'll be Loretta Lynn – I've not got the boobs for Dolly. One glass of plonk coming right up, Jessie.' And with that, the force of nature that was Loretta went off to seek a medicinal refreshment for her.

'Sorry, Moira. It's been an emotional day. I'm not great at goodbyes, and I've been saying a lot of them lately,' Jessie explained.

'That just shows you all the smashing folk you have in your life, Jessie. It's hard to leave people you love. I was singing on the cruise ships for sixteen years and there wasn't a day that went by that I didn't miss my Ollie and my pals.'

'He's a lovely lad, Moira. You did a great job with him.'

Moira beamed. 'Aye, but not because he's famous, because that's the least of it. He's just a decent man, and that's all any of us can ask for really, isn't it? That our kids turn out to be good people. Your Georgie is the same. I think that's why those two hit it off together.'

Jessie nodded, knowing what a thrill Georgie got from having her one celebrity client – if you didn't count old Mr Collins from Craigielea Road, who was once on *Antiques Roadshow* and got told his granny's tea set was worth over a grand. He splashed out and gave Georgie a two-pound tip on his next visit.

She was so distracted by that memory, she misheard what Moira said next. At least, she must have picked it up wrong, because it didn't make sense. Something like...

'They'll be great company for each other over in Colorado.'

'Sorry, Moira, I didn't catch that. What did you say?'

'I said they'll be great company for each other over in Colorado. Ollie was so chuffed when she said she was interested in the job.' Moira must had spotted Jessie's perplexed expression, because she suddenly caught herself. 'I hope I'm not speaking out of turn. Someone from the studio was calling her to confirm everything today. I just assumed...'

Whaaaaaat? She could swear that brain cells were exploding in her head right now. But Jessie McLean hadn't worked with the public for a lifetime and not learned how to act fast and fake it. Big smile. Cheery voice. 'Ah, she mentioned that, but I haven't heard the latest. She'll be here soon though, so fingers crossed.'

'Here you go, Jessie,' Saint Loretta of the Holy Thankful Interruptions appeared, brandishing a large glass of something bubbly, allowing Jessie to shift the focus. She took it, then, balancing it carefully, hugged the two of them in turn.

'Off you two go and get a drink of your own. I'm looking forward to that duet!'

Somehow, she managed to keep the smile up until they turned away, then it dropped like a stone. What the hell? A job in Colorado? What was that about? And why hadn't Georgie told her?

She took a large slug of her bubbly.

As soon as Georgie got here, Jessie was going to find out exactly what was going on. And she had a feeling she was going to need something stronger than Prosecco.

22

GEORGIE

Georgie knew she was going to be a little late for the party, but she also knew that her mum would be in shindig-heaven, surrounded by all her pals, and wouldn't even have noticed that she wasn't there yet.

As soon as Flynn had bolted out, sparks coming off his heels, she'd headed for the shower and soaked under the hot jets until she'd washed the duplicity of their conversation from her mind.

As she'd rinsed off her favourite mango bodywash, the little angel that lived on one of Georgie's shoulders, the mature, conscientious, paragon of positive co-parenting, had told her that by handling it the way that she had, without full disclosure or accusations, they would have a healthy, friendly relationship moving forward. In a couple of years, they would celebrate Kayleigh's twenty-first as a family, they would link arms and beam with pride when she graduated, if she chose to get married (and right now Georgie would strongly advise against it), they would dance at her wedding and they would cry happy tears if she made them grandparents.

However, the little devil on her other shoulder hadn't been able to get past hoping that Monica would dump him on his arse and he'd wither away, loveless and sexless until his penis fell off. The devil watched too many crime shows.

When she'd got out of the shower, Georgie had pulled the rubber cap off her head and let loose her wild, tangled mane of copper curls, giving thanks that big hair was back in fashion and she didn't have to spend the next hour of her life straightening it and forcing it to behave. Instead, that time had been spent whipping on a smoky eye, a matte base, a bit of contour and a nude lip, figuring that maybe if she was worried about spoiling carefully applied make-up, she wouldn't cry when she thought about the job she was giving up, or the fact that she was saying goodbye to her mother. She still wasn't sure which one was breaking her heart more.

Face done, she'd pulled her favourite silver slinky frock from the wardrobe, deciding it was close enough to Christmas to go out looking like a disco ball from the eighties. Besides, she didn't get out much and it had been a tough week, so for once she'd been going for a bit of glamour.

She'd hung the dress on the front of her wardrobe, while she'd slapped on some Chanel No. 5 body lotion, then pulled on her dressing gown, just as there was a knock on her bedroom door. Her stomach had flipped. If that was Flynn back, saying that he'd reconsidered and wanted to sign up for more fatherhood, she was leaving the country in her mother's suitcase tomorrow.

Thankfully, it was Kayleigh that had popped her head round the door.

'Mum, it's time to go. Oh. Not ready.' Her daughter had pointed out the obvious.

'I'm running late, sweetheart. You and Uncle Grant go ahead, and I'll meet you there.'

'Are you sure?'

'Yes! Cover for me and hopefully Gran won't notice I'm late. It would be embarrassing to get grounded at thirty-eight.'

'I'll create a diversion, don't worry. I'll tell her I'm pregnant or on bail for something juicy.'

Georgie had chuckled. 'I said cover for me, not kill her.'

'Okay, maybe something not quite so dramatic then. We'll see you when you get there.'

The next thing she'd heard were shouts of goodbyes and the front door opening and closing.

Still in her dressing gown, she'd sat down on the edge of the bed and pulled her laptop out of the drawer beside her. The producer from *The*

Clansman had told her they'd be sending over all the details of the job offer today, but she'd been too busy dealing with an ex-husband, his girlfriend, three dancing retirees, and trivial things like her existential crisis about the future of her life, to check her emails.

The decision to refuse the job had already been taken. She wasn't going to risk the future of a salon that was her mum's life's work and greatest gift to her, but she might as well torture herself by seeing what she was missing.

After she'd fired up the laptop, she'd scrolled through multiple emails offering discounts on everything from skin care to fashion to – slightly worryingly – a three-day course to explore her inner goddess. Her inner goddess decided that all she wanted to do was find the bloody email from...

Clansman Productions. There it was.

Just seeing it had made her skin tingle. The fact that a company like that knew who she was blew her away, even if it was via the star pulling some strings.

As she'd begun to read it though, Georgie had realised that opening the document had been a mistake. It was a six-month contract, but the salary was more than she'd earned last year. She'd be provided with accommodation in a hotel or apartment of a commensurate standard. Yes, she'd be expected to be on set for approximately ten hours per day, five days per week, but all food and expenses would be taken care of, including return business-class flights from her home city to the location of the shoot.

Holy. Swanky. Shit.

The rest of the pages on the document were a Non-Disclosure Agreement (both compulsory and standard), contract terms and conditions and a medical questionnaire. But none of the bureaucratic stuff had stuck in her brain, because she'd kept going back to the highlights of the offer.

It was a great package. Stunning. And while the thought of doing something so far out of her comfort zone filled her with absolute terror, at any other time in her life she'd have jumped at it.

Just not now. And the knot that had been twisting her gut since Ollie first broached this with her had become unbearable. For her own sanity and wellbeing, she had to shut this down. Close it off. Put it behind her and move on. She'd resolved to speak to Moira later and get Ollie's contact details so that she could call him to thank him and explain her reasons for declining. Moira had told them about the time that he'd flown from LA to Hong Kong because she'd been in an accident, so Georgie was pretty sure that he was the kind of guy who would understand her family loyalties and her reasons for staying here.

Before that, though, she had to formally reject the offer. She'd skimmed back down to the covering letter, looking for the response method. 'Please reply with urgency to this email indicating your acceptance/refusal of this offer. Alternatively, please call…' Georgie had checked her phone and seen that it was the same number that had called this morning. She'd briefly considered the options and decided to call, checking the time difference first. They were eight hours behind in LA. Almost lunchtime. Okay, so she wasn't going to get the woman out of her bed to deliver the news.

Her fingers had trembled a little as she'd clicked on her recent calls again, located the number and pressed connect. She'd been hyped up and ready to speak, when it went straight to voicemail.

'Hello, this is Bonnie Katowski from Clansman Productions…'

Listening to the recording, Georgie had begun to panic as she'd tried to decide whether to leave a message or call back. A message. Definitely. It was the only way to get this over with, so that she didn't have to think about it again. For some reason that she didn't quite understand, she'd squeezed her eyes shut as she'd begun to speak.

'Hello Bonnie, this is Georgie Dern. We spoke this morning when you very kindly let me know about the offer of a position as Ollie Chiles' hairstylist on *The Clansman*.'

The angel and devil had returned to her shoulders and this time the angel was telling her that she was doing the right thing, being a loyal daughter and making a decision that would allow her to thrive as the successful owner of her own business. Meanwhile, the devil had slapped his hand to his forehead and told her she was a total tit for passing up the opportunity to do something wild.

'You did say that you would like a swift decision, so I just wanted to let you know…'

That was it. Last chance to go one way or another.

'I'm afraid I am unable to accept the position, but thank you for the opportunity.'

Eyes still closed, it had taken her three attempts to hit the button to hang up, but she got there in the end.

It was done. Over.

She'd done a quick check to try to ascertain how she was feeling, and the result was... relieved. A bit sad too, but mostly just relieved. No more secrets. No turmoil. No dilemmas. She wasn't like Grant, who relished a risk and thrived on adventure. She was a creature of habit, of familiarity and the whole thing would probably have scared her to death anyway, so she'd just saved herself a whole lot of heartache. At least, that was what the wee angel on her shoulder was saying, so that's what she was going with.

The very short chapter in her life was closed, and one day she'd be able to tell her grandchildren that she was once offered a swanky job in Hollywood. That would definitely put Grandad Solar Panels in second place in the cool grandparent rankings.

Now, a minute or two later, she exhaled, letting all the stress slide from her shoulders. It was time to go celebrate her mum.

Rising from the edge of the bed, she quickly pulled on her dress, put her heels in her handbag and her exceptionally un-sexy wellies on her feet, and in no time at all she was out of the door and walking to the café. The pavements were still thick with snow, but the gritters and ploughs had been out on the road, so it took less than five minutes of trudging through slush, only stepping back onto the pavement when a couple of cars passed, to get to Main Street.

Even from across the road, she could see that the café looked beautiful – all twinkly lights in the windows, and lots of chatting, smiling people inside. That sight of the crowd made her beam – her mum had been worried that no one would come out in this weather, but, of course, she'd been wrong. Georgie knew that it would take a lot more than a snow storm to prevent most folks in this village from celebrating Jessie McLean.

She was halfway across the road, when she heard the unmistakable sound of her Aunt Loretta belting out 'Mustang Sally' and she allowed herself a little bubble of excitement. She loved a party and tonight was going to be such a respite from the stress of the last few days.

As Georgie stepped onto the pavement, she saw that Jessie was standing just inside the door. Okay, shoulders back, smile, best foot-in-a-wellie forward. She was going to go in there and be nothing but smiley and happy all night.

She pushed the door open and walked into the warm, sparkling, beautiful interior feeling nothing but positivity… until her mother rounded on her with a look that she hadn't seen since she was fifteen and got caught sneaking out her window at midnight on a Saturday night to go meet her boyfriend.

'Georgette Catherine McLean…'

Oh bollocks. Like every mother of her generation, Jessie used Georgie's full moniker when she was seriously pissed off. And also, apparently, forgot that she was married and her surname had been Dern since 2006. What the hell had she done to deserve this? The answer was rapidly forthcoming.

'When were you going to tell me that you've been offered a job on a TV set in America?'

23

ALYSSA

It was both heartbreaking and ironic to Alyssa that tonight her gorgeous café was more beautiful than it had ever been, and yet this had also been the day that she'd discovered it was being taken away from her.

The room was packed, the music was playing, guests were raving about the food and everyone looked so happy. Except, maybe, Jessie's husband, Stan. He'd been standing over at the bar since he came in, and the only time Alyssa had seen him smile was when his granddaughter, Kayleigh, and his son, Grant, had gone to chat to him. Alyssa didn't know Stan very well, and as far as she could remember, he'd never once set foot in the café. Alyssa only knew who he was because she'd seen him around the village with Jessie over the years. Maybe he didn't do coffee. Or perhaps he was gluten-intolerant and didn't want to be faced with the sight of all the cakes she had on display. It was hard to imagine that the bubbly, warm Jessie would be married to someone grumpy, though, so he must just be having a bad day.

Well, he could get in line. Although, if she did lose the café, at least tonight would give the whole village something to remember her by, she thought mournfully, letting the toll of all the disappointments and traumas of the day edge her a little further towards acceptance that she might not be able to avoid defeat. How could she win against people like the guy who'd sat in here just hours before and told her he couldn't... no, *wouldn't* help her? If the rest of his family was as dismissive and devoid of compassion, then she didn't stand a chance. Her doors would be closed in fifty-nine days and she'd have to start all over again somewhere else. She knew that her grandad would love to have her move in with him until she got back on her feet – and that was definitely the preferred option over her mother's house. But there was no easy solution to losing her business. She didn't even know where to begin.

'You all right there, pet?' She'd been so deep in thought that she hadn't even noticed that her grandad had come up beside her.

She mustered a smile. 'I'm fine, Grandad.'

'What a night you've pulled off here. You know, when you first opened this café, I was worried about whether it would take off – didn't want you sinking all your hard-earned cash into a money pit – but just look what you've done. I couldn't be prouder of you.'

Her heart cracked and she let her head fall onto his shoulder, mostly so that he wouldn't see that she was blinking back two big fat tears. She wasn't a crier. When she was growing up with a mother as dramatic as Dorinda, someone else had to be the calm one, so if she started sobbing, her grandad would know something awful was afoot. He wouldn't be wrong. Besides herself, Hugo was the person who'd be affected most by the closure and Alyssa didn't know how she was going to break it to him.

Tomorrow. That was a problem for tomorrow. Right now, the most important thing was that they made tonight wonderful for Jessie.

'Thanks, Grandad. I'm pretty proud of you too.'

Their conversation was ended there by Ginny, who was speeding towards the counter, and when she reached it, flopped down on it in a theatrical fashion.

'I'll give you everything I own in the world if you save me from our mother,' she wailed.

'You already promised me your internal organs for taking you to the interview this morning and you don't own anything else,' Alyssa pointed out, glad of the distraction.

Ginny straightened up. 'I feel that was unnecessarily harsh and I'll be speaking to the Shit Waitress union regarding your attitude in the workplace.'

Despite her admittedly woeful waitressing skills, Alyssa would miss Ginny being here too, making sure there was never a dull moment. Case in point, right now.

'Anyway, what's Mum doing that's bugging your happiness, Ginny?'

'Nothing! That's the point. The place is mobbed and I asked her to help me go round topping up drinks and she refused. Says she wasn't "being seen doing manual labour". And she's acting all weird. I've no idea what's going on with her. You know that way she was when she had a thing for the Amazon delivery guy, and she ordered a new set of scrunchies every day and then made sure she was wafting around looking sultry when he delivered them...?'

Alyssa nodded, getting the picture. There was never any doubt that her sister had an artistic flair and a gift for a tall tale.

'Well, she's definitely got the hots for someone in here, because she's got that same look on her face.'

A theory suddenly popped into Alyssa's head. 'I reckon it's because Moira Chiles is here. Mum is hoping Ollie Chiles will walk in and she can cougar him to death.'

'I've never wanted to leave a conversation more,' her grandad winced.

'Sorry, Grandad,' Alyssa giggled, her first authentic laugh since that letter had arrived this morning.

Ginny stepped in to save him. 'Come help me, please, Grandad. It might even persuade me to forgive you for making our mother such a nightmare.'

Amused and happy to help, Grandad grabbed two bottles of fizz from the ice buckets on the counter and off they went, passing Kayleigh Dern coming the other way.

'Kayleigh!' Alyssa exclaimed, giving her another hug. 'How are you? How's university going?'

Several of the village teenagers had worked in the café over the years, but Kayleigh had been one of her favourites. She'd been around her gran and mum's salon since she was a toddler, so she worked hard and had a natural gift for chatting to customers.

'It's going great. Bit wobbly at first – took me a while to get used to being on my own and being able to walk down the street without bumping into forty people I know.'

Alyssa chuckled. 'That could have pros and cons.'

'It definitely does. And not having my gran's place or here to pop into every day feels weird too.'

The unintentional link to the problem that was plaguing Alyssa was too clear to ignore. Soon there wouldn't be a café for anyone to pop into. 'Actually, Kayleigh, can I show you something?'

Kayleigh raised an eyebrow. 'Will I have to lie to the police or deny it under oath?' She also had her grandmother's dry sense of humour.

'Unlikely, but you never know.'

Kayleigh shrugged. 'Then sure.'

Alyssa beckoned her into the kitchen and pulled Jeremy Sprite's letter from the drawer she'd been hiding it in so that Grandad or her mother wouldn't see it.

'Can you read this, please? I know you've only just started studying law, but I wondered if you'd have any ideas about who I could speak to, or if any of your professors would know about this kind of thing. I don't really have the funds to get my own lawyer, so I'm just looking for other ways to get help.'

She watched as Kayleigh began to read, her eyes widening with every line until she got to the end and gasped. 'Shit, Alyssa, this is awful.'

'I got it this morning.'

'Oh no, I'm so sorry. Did you try to speak to them? Find out what's going on?'

'Yep, but it's hopeless. The lawyer is impossible to get hold of, but I spoke to the son of the owner who died and asked him to help.'

'And?'

'Horrible person. Wouldn't even consider helping me. Said it's a done deal and there's nothing he can do about it.'

'You should have taken my gran. Jessie would have kicked his arse.'

'That might be my next plan.'

'Okay, let me think...' Kayleigh said, reading the letter again. 'I don't know anything about this kind of stuff yet, but there's a paralegal on my course who is retraining to be a lawyer and she knows everything there is to know. And I've got a property law class on a Friday, so I'll ask my professor if he'll take a look at this. Can I come by tomorrow and get a copy of this letter and a copy of your lease and I'll see what I can do? I'm not sure I can help, but I'll give it a shot.'

For the second time tonight, Alyssa had to blink back tears. Lachlan Morden wouldn't so much as give her the time of day, yet here was Kayleigh, prepared to do whatever she could to help. 'Thank you so much. I'd be so grateful.'

The alarm started to go off on the cooker, interrupting them.

'Do you need a hand in here?' Kayleigh asked, before joking, 'I was a much better waitress than Ginny.'

'That's not a very high bar of achievement. But no, you go on back out and enjoy your gran's party. And, Kayleigh, thanks again.'

'No worries. Still think you should get Jessie to kick his arse.'

'It might still come to that.'

Only after she'd gone did Alyssa realise that she'd forgotten to ask Kayleigh not to tell anyone about this. As soon as she'd organised the hot food for the buffet, she'd go and find her again and swear her to secrecy. Gossip went round this village like a tornado, and she didn't want Grandad hearing before she'd told him herself.

As she pulled the mini steak pies out of the oven, and began arranging them on a bamboo serving platter, Alyssa thought about what Kayleigh had said about the strangeness of living an anonymous life, and had the sudden realisation that she'd have that same experience if she went anywhere else. In Weirbridge, she went to the corner shop and knew everyone on the way. If she was in the post office, chances were she'd served up a bowl of soup to the customers in front and behind her in the queue.

Sure, there were downsides too. If she nipped into the doctor's surgery, there would be ten people in the waiting room asking after her grandad while trying to work out what ailment had brought her there. And, of course, that could start rumours. Twice, she'd heard she might be pregnant, and there was an allegation of a boob job being in the works.

The point was, all of that only happened because she'd lived here all her life. If she went somewhere else, maybe got a job working in the city centre or perhaps down by Loch Lomond, she'd know no one.

The thought of starting her own catering company had crossed her mind when she'd been setting up for the party. She already had the van, so she would just need to find premises to work out of. At face value, that could be an option, but it would require investment in equipment and advertising, and she'd have to work hard to build a customer base that could sustain it. And, at the end of it all, she still wouldn't have the joy of the toddler groups coming in for their Wednesday afternoon reading sessions, or the enjoyment of chatting to the ladies in the running club who met every Tuesday to discuss their plans to run a marathon in memory of their lovely friend who'd passed from cancer. The whole village had turned out for that lady's funeral.

Alyssa lifted the tray and made her way out of the kitchen and into the café, still deep in thought.

It wouldn't suit everyone, but this was the life that Alyssa wanted. Right here. Even if Kayleigh didn't have a friend who could help, Alyssa couldn't give up without fighting for this. She would start a petition. Somehow find the money for a good lawyer. Hell, she would picket Jeremy fricking Sprite's office if that would shame him into listening to her.

Her spirits temporarily bolstered by her resolve, she laid the steak pies down on the buffet table and, with a tug of relief, noticed that her mother wasn't stalking Moira Chiles after all. Instead, she was over at the bar, chatting to Jessie's husband, Stan.

Ah well, at least her mum was serving a purpose now. Maybe her mother's trademark flirty chatter would cheer him up a bit and he'd get into the swing of the party and make this a night Jessie would never forget. Just as that thought went through her mind, she saw that nope, he was still frowning.

Maybe there were some men that were oblivious to Dorinda's charms after all.

24

LACHLAN

The living room was different from how he remembered it. When Jason lived here alone, it had been a true bachelor pad, with huge, oversized sofas, a glass and granite bar against the far wall and a pool table where a white chaise, with artfully placed cushions, now sat. Even if he didn't know that Tanya lived here, he'd recognise her in the casually elegant style of the room, the whites and creams of the décor, the frames of her abstract art on the wall where the bar used to live.

Tanya. She looked different too. Her hair was shorter, still caramel blonde, but sitting just on her shoulders now. The old sweats that she used to change into as soon as she got home from work had been replaced by a matching cream knitted jumper and trousers, that looked so expensive they could only be cashmere. There were small diamonds in her ears and a huge rock on the third finger of her left hand. But, of course, it was the other difference that was most notable of all.

'You're pregnant,' he said softly. 'Congratulations.'

'You didn't know?' He wasn't sure why she seemed surprised at that. 'I'm eight months along. It was why I couldn't come to your father's funeral in Monaco. I thought Jason would have told you. I'm... sorry.'

Lachlan managed to hold the smile. 'Nothing to be sorry for. I'm happy for you Tanya. Truly.'

'Thank you.'

Silence.

'Can I get you a drink?'

'No, thanks.'

Silence. This was excruciating.

She raised her gaze upwards. 'He's up in the shower, but he'll be back down soon. Have you got time to wait?'

'Yes.'

More silence.

He knew he couldn't sit here for that long, on opposite couches, a few yards and a million miles between them, so he was the first to break. 'Actually, I'll have a coffee if you don't mind.'

Tanya's relief was instant. 'Sure. But the awkwardness of this is killing me, so why don't you come talk to me while I make it?' That was a flash of the old Tanya, the one he'd thought he'd spend his life with.

Tanya. The love of his life. Their future was the thing that Jason had taken from him that hurt the most. And Lachlan had let that happen.

After they lost the baby, Thomas, when Tanya was twenty weeks pregnant, they'd both been devastated. They'd cancelled their wedding, only two weeks away, knowing that they wouldn't be able to celebrate anything for a long time to come. Tanya was broken by the loss and Lachlan would fall asleep at night and wake up at 2 a.m. from a dream about the child he'd never know. The injustice of it would tear at his soul, make him angry, then desolation would set in and make him want to push the world away.

Including Tanya. For some couples, he knew that grief pulled them together, but that hadn't been the case for them. Lachlan had shut down, Tanya had retreated from him, and that had created a vacuum that had allowed his brother to do the thing he was best at – taking what he wanted.

Months later, after analysing it all with the benefit of perspective and hindsight, he'd seen that Jason's feelings for Tanya had always been there. The way that his brother was always on his best behaviour when he was around her. The relentless charm. The attentiveness. The conversations he would initiate with Tanya at family gatherings. How had Lachlan somehow overlooked what he knew was true – that Jason only showed an interest in something when he wanted it for himself.

Maybe Lachlan hadn't spotted the threat because Tanya saw Jason for what he was. At least, in the beginning. She'd been unimpressed by his wealth. Indifferent to his accomplishments. Incompatible with his relentless drive for success and control.

But then, as Lachlan had slipped further into the solitude of his own grief and wasn't there to share Tanya's, he'd missed the most obvious truth of all. When someone is lost and they're offered a safe place to be, they'll take it.

Jason became her safe space. When Lachlan was staying late at work because he couldn't deal with the pain of their loss, Jason was the one who went to their flat to check in on Tanya. He'd listen to her. He'd say the right things. He gave her the support and the friendship that Lachlan had withdrawn.

It would be easy to blame Jason – and sure, Lachlan had no doubt that he'd known exactly what he was doing – but the truth was this was Lachlan's fault. And that was the reality that hurt most of all.

Tanya hadn't done anything wrong. There had been no tawdry affair. They'd hung on for almost a year, the gulf between them opening and closing, until they were too exhausted and drained to keep trying and she'd called it a day. Two months later, she'd phoned him to tell him that she had feelings for Jason and that they'd started dating. Lachlan had respected her honesty. And he'd wanted to kill his brother. But, instead, he'd just walked away. Dax had just been transferred to the London team, so Lachlan had agreed to go with him to work on his new property. As for everyone here? He'd turned his back on them all.

In the kitchen, he sat on a black suede bar stool at the long stone island, while Tanya made a coffee he'd asked for but didn't want.

'Are you good?' she asked. 'I heard you moved to London.'

'I did.'

'Like it?' The raise of her eyebrows, the amusement at the corners of her mouth, told him that she already knew the answer to that. She was well aware that he wasn't a city guy. They'd always talked about going out to live in the countryside when they had a family, and they'd already put their Glasgow flat on the market before they lost Thomas, with the plan to move to a more rural area.

'As long as I stay out of the busy bits, I'm fine.'

That made her chuckle, and he had a twinge of pleasure in seeing her smile. After the trauma of what had happened, he'd wanted that for her, hoped she would find joy again. He just didn't think it would be here or with his brother.

'Babe, who are you talking to?' Jason came in, wearing a T-shirt and joggers, bare feet, drying his hair as he walked until he saw Lachlan and stopped. 'Oh...'

The most loaded 'oh' of all time.

Lachlan watched as Jason's gaze went from him, to Tanya's smile, back to him.

'What are you doing here?' There was a hint of a challenge there. 'If you'd told me you wanted to meet, I could have come to you. I tried to talk to you this morning.'

Lachlan nodded. 'I know. I guess I didn't have anything to say then.'

'And you do now?' Jason's eyes narrowed, like an animal that was wary and anticipating attack.

'Yeah.'

Tanya put an earthenware mug of coffee on the island in front of him and pulled out a chair, so that she was sitting at right angles to him.

'Are you okay with me staying for this?' She directed the question at Lachlan, and he wondered if she thought he was here to settle scores or to hold them to some kind of belated account for what had happened.

'Sure. It won't take long. I just want to talk about Dad's will.' He put that out straight away, hoping it would defuse any defensiveness Jason was feeling. If he was going to get anywhere with his brother, he had to come at this from a place of peace.

'Yeah, I'm not fucking happy about it either. I can't believe all we got was one crappy property and some change.'

Lachlan wondered in what world £125K could be called 'change'. And he'd seen for himself that Alyssa's café was far from 'crappy', but this wasn't the time to argue.

He tried to keep his tone even and non-confrontational, even as he said, 'I didn't say I wasn't happy about it. To be honest, I didn't expect anything, so it made no difference to me.'

'Always the Boy Scout,' Jason jibed, with a bitter smile, as he reached into a drinks fridge on the far wall and pulled out a beer. He came back and stood at the other side of the island from where Lachlan was sitting so that he was directly opposite and in front of him. Lachlan knew it was a classic power move. Stay standing. Be the tallest in the room. Command the space.

He wanted to reply, 'Always the dickhead,' but he managed to refrain.

Out of the corner of his eye, he saw Tanya lower her gaze so that she was staring at the island and wondered if she regretted staying to listen.

He had to get this back on track, so he ignored the dig and rewound a few seconds.

'The thing I wanted to talk about was the Weirbridge building.'

'I used to hate it when Mum would drag us out to the sticks to go to that place every summer,' Jason sneered.

Of course he did. It was one of Lachlan's favourite memories, so naturally Jason had a completely opposing view. But again, now wasn't the time for arguing. 'I went there today. Do you know much about it?'

Jason's mannerisms were telling him that his brother's brain was whirling, trying to work out what was coming. Always trying to be ten steps ahead.

Jason took a slug of his beer before he answered. 'Yes. Café on the ground floor, with a flat above it. Would be worth a fortune in the city, but not out there. Like Jeremy said, the building is worth about £360K. I had my guys give me a report on it this afternoon. We made some calls to a couple of other developers I know, and I reckon we can offload it in the next week or so. If they do it right, they'll get three flats out of it and a decent profit. I'd do it myself, but I'm stacked with other projects right now and don't have the time.'

Lachlan caught the boast – his brother was clearly doing well if he didn't have time to take on this redevelopment. Maybe that could work in his favour.

'What if we didn't sell it though? If you're too busy right now, what if we hung on to it a while longer? I met the woman who runs the café and lives in the flat today. That's why I'm here. That place is her life, Jason, and we've given her sixty days to wrap it up. I want to help her find a way to keep her business, or at least give her longer to work something out.'

Jason's reaction was instant. 'What, and risk the market going down and we lose money? Are you crazy? We can get cash for that right now, and we'd be mad not to go that route. I mean, sad for the café chick, and hate to sound brutal, but these things happen in business. So no. I'm not holding off.'

The next argument was out of Lachlan's mouth before he'd even thought it through. 'What if I bought you out?'

Jason at least paused to run the numbers on that before he challenged it.

'The value is £360K minimum. So that's £180K you'd owe me. Even if you use the £125K Dad left you, you'd still come up short. Unless, of course, you have £55K lying around somewhere.'

They both knew he didn't.

'I could look at getting a mortgage...'

What the hell was he doing? Why would he take out a mortgage on a café in Weirbridge when he lived in London and had solid intentions never to come back here? There was just a sudden and unassailable need not to let his brother win.

'And that'll take months. We're already going to have to wait for it all until probate is finished, and a mortgage could take six, maybe eight weeks to arrange. I can have a cash offer on that next week. Sorry, bro. It's not happening.'

'Come on, Jason. At least meet her...'

'How many times do I need to hit you before you lie down here, Lachlan? This isn't your world. You're a decent builder, but you know nothing about finance. You stick to your stuff and I'll stick to mine. This conversation is done.'

There was still an urge to argue, but Lachlan could see it was pointless. Instead, he got up, walked towards the door, but only after he said, 'You know once upon a time I wanted to be just like you... but that was before you turned into a colossal prick.'

He was at the kitchen door, when, behind him, still standing at the island with his beer, Jason said, 'Always trying to rescue people, little brother. Problem is, you pick the wrong people to help. Maybe if you'd worried about the people close to you, you wouldn't have fucked up your life.'

Lachlan stopped, every single cell in his brain begging him to go back and punch that asshole until he couldn't stand. Then he turned, and he saw Tanya was right behind him, her eyes pleading with him, her hand resting on the top of her swollen belly.

He didn't know if it made him a good guy or a coward that he kept on walking.

When he reached the front door, Tanya stepped in front of him to open it. 'Lachlan, don't hate him.'

How could he not? But, again, he said nothing. He wasn't going to drag her into this or upset her, especially now.

She kept her voice low as she went on. 'He's broke. Lost almost everything on a big deal that tanked and he's trying to pull it back. He needs the cash from the sale of this property to clear his feet and let him get back to a position where the banks will loan to him again. That's why he won't hold off. He needs the full value of the building, and he needs it quickly. And he's not aware that I know any of this, so it stays between us.'

Everything now made sense. The urgency. The arrogance. The lashing out. Jason always came out fighting, especially when his back was against the wall.

Lachlan understood it now, and most of all, he was 100 per cent sure that there was nothing he could do to change it.

Stepping out of the doorway, he felt the snap of the cold air, before he turned back to her. 'Good luck, Tanya,' he said softly. 'I mean that. I want you to be happy.'

Her eyes were glistening under the door light as she nodded. 'You too, Lachlan.'

As last goodbyes went, it was a sad, but maybe a needed one. Goodbye. I wish you well.

When he climbed into the car, he felt a sense of finality. They'd put a full stop on the end of their chapter.

But the last hour had also put a full stop on any hopes he had of helping Alyssa.

He glanced at the time on his watch. Almost eight o'clock. Still an hour until he needed to be at the airport for his flight. He went on to the airline app to check in online, and that's when he saw the notification – the flight had been delayed until 11.30 p.m. He checked in anyway, so he now had almost three hours to kill and the airport was only twenty minutes away. He thought about calling Margaux, but there was a text there from her too.

> Ok – first impressions of date – he has no interest in true crime shows, so think he's not a serial killer. Good sign. Did you get earlier flight or are you still here?

He texted back, determined not to say anything that would give her an excuse to flunk out on her date.

> Glad non-serial-killer vibes established. All good with flight. Will call you in morning. Love ya! Xx

It was almost true. It was only a short delay. He could go straight to the airport now, or…

His thoughts returned to his mum's mantra of doing one good thing at the end of a bad day.

He wanted to go back and see Alyssa, but he figured the café would be closed by now. That's when he remembered her saying that she was hosting a party there tonight.

There might not be anything he could do to change what was happening to her – but he wanted to let her know that he'd tried.

8 P.M. – 10 P.M.

25

JESSIE

Jessie wasn't sure what stung the most – the fact that Georgie would keep something this important from her or that Stan was at the bar and Dorinda Canavan was all over him like a rash. Actually, that wasn't even a close contest – it was definitely Georgie's secrecy that stung more.

Her daughter hadn't even got her coat off before Jessie had challenged her about it and immediately saw that it wasn't all some big mistake or misunderstanding on Moira's part.

Georgie let out a long, slow sigh. 'Oh, Mum, I'm so sorry you found out. I didn't want you to know.'

Jessie felt like she'd been slapped. 'But why? Why wouldn't you tell me about it?'

'Because I didn't want the job. It would have been crazy. Who wants to go to Colorado in winter?'

If that lass thought that she could get away with lying to the woman who had been her mother for thirty-eight years, she must have inhaled too much hairspray doing Cathy's hair today.

Jessie pursed her lips. Raised her right eyebrow. Waited. And, of course, Georgie had cracked. She'd always been a terrible bluffer.

'Argh, okay! I didn't tell you because you're finally getting to retire, Mum, and I knew that if you heard about this, you'd put your life on hold and try to make it happen for me. You've already given me your salon and I know how lucky I am to have that, so there was no way I was going to ruin the plans for you and Dad to go off and live your best lives. But, at the same time, I couldn't just shut up shop for six months and bugger off. The salon would take years to recover from that. So there was no option but to refuse the job. But I'm totally fine with that decision – I'm not the adventurous type anyway.'

Jessie was flabbergasted. Stunned. This whole time, there she'd been, dreading going off into the sunset and now, Georgie had given up what sounded like the opportunity of a lifetime, because Jessie wasn't going to be here. This discussion wasn't over by a long shot.

'But, Georgie, if you'd told me about it, we could have come up with a plan. I could have stayed here longer. Another six months working in the salon wouldn't have made any difference to me.' Jessie could hear herself and hoped that Georgie didn't realise that this time it was her who was lying. The truth was, she'd been on her feet since she was eighteen – that was forty-seven years of standing all day tending to people's locks. She was done. Exhausted. It was time to put her feet up. The problem had never been that she was being forced to retire – she was wholeheartedly looking forward to that. If she never spent another day standing behind a chair, clutching a comb and a pair of scissors, that would be just dandy. The problem was that she was going to be spending that retirement in a place that didn't have... She looked around her, as if making the point to herself. Tenerife didn't have this. Friends. Family. Her community.

'Mum, please forget about it. I turned it down and it's over with, and I'm happy. Let it go and just enjoy your night. You deserve it.'

Jessie recognised that she was being brushed off, and she knew that Georgie was doing it with the best of intentions, but this wasn't sitting right with her at all.

Although, perhaps here and now wasn't the best time and place to have this conversation, because the door kept opening and more people were arriving every two minutes.

'Helena! Eve!' Jessie exclaimed. 'Och, the two of you are radiant, so you are.' Cathy's daughter and granddaughter made their entrance – two lovely ladies who couldn't be more different. Helena was a terrifyingly astute criminal lawyer, and Eve was a talent agent who loved a party. Georgie adored her cousins, and the cheeky madam was now using them as an excuse to get out of this conversation, saying, 'Ladies, come with me and let's get you a drink. I think Aunt Cathy and Richie are over at the buffet.'

She then turned back to Jessie and said in a smiley singsong voice, 'Mum, we'll chat later, but don't you worry about a thing. Everything is exactly the way it's supposed to be.' With that, she kissed Jessie on the cheek and shepherded her cousins through the crowd to the other side of the room, passing her brother on the way. Grant reached Jessie, threw his arms around her and then pulled back, took one hand and twirled her round as Loretta belted out 'Man, I Feel Like A Woman'. Loretta and Moira were having a ball – over next to the area that had been cleared for dancing, they'd pushed two coffee tables together to fashion a makeshift stage that would never pass a health and safety inspection, and the crowd was loving it.

'Great party, Mum. Although, if there's a crime spree in Weirbridge tonight, they'll clean everyone out because the whole village is here.'

'True. The head of the Neighbourhood Watch is over there, line dancing in the opposite direction to everyone else.' He followed her eyeline and then howled when he spotted Val, who was indeed going left when all the other Shania Twains were going right.

Jessie stretched up on her toes, so that she could speak to him without shouting over the music. 'I need to talk to you, son.'

'Oh, no. I wasn't there, it wasn't me, and I didn't do it,' Grant retorted, parroting the same line he'd frequently used as a teenager to deny all culpability for any misdemeanour, especially if he *was* there, it *was* him and he *did* do it.

Jessie gave him an unimpressed nudge and got back to the point. 'Does that sister of yours still tell you everything that's going on in her life?'

He eyed her with suspicion. 'Maybe. Perhaps. I can't confirm or deny. Why?'

'Because if she does, then she might have told you that she got offered a job in America working with Ollie Chiles.'

Jessie was studying his face intently. Like Georgie, he was a terrible liar, and she could spot a porky with her eyes shut. Grant knew that, which was probably why he was going for vague acknowledgement but confirming nothing.

'I may or may not know something about that situation, but I'm not a grass, so I can't possibly say and you'll never break me.' He'd never been the same since he binge-watched *Chicago PD*.

'And if she told you about it, then she probably told you that she turned it down.'

That appeared to be news to him because his surprise gave the game away. 'She did? Bugger. I've been trying to talk her into taking it all day. Six months on a TV set is a brilliant gig. If he'd asked me, I'd be there in a heartbeat. Don't ever tell Gabriel I said that.'

Okay, now that he'd dropped the coy act and become an official informant, she needed him to cough up the crucial info.

'Grant, did she want the job? Did she say no to it because she didn't want to trouble me?'

'No!' There was a short pause, before he surrendered. 'And by that I mean yes. Okay, yes. To both questions. She would have loved to have taken the job, but the timing didn't work with you retiring, so that was her dilemma.'

That was what she wanted to know. The whole point of giving the salon to Georgie had been to set her up for life. She hadn't considered for a second that Georgie might have wanted other options.

'Am I excused, or do you want to shine one of those candles in my eyes and grill me for more information?'

'No, I want you to mind the door here while I nip to the loo and be sparkling and gracious to everyone who arrives.'

She left him behind and made her way through the throng towards the ladies. She was halfway there when she was sidetracked for a couple of minutes by Val and Cathy, who coerced her on to the dance floor for a quick shuffle to Loretta's version of 'Waterloo'. Which wasn't really the song Jessie wanted to hear when she was dying to get to the toilets.

Thankfully, there wasn't a queue when she got there, but when she came back out, she spotted Kayleigh, leaning against the wall, next in line.

'Are you okay there, sweetheart?'

'I'm fine, Gran.'

'So why the serious face? You look like someone stole your Harry Piles album.'

'Harry Styles, Gran. And we don't call them albums any more.'

'That's why you look miserable. A new Osmonds record could keep me happy for weeks at your age.'

She flattened herself against the wall as Linda Nesbit from next door stormed past Kayleigh and into the loo, skipping the line. Thankfully, Kayleigh didn't seem to mind.

'Anyway, I'm not miserable – I'm just waiting for a uni friend to text me back about a legal thing.'

That didn't make sense to Jessie. 'At nine o'clock on a Monday night? Are you in some kind of trouble?'

'No, no, not for me! For Alyssa. When you were here this morning, did she tell you about the letter she got?'

Jessie was none the wiser. 'Letter about what?'

'This building is being sold and she's losing the café and her flat. I'm gutted for her. I'm going to try to help, but I'm not hopeful.'

Jessie was wondering if she'd had one too many glasses of plonk to process that. Or maybe she didn't hear it properly over the glorious sound of Moira Chiles, standing on a coffee table singing, 'Proud Mary'.

'Hang on, did you say she's losing the café? That can't be the case, surely?'

'It is, Gran.'

Holy hell, she had heard right.

'And who's doing this to her exactly?' Jessie could feel a combination of rage and horror rise in her chest and make her bra strap feel too tight. That lass had worked too damned hard, and this café was too important to the village to close. Where would all the old dears go for their tea and a heat in the winter? Where would the customers in the salon go after their highlights? Or the monthly speed dating group, that they'd nicknamed 'Not So Speedy Dating' because Agnes, the optimistic singleton from the fish shop, took twenty minutes to get to the point of any story.

No. No. No. Sod that.

Kayleigh was leaning into her ear now, so that she could be heard over the sound of the crowd cheering for Moira.

'The landlord. Actually, not the landlord, because he died. From what I can gather, the café is part of his estate, and his beneficiaries are selling it off. Only sixty days' notice, Gran – it's terrible. Alyssa says one of the man's family came in today and she begged him for help, and he refused. I wish you'd been here when it happened. I told her you'd have kicked his arse.'

At that, Linda vacated the toilet and Kayleigh moved to go in.

'Anyway, don't worry, Gran, I'll figure it out.'

Jessie swiped two mini steak pies and a glass of plonk from the buffet as she passed to relieve Grant over at the door. There couldn't be too many more people coming in at this time, so she'd give it five more minutes and then mingle – just long enough to ponder the revelations of the last couple of hours.

How could she leave? She wasn't even out of the country yet and the café was closing down, Georgie was keeping secrets and Dorinda bloody Canavan was over there talking to Stan like they were long-lost lovers. Which, technically... She watched them for a moment, wondering what they were discussing and why. In almost thirty years, since that night at the golf club, she'd never seen them speak to each other. In fact, as far as she knew, they'd never even been in the same room. Stan avoided the café and Dorinda didn't frequent the golf club, so there were no crossover points. So why was Dorinda speaking to him now? And was Jessie going to ignore it, or march right over there and find out what they were discussing?

Before she could decide, the lovely Hugo Canavan came through the crowd towards her holding up a bottle of fizz. She knocked back the wine in her glass then held it out towards him. 'Top it up please, Hugo. I think I'm going to need a bit of liquid courage for what's ahead tonight.'

26
GEORGIE

The party was in full swing and the space occupied by those having a dance was getting wider and wider as more people let their inhibitions drop and their pants boogie. Moira and Loretta had the whole crowd in the palms of their hands, acting like a tag team to throw down hit after hit from the seventies and eighties. They were currently duetting to 'Islands In The Stream' and Moira's ability to replicate Kenny Roger's low notes was notably impressive.

Georgie hadn't had a chance to get her dancing shoes on yet because she was too busy catching up with her cousins, Helena and Eve. They'd been blethering for the last twenty minutes, and she was deeply aware she may also be using them as a human shield against the advances of her mother.

She didn't blame Moira for letting the news of the job offer come out – by all accounts it had been an honest slip-up. But her mum's reaction had been the very reason that she hadn't wanted her to know. Hopefully now that Georgie had reassured her she wasn't taking the job, her parents could just fly off tomorrow morning and put all their energies into having a blissful retirement.

Although, looking at her dad now, stuck over at the bar table and deep in conversation with Dorinda Canavan, she wasn't sure he'd quite got his 'bliss' face down perfect yet. Georgie decided to go and rescue him just as soon as she'd finished getting the scoop on Helena's wedding plans.

Georgie had always loved Eve, Helena's daughter and Cathy's granddaughter. They were only a few years apart in age and had been the two kids sitting giggling under a table at family functions for most of their childhood. Helena, however, had always been mildly terrifying, but she'd mellowed slightly since rekindling her relationship with Eve's father, and now they were set to marry.

'You know, Helena, I don't think I've ever asked – how did you meet him the first time round?'

Georgie watched Eve react to that question with 'Oh no,' and then put her hands over her ears. 'Okay, Mum, I'm not listening to this bit – on you go.'

Helena rolled her eyes. 'This one is such a prude. Anyway, I don't mind admitting it – he was a one-night stand when I was twenty-five, and Eve was the result. Didn't see him again for almost thirty years.'

'Noooooooo,' Georgie exclaimed. Helena McLean, one of Scotland's top solicitors, and perhaps the most strong, powerful and intimidating woman that Georgie had ever known, had not just said that.

Eve cagily took a hand away from one ear. 'Is it over? Has she told you?'

'I'm shook. Shook!' Georgie told her, chuckling. 'Helena, I'd never have believed that of you! If I was wearing pearls right now, I'd be clutching them and demanding my smelling salts.'

'There's nothing wrong with exploring healthy sexual urges, ladies,' Helena preened defiantly, making Eve wince again.

'You know...' Helena's comment had struck a chord with Georgie. 'I've never had one of those.'

'A mother who overshares?' Eve asked.

'No, I've definitely got one of those. I've never had a one-night stand. Or a two-night stand, for that matter.'

'I'm refusing to share my status on that, given that my mother is present,' Eve declared, chuckling. 'But don't sound so disappointed when you say that, Georgie. It's not like it should be a bucket list item.'

'Well, maybe it should be,' Georgie declared, emboldened by the full glass of champagne she'd already downed since she arrived. 'Flynn and I got together when I was seventeen and I'd had one boyfriend and a few fumbles before him, but that was it.'

'And since then?' Helena asked with an intense gaze. Georgie saw now why witnesses crumbled under her stare.

'Erm, nothing. No one.'

'No one?' Eve looked surprised, then immediately rallied and attempted to make her feel better. 'Well, it's not been long since your marriage ended.'

Georgie loved her for trying, but... 'Eve, it's been three years. And in that time, the only hot hip action in my life has been watching *Strictly*.' After the events of this afternoon, she was choosing to remove her occasional indiscretions with Flynn from the hot hip-action category.

'Then I suggest you get out there and do something about it,' Helena said, no-nonsense as always. 'If you'd like to have a man, that is. Or a woman. I truly think I could have gone either way, depending on the person. However, that's only if you want to be with someone. I don't think for a single second that a person needs to have a relationship to validate their worth.'

'Watch you don't slide off your soapbox there, Mum,' Eve teased her, but they were saved from Helena's inevitable scathing retort by Kayleigh passing by, holding a tray of sausage rolls aloft.

'Mum, Alyssa has put me to work,' she grinned, then stopped suddenly when she realised who Georgie was speaking to. 'Aunt Helena!' she gushed.

Georgie wasn't surprised by the reaction. Helena was one of the women who'd inspired Kayleigh to go into law in the first place.

'I didn't realise you were coming. Hang on.'

She put the sausage rolls down on the nearby buffet table, then came straight back over and hugged both Helena and Eve in turn.

'Aunt Helena, I can't believe you're here. And I can't believe I didn't think of you!'

Georgie had no idea what her daughter was rambling about, but she seemed fairly giddy about something when she asked, 'Do you know anything about property law?'

Helena shook her head. 'Not much. Only what I can remember from university and perhaps a few titbits I've picked up since then.'

Georgie doubted that very much. Helena was a criminal lawyer, but she was so smart in every area of life – including, apparently, relationships and the value of a one-night stand – that she would definitely be Georgie's pick for the 'phone a friend' if she ever went on *Who Wants to Be a Millionaire*. Having Helena onside would be the perfect complement to Georgie's specialities of cocktail recipes, the history of hair, and the entire works of Westlife.

'Would you mind coming and having a quick chat with my friend, Alyssa? She owns this café and I'm trying to help her with a legal issue to do with her lease.'

For a second, Georgie wondered what Helena's reaction would be. Being a lawyer must be like being a doctor, she imagined. As soon as people at dinner parties knew what you did, they wanted to ask your advice on their speeding ticket or their piles.

She needn't have worried. The lawyer and the feminist in Helena had never yet refused her niece, or any woman in legal jeopardy, even while at a party with a drink in her hand. 'Of course, I will, but I'm expensive. You may have to come intern for me all summer to pay me back.'

Kayleigh's beaming grin made it clear that wouldn't be a hardship.

Just as Helena left, the song changed and the crowd cheered as Moira broke into 'I'm in the Mood for Dancing' by the Nolans, and Georgie and Eve were treated to the incomparable sight of Aunt Cathy boogying towards them. 'Right, you two – my Richie's back is playing up and this is one of my favourite songs, so who's dancing with me?'

'If you don't take this one, I'll talk about your mother's one-night stand again,' Georgie warned Eve, who capitulated immediately, giggling, 'Right, Gran, let's do it,' as they danced off.

Georgie was about to go mingle, when she saw that Dorinda Canavan was still chatting to her dad and there was something about his pained expression that made her feel sorry for him. Dad hated things like this. Mum was the social butterfly, and Dad was the one who was happier out on the golf course, being unbothered by anyone, especially someone as full-on as Dorinda. Dad probably didn't even have a clue who she was, and he'd definitely have run out of small talk by now. There was nothing else for it than to be the social equivalent of a SWAT team. In. Rescue. Out.

She sidled over. 'Hi, Dorinda! Sorry to barge in, but can I have a quick word with my dad? Just need to organise Mum's birthday cake.'

The rude cow didn't look too happy, but she took the hint and left them anyway.

'You're welcome, Dad,' Georgie said with a wink. 'You looked like you needed saving.'

She'd thought that her dad would have found that amusing, but he was still strangely sullen-faced, as he muttered, 'Thanks, love.'

Something was off. 'Are you okay, Dad? Oh God, tell me Mum hasn't changed her mind about going because I got that job offer? I've already told her I turned it down.'

To her relief, he clearly had no idea what she was talking about. 'She never mentioned a job offer to me,' he said. 'Truth is though, love, she didn't want to go to Tenerife in the first place. She's only coming because I wanted it.'

The conversation had definitely taken a turn she hadn't expected, but she swallowed her shock and attempted to set him straight.

'Dad! That's not true. Mum is looking forward to it and she'll be happy anywhere if you're there.'

'I'm not so sure about that.'

Georgie opened her mouth but couldn't find the words to reply. This was so out of character, that Georgie was stumped. Her mum and dad had always been the happiest, most solid couple that she knew. What was going on?

'Why would you say that? You're a great husband. A brilliant dad too. Of course Mum is happy.'

'No, love. I've not always been the best husband.'

Oh lord, her solid, dependable, steady dad was in full crisis here. Had someone spiked his drink? Did men go through some version of the menopause?

'But, Dad...'

She didn't get the rest of that out, because her mum swooped in from behind her.

'Stan, can I have a quick word with you outside? Sorry, Georgie – I'll just steal him for a minute.' Curt. Serious. Taking no objections.

Before Georgie could reply, off they went, leaving her speechless.

What. Just. Happened? Mum had seemed pretty pissed off with something, and she just hoped it wasn't her. No. That wasn't her mum's style. If Jessie McLean was annoyed with you, she told you directly to your face. She had no idea what Dad had done, or why he was so miserable, but if there was one person who would have the gossip...

Georgie cast a glance around the room searching for Grant, until she spotted him at the edge of the dance area, twirling Val around. In Aunt Cathy style, she shuffled over towards them, but as she got there, the Nolans took a break and were replaced by Whitney Houston declaring that she wanted to dance with somebody.

Val conceded defeat. 'Grant, son, I can't do two fast songs in a row without hydrating, so I'm away for a Porn Star Martini,' she announced, heading off in the direction of the bar. Georgie took advantage of the moment, grabbing Grant's hand and leading him over to a quieter spot by the door. Lovely old Mrs Dawson and her equally sweet sister were sitting there, multi-tasking by tapping their feet in time to the music, smiling as they watched the dancers, and knitting furiously with hands that seemed to work independently of the rest of their bodies. Mrs Dawson appeared to be knitting a scarf that would fit around an elephant, one that liked a bright pink woolly number that stretched for miles.

Georgie knew from their visits to the salon that they were both extremely hard of hearing and couldn't pick up the din of a brass band unless it was playing in their living room, so she wasn't worried about them listening in.

'What's going on with Mum and Dad? Dad said something about not always being a good husband and now Mum just came and swept him off and she's got a face like thunder.'

Grant shook his head. 'I've no idea. Genuinely. But I have to say, I'd forgotten what life was like in this family. I work in a frantically busy Kensington salon, employ thirty-five people, tend to the demands of more divas than I can count, and I still think there's more drama going on up here. Talking of which, tell me you're not getting back with Flynn.'

'I'm not getting back with Flynn,' she repeated.

'Oh, thank God. If I had to have another conversation about solar panels, I'd have bought earmuffs.'

That made her chuckle, so she decided to say something that would really make his day. He wanted drama, so…

'But I've had a long chat with Helena, and I've decided one-night stands are the way to go.'

That evoked such a cackle that if he'd had a drink, he'd have spluttered it across the room.

'What? I mean, I'm thrilled for you, but I think I need a bit more information.'

'Well, I've been with Flynn for my entire adult life, so I've decided I need to—'

'If you say "spread my wings", I'll die,' he warned her, wiping away tears of laughter.

'*Get out of my comfort zone*,' Georgie countered haughtily, before giggles consumed her too. These were exactly the kinds of conversations that made her love her brother more than words. 'I need to date. To socialise. To venture out of the village every now and then and, yes, maybe explore all that sweaty, bendy stuff with an attractive member of the male species.'

The words were barely out of her mouth, when she had to move to the side because a new arrival was coming in the café door.

Georgie turned, ready to extend a greeting to another villager, but was surprised to see a stranger there. A guy. Tall. Broad. Long blond hair swept back off his face. If he had an Australian accent, she'd bet a fiver he was related to the Hemsworths.

'Hi,' was all she could manage at short notice.

'Hi. Sorry to gatecrash, but do you know where I'll find Alyssa?'

Not Australian. Scottish. Glasgow. Sexy voice.

Georgie scanned the room, but couldn't see Alyssa, which gave her the answer. 'Erm, yes. If you go right up to the back of the café, past where that lot are doing the Macarena, she's probably through the door behind the counter.'

'Okay, thanks.'

As he went off to follow her instructions, she realised that both she and Grant were watching him go.

'Sis, if you're looking for an attractive member of the male species for that sweaty bendy stuff, you might want to start there.'

27

ALYSSA

'Ginny, can you give the thirty-second warning for the birthday cake? Georgie asked me to bring it out at nine o'clock and it's almost time.'

Alyssa was firing the candles into the hairdryer-shaped cake, unsure whether sixty-five of them were going to fit, and, worse, if the heat would set off the smoke alarms. She'd seen that happen in a video on social media and it had been a pathological fear ever since. What did it say about her life that her sprinkler system being activated, soaking a room full of revellers and the interior of her gorgeous winter wonderland café wouldn't be the worst thing to happen to her today?

No, the most recent contender for the worst thing to happen to her today had kicked off just a short while ago, when Kayleigh had come into the kitchen with a tall, red-haired, striking woman in a stunning black velvet trouser suit.

'Alyssa, this is my Aunt Helena. She's Aunt Cathy's daughter.'

Alyssa had to dig deep for a smile and a cheery greeting. It was nice that Kayleigh wanted to introduce her family, but right then, she had a whole lot of other things taking up her time and her mind.

Alyssa had halted the candle insertion and held out her hand. 'Lovely to meet you, Helena.'

Okay, time to get back to work. Things to do. People to serve. Candles to light.

'Aunt Helena is a lawyer. A pretty brilliant one, actually.'

Alyssa had frozen, suddenly unaware of a single other thing she had to do.

Had she heard that right? 'A lawyer?'

Helena had answered that, her voice modulated and posh. 'Yes. Actually, I'm a criminal solicitor. Kayleigh explained that you're having a problem with your lease, and I'm afraid I'm not well-versed in property law, but I can certainly give you my thoughts. Kayleigh said you received a letter? Can I see it?'

Alyssa had known Cathy since the café opened, and she'd come in every Monday with Jessie on her day off from the salon. She was the loveliest lady, but she sure didn't have these cut-glass vowels and the assertive presence of her daughter.

'Yes, I'll just get it and thank you – I can't tell you how grateful I'd be. I've been totally blindsided by this to be perfectly honest, and I don't have a clue what to do.'

Alyssa had said all that while going to the drawer and pulling out the letter and the lease yet again. Even looking at it had made her stomach churn, but at least this time there was a flicker of hope that this lady could help. She'd handed it over and then held her breath.

Helena's first reaction had been to the company name at the top of the letter.

'Huntington Farrell. They're a good company. Expensive.' She'd then lowered her gaze to the bottom of the letter. 'Jeremy Sprite. Okay, I know him too. Bit of an arrogant git, and a reputation for being a rottweiler for his clients. Not the best start,' she'd observed, before her gaze went back to the top of the page and she'd fallen silent as she read the contents.

Alyssa had felt her hands shake as she'd shot a silent but grateful glance at Kayleigh, who'd responded by holding up crossed fingers.

After a few seconds, Helena had paused, lifted her head again. 'Your landlord was Martyn Morden.' It wasn't phrased as a question – more of a notable observation.

'Yes, do you know him too? Sorry, *did* you know him. I believe he died a couple of months ago. Which was sad. Obviously. For his family. And his friends. And… people.'

Aaagh, she wasn't sure if she was more intimidated by Helena's steely gaze and authoritative manner, or terrified about what Helena was going to tell her, but her brain had turned to mush and she'd lost the power of articulation.

'Yes, I knew him. Met him many times over the years. A good businessman – a property developer, and a bit of a pillar of the community. Although he raised a few eyebrows among the stuffed shirts when his wife died, and he married a thirty-year-old and went off to live out his twilight years in Monaco.'

Alyssa had thought back to Lachlan Morden's visit earlier in the day.

'Do you know his son?'

'Not personally. Bit of a twat, by all accounts.' Her lips had pursed as if she were trying to recall something, before saying, 'Jason Morden, that's it. He's a property developer too, but a separate entity from his father.'

By this time, tension had raised Alyssa's shoulders to the level of her ears.

'Oh. No, that's not the one I met today. The one who was here was called Lachlan.'

Helena had an immediate response to that. 'Wait, he came here? Was it some kind of intimidation tactic? Some of these alpha male fuckers think they can railroad anyone into doing what they want.'

'No, no! Actually, he'd come because… I'm not even sure. Something to do with his mum working here when she was younger. He didn't even say who he was until my daft sister tried to…' She hadn't been able to say it. How pathetic would Helena think she was if she told her about Ginny's plans for a romcom moment? Instead, she'd finished with, '…to engage him in conversation and pried it out of him.'

Helena was clearly not impressed by this development at all. 'And what happened?'

Cue Alyssa's second opportunity to sound pathetic. 'I basically begged him to help me keep the café and he said there was nothing he could do. He wouldn't even try.'

'Mmm.' That was all Helena had said, before resuming her study of the documents. When she'd read the letter, she'd gone on to the lease. After what felt like a week and a half, but was probably only a couple of minutes, she'd raised her head again. 'Alyssa, I'd love to give you good news, but as far as I can see, this all seems to be in order. The difficulty is that you signed this lease – in effect a contract – and one of the clear terms was that in the event of the death of either party, there would be a sixty-day termination period.'

'I didn't even register that when I signed it.'

Helena had nodded thoughtfully. 'That's understandable. It's more usual that the owner of a commercial property would be a limited company, but for some reason this building was owned personally by Mr Morden. Probably why his lawyer inserted this clause. As I said, I don't know enough about property law to advise you. What I would say is that you need a good lawyer…'

The air had seeped out of Alyssa's body. 'I can't afford a lawyer. Not one that could challenge something like this.'

Helena must have taken pity on her. 'I understand. Look, send me copies of all this tomorrow and I'll ask a colleague that specialises in this field to take a look at it as a favour. No promises, but I'll see what I can do. My mother would be horrified if I didn't try to help – she says your prawn toasties are the best things she's ever tasted.'

'Thank you. Thank you so, so much.' Alyssa could have cried. She almost did, but Helena's generosity had been dampened by her next statement.

'You're welcome. But, Alyssa, I do want to manage your expectations, so I have to say that I'm not optimistic that there's a way out of this. In a fair world, there would be, but…'

She hadn't had to finish the sentence. Instead, she'd handed the documents back to Alyssa and given her a sympathetic smile. If Alyssa were ever to be convicted of a crime, she'd already decided that this woman would be her first call.

When they'd left, she'd finished the candle placement, then slumped down on the chair, grateful for a quick minute of solitude, replaying the conversation in one of the few moments of peace she'd had all day.

Maybe it would be pointless after all. Perhaps it was time to accept that this was her new reality and come up with an alternative plan. If the catering company idea didn't work, maybe she should just sell everything off, take a year out, go travelling. She'd grafted solidly since she was a teenager and hadn't done the gap year thing, or the university summer holiday trips. She'd been too focused on saving up to open her own place, and then too busy running it to take a holiday.

And yet… the thought of sunny beaches and carefree days didn't even come close to the happiness that she had here, day in and day out.

The tip-tap of heels had burst through her thoughts a few moments later, when Dorinda had come in, clutching a half-full glass of champagne and wobbling, decidedly unsteadily, on the six-inch stiletto sandals she'd paired with a scarlet, off-the-shoulder, calf-length pencil dress. Alyssa's first thought had been that if it were her, she'd have had to diet for a month to get into that dress. Her second was that she would break her neck in those heels. Her third was that her mum was clearly tipsy.

'Darling, I was just thinking I should take the cake out. I mean, it would be a waste of this outfit if I didn't.' At that, she'd twirled around, slopping champagne over the side of the glass.

Her next thought had been that 'tipsy' didn't even come close. Her mum was actually pissed as a fart. And Alyssa sooooo didn't need to be dealing with this.

'Why would you want to take the cake out, Mum?'

Alyssa didn't get it. Her mum and Jessie weren't pals. In fact, she'd always sensed that they didn't particularly like each other. Then a realisation had dawned on her and suddenly, Alyssa knew exactly why her mother wanted to deliver the cake – she couldn't help her insatiable need to be the centre of attention.

'Mum, you're not taking the cake out.'

'Why not?'

'Because there are about to be sixty-five lit candles on here, and if you fall flat on your face, we'll all go up in flames and I'm too young to die.'

That had sent her packing, muttering something about 'ungrateful daughters' and Alyssa had to stand perfectly still for a second and push all the air out of her lungs, then take a new breath and carry on.

Now, five minutes later, she'd just finished lighting the last candle when

Ginny reappeared at the door. 'Okay. The singers are about to take a break, and Grandad is over at the microphone ready to kick off "Happy Birthday". Kayleigh has tracked down Jessie and made sure she's there, and I've just given a thumbs up to Georgie and Grant. Are you good to go?'

Slowly, carefully, Alyssa lifted the blazing sponge. 'Good to go.'

'Okay, hang on.'

Alyssa watched as Ginny peeked her head out of the kitchen, gave Grandad the okay signal, then stretched around to the control panel and switched off the café lights, leaving just the candles on the walls, the twinkle of the Christmas tree and the garlands of fairy lights in the windows to illuminate the room.

'Happy birthday to you...'

Despite feeling like her heart had been ripped from her chest today, the sound of Grandad's voice belting out 'Happy Birthday' made her smile.

Holding the cake in front of her, she walked slowly out of the kitchen door.

'Happy birthday to you...' The rest of the guests had spotted her now and started singing along.

'Happy birthday, dear Jessie...'

She crossed the space behind the counter, veered carefully around the serving area.

'Happy birthday to yooooooo...'

In the dim light, she saw Jessie and stopped right beside her.

'Hip hip hurray!'

That was the cue to put the lights back on, and Ginny, always great with a production, was bang on time.

'Hip hip hurray!'

As the lights flashed back on, Alyssa turned her head to scan the room and take in everything, devastatingly aware that this would probably be the last big party she'd ever throw in this room.

She saw her grandad, beaming as he roused the crowd. She saw a packed house of guests, all wide-eyed and happy. She saw Jessie, clearly overcome with emotion, tears in her eyes. And Alyssa felt an overwhelming wave of gratitude...

'Hip, hip, hurray!'

...until she spotted Lachlan Morden standing right in front of her.

28

LACHLAN

This wasn't exactly the subtle, low-key arrival that Lachlan had hoped for. The plan – as much as he'd had one – had been to quietly arrive at the party, unobtrusively track down Alyssa, then have a quick, but quiet chat with her and be out and on the way to the airport ten minutes after he'd arrived.

Instead, he'd walked into the small Scottish village equivalent of Mardi Gras. A couple of guests at the door had pointed him in the direction of the kitchen, and he'd very politely worked his way through the room, dodging tables, swerving round people singing at the top of their voices, then skirting past a crowd that were doing some kind of synchronised dance. All of a sudden, he'd made a wrong move, and his path had been inadvertently blocked by a crowd of older women, one with a blonde bob, who'd somehow – and until the end of time, he would refuse to replay the memory of this – coerced him into staying on the dance floor until the end of the song. Thankfully, it was mercifully short, and when the music had stopped, he'd spotted the door behind the counter, taken a few steps towards it, when the lights had gone down and the whole room had erupted into a chorus of 'Happy Birthday'.

At this point, his will to live had deserted him, and he'd had to stand there, reluctantly joining in, while Alyssa brought out a cake and did a whole birthday candle-blow out thing. Then the lady who was having the party burst into tears, gave a sobbing speech of thanks and everyone clapped.

Everyone, that is, except Alyssa, who was staring at him with unmistakable fury, while holding a cake in the shape of a hairdryer. And now, as the applause subsided, he was questioning both his choice to come here and his sanity.

With a subtle nod to the side, Alyssa gestured to the door behind the counter, her meaning clear. As the music started up again, and the party resumed, he followed her and she led him into a room at the back that was obviously the kitchen and prep area.

Alyssa had just put the cake down when her sister stormed in, saying, 'Lyss, I could swear I just saw that prick from earlier and...' She spotted him and went with an admirably direct, 'Yup, he's here.'

He decided that brevity was the route to take. 'Hi.'

Alyssa looked so much wearier than the fired-up version he'd met earlier, but still she took the lead. 'Are you here to tell me that you've had a change of heart and I can keep my café?'

'No. Sorry. I'm—'

She cut him dead. 'Then please don't take this the wrong way, but piss off. Truly. I have about a hundred guests out there, a party to run, a cake to cut, I've had the shittiest day of my life and I don't have the energy for you.'

He hadn't come all this way to give up without trying to do something positive for her though, even if it was just giving her all the facts. 'I understand. I swear I do. But I just need ten minutes of your time to explain a few things. And I'd come back when you're less busy, but I'm flying home in a couple of hours, so I need to get to the airport. And trust me when I say I don't intend to return for a very long time. Like, when hell freezes over.'

Something in his voice – probably sad desperation – must have struck a chord with them because he caught the glance that went between the sisters, and they seemed to reach some kind of silent agreement.

'Okay, have a seat,' the younger one said, as they pulled out chairs on the other side of the table and sat down. He searched the memory of this crap day for her name. Ginny. That was it. She reminded him of Margaux. Funny. Quick. Quirky. Bold in all the good ways. Especially – going by the hostility her gaze was throwing in his direction – when defending the people she loved.

'Ten minutes,' Alyssa said. 'And I need to cut this cake while we're speaking or there'll be a mutiny out there.'

'That's all I need,' he promised, pulling out a chair opposite them. 'First, I want to apologise for earlier. You caught me off guard, and I handled it really badly.'

'You did,' Ginny agreed.

'So I wanted to explain why I couldn't help, and I'll just give you the important details – if there's anything else you want to know, just stop me.'

Neither of them spoke so he carried on.

'I flew up here this morning for the reading of my dad's will. There are three beneficiaries to my dad's estate: his second wife, my brother, Jason, and me.'

He thought he saw a flicker of recognition in Alyssa's face when he said Jason's name, so perhaps she'd done some research.

'The majority of the estate was left to my dad's wife…'

'Your stepmother,' Ginny corrected him.

'Yeah, I guess. I've never thought of her that way – probably because I'm thirty-four and she's only a year older. Dad only married her a few years ago, and they lived abroad, so I've only met her a couple of times.'

He paused for questions but there were none, so he carried on.

'Anyway, we only found out this morning that this building was left to my brother and me. Like I said, I had no idea my dad owned it. I can't remember if I told you this earlier, but apparently, he bought this place as a gift for my mum on her fortieth birthday because it had such sentimental value for her.'

'That is so romantic,' Ginny conceded. 'Better than bed socks and a box of Quality Street.' Something in her tone told him that one came from experience.

'Yes, I guess it was. When my mum died, everything she had was left to Dad, and now he has passed this place on to us, with instructions to sell it and split the proceeds between us. I'm pretty sure my dad made that clear in case my brother and I disagreed on what to do with it. My brother wants it sold immediately and, for his own reasons, won't delay under any circumstances, won't negotiate and won't consider any other options. I promise I tried. I even went to his house tonight to ask him to cancel or postpone the sale, but he wouldn't budge.'

'Even though his own brother was asking him?' Alyssa had sliced half the cake while he'd been speaking.

'My brother and I... we don't have a good relationship. Or any relationship for that matter.' He was trying to be as discreet as possible on that one because talking about his personal issues made him squirm.

'Why?' Ginny asked, clearly not sharing his boundaries. He couldn't tell them. Wouldn't. Shouldn't. But...

'Because six weeks after my fiancée and I split, he swept in and now they're married.'

Ginny gasped. 'No way! Lyss, if you do that to me and Caden I'll never forgive you.'

Alyssa ignored her and spoke to him. 'I'm sorry. That's a shitty thing to go through.'

He shrugged, desperate to get off the subject of his private life. 'It is what it is. Anyway, I just wanted to give you the bottom line. The building is worth £360K. He reckons he has a buyer who will offer that for it next week and turn it into flats. The only way to avoid this is to buy it before then. It's the only option.'

'Unless I won the lottery tonight, I don't have that kind of money. And I'd only get a mortgage for a fraction of that.' Alyssa slumped back in her chair. 'There must be a way to fight this.'

Lachlan felt awful for her, but there was no point fudging the truth. 'I wish it were different, but if you fight it, the reality is that it'll cost you money, time and so much stress and you'll lose anyway, because he has the resources and he's ruthless. I'm so sorry. I swear if there was anything I could do, I would.'

Silence. More silence. Before either of them could find the words to respond, a woman in a tight red dress came to the doorway.

'There's no wine left, and I'm getting ready to riot.' Even to the untrained eye, the slur and the animated mannerisms would indicate that she'd imbibed a considerable amount of the missing wine.

Alyssa sighed and spoke to him as she stood up. 'Okay, Mum. Lachlan, give us two minutes. Ginny, you grab the cake, and I'll get the wine.'

While they were gone, he had a quick glance around and saw how much work and care had gone into this kitchen. It was spotlessly clean, and the yellow walls looked as if they were freshly painted, while the pale wood floor was either new or just scrupulously maintained. The cupboard style was dated, and the appliances weren't top of the range, like the kind of high-end brands that he'd installed in Dax Price's house. Dax hadn't fried an egg or switched on an oven in his life, yet apparently it was essential that he had a La Cornue range, a snip at just under £10K. However, what this kitchen had was lots of personal touches and it was obvious that the people who worked here took pride in it, which made him feel yet another level of crap over what was happening to them.

He pulled his phone out of his pocket to check the time – almost 9.30 p.m. He had just over an hour to get to the airport before his gate closed. It was a twenty-minute drive, and the car hire drop off was a two-minute walk from the terminal building, so as long as the snow had been cleared from the roads, he would still make it if he left in the next ten minutes.

He was about to put his phone back in his pocket when he noticed a voice message notification. He clicked on it and saw it was from Dax Price. There was still no sign of Alyssa, so he pressed PLAY.

'Mate, got your message. Need to postpone the job this week. Looks like the fuckers might be selling me to Milan. Flying there tomorrow morning for talks, back Friday. Will buzz you when I'm sorted and I know the score. Cheers, bro.'

He'd just locked his phone again when Alyssa and Ginny came back in.

'Sorry about that,' Alyssa apologised, and he wanted to say that she was the last person that should be saying sorry to him.

'That's okay.' He stood up, ready to get out of there and fairly convinced they'd be happy to see the back of him too. 'I'm going to go. I'm sorry again about all of this. I wish it wasn't happening, honestly.'

'Makes two of us,' Alyssa replied, but there was no aggression or reprimand in her tone, just sadness.

'I've left my mobile number on the napkin there. If you get a lawyer, and you need any more information, or if there's anything else I can do, just call me.'

He couldn't think what help he could give, but it didn't feel right leaving without offering.

Alyssa somehow managed to be gracious. He wasn't sure he'd do the same if the roles were reversed. 'Thank you. I'm sorry I shouted at you earlier. And, you know, about the "piss off" comment. It's been a long day.'

She looked as exhausted as he felt, and he hated that his family had caused that.

'I get it. I'd have told me to piss off too.' He took a step towards the door but was immediately blocked by the arrival of the older man who'd been at the microphone singing 'Happy Birthday' earlier.

The gent staggered a little as he crossed to the table, clasped onto the back of one of the chairs, supporting his weight before he dropped down onto the seat. His breathing was laboured and there was no mistaking the sheen of sweat on his face, or the hand that was circling his chest.

Alyssa jumped up, her face a mask of panic. 'Grandad! Are you okay? You're sweating! Were you dancing?'

The man managed to shake his head but still struggled to catch his breath.

'Oh God, Grandad, are you having a heart attack? Are you having chest pains? Ginny, run out to the square and get the defib from the front of the community centre while I call an ambulance.'

'Alyssa!'

For someone who was having a heart attack, Lachlan decided the grandad's voice was pretty strong. 'I'm fine, pet. Just give me a minute to get my breath back. I'm not having a heart attack.' He took a couple of deep breaths before going on. 'I've just been chasing the Nesbit triplets. I spotted them outside at some big Range Rover and the wee buggers have let down the tyres of every car in the street.'

Lachlan took in this information, glanced at his watch and then sat back down.

A minute ago, he'd calculated that he only had an hour to get to the airport.

Now it was pretty clear he wasn't going anywhere.

10 P.M. – MIDNIGHT

29
JESSIE

Jessie McLean had locked herself in the loo and she wanted to cry. Again. She'd already been pure mortified that she'd made a show of herself when the birthday cake had come out and she'd tried to make a speech. All she'd wanted to do was thank people for coming, tell them how much she treasured every one of them, but it had all got too much for her and for the first time in her life, she hadn't been able to put a face on it.

It was the emotion of it all. The shock. The absolute devastation of realising the full extent of the carnage caused by Stan and Dorinda bloody Canavan.

She reached for a piece of toilet paper, blew her nose, then closed her eyes, trying desperately to block out the conversation she'd just had with them. It didn't work. It was all still there, replaying in her mind, every word of it.

It had started when she'd interrupted their cosy chat and dragged Stan to the end of the corridor outside the toilet she was sitting in now.

'Stan, what's going on?' She'd faced it head on.

Of course, he'd tried to lie about it, but it was so half-hearted, it was almost pathetic. 'Nothing, love. Nothing at all.'

She could have left it for later. Decided to discuss it tomorrow. Got on with her party and talked it over at breakfast at the airport tomorrow morning, but the sickening knot in her stomach wouldn't let it drop because her intuition had told her that something was off. She'd seen it in his face, when Dorinda had him pinned in a corner. Fear? Fury? She wasn't sure, but what she did know was that Stan McLean was the coolest, most laid-back man she'd ever encountered, so if he was reacting like that, something was going on and Jessie could only come up with two possibilities – either Dorinda was taunting him about an affair that happened decades ago, or – and this was the one that had been making her unravel – maybe they were still seeing each other. Maybe it had never ended. Maybe she was the village fool, and they'd managed to hide an ongoing affair for all this time.

'Stan, I have loved you my whole life, but I swear to God if you don't tell me what is going on—'

'Have you told her yet, Stan?'

Dorinda. Bloody. Canavan. She'd come up behind them and inserted herself right in their space. Half-pissed. Swaying. And with a smug expression on her face that made Jessie want to explode. But she wouldn't give that woman the satisfaction of seeing her bothered.

'Dorinda, don't...' Stan had warned, but they both knew it was futile, because whatever Dorinda wanted to get off that pushed-up chest was coming out whether they liked it or not. That's when Jessie had snapped. There was no way on this earth that she was going to let this tart think she'd got one up on her.

'Told me what, Dorinda? That you and my husband had an affair back in the day?'

In the corner of her eye, she'd seen Stan wince as he'd whimpered, 'Jessie...'

She'd put her hand up to stop him, not even looking his way, blazing eyes still on Dorinda. 'Stan, don't. I'm not a damn fool, so don't treat me like one.' Back to Dorinda. 'So there, happy now? Are we done? I've known about it all this time and I ignored it because... well, it doesn't matter. *You* don't matter.'

A part of her had been well aware that most of her anger at that moment was directed at Dorinda, when Stan was the one who had betrayed her, jeopardised their marriage and their family, but she'd decided that now that it was out, she'd deal with him later. In private. Right then, it was Dorinda who was threatening her, and Jessie had never backed away from a confrontation in her life. Especially when the shameless tart still – for some inexplicable reason that Jessie couldn't even begin to fathom – had a smug expression of triumph on her face.

'Actually, I think you'll find I do matter, don't I, Stan?' Dorinda had leered, and Jessie had to fight hard to control the volcano of anger that was rising inside her.

'Dorinda…' There had been no mistaking the agitation in Stan's tone, and Jessie had instantly guessed why. Her worst fear. They had indeed been seeing each other all these years and they'd somehow managed to hide it from her, the world and – more shockingly – the all-seeing eye of the village oracle, Val Murray.

'Stan?' Dorinda wasn't letting it drop. 'You tell her or I tell her. Simple.'

Jessie had seen that Dorinda was relishing every second of this. That's when she'd slowly turned, volcano almost ready to blow, back to her husband, whose shoulders were slumped in defeat, his handsome face now redder than Dorinda Canavan's frock.

'Jessie, I'm so sorry…'

She had no time for his apologies. Too little and too late. 'Get to the point, Stan.'

He'd hesitated, then let it spill out and smack her right in the face. A knockout punch. 'She told me tonight that she wants me to do one of those paternity tests that you see on the telly. She says Alyssa might be my daughter.'

She'd immediately felt like she was concussed. Stars began spinning above her head. She'd struggled to breathe. Dear Lord, not this. She hadn't seen that one coming at all. She'd tried to make sense of it, to remember. Shortly after that night at the golf course, Dorinda had gone off like she was prone to do back then. Poor Hugo and Effie had been devastated as they always were when she pulled a disappearing act. A few years later, she'd appeared back with a boyfriend and two wee ones, and… Why hadn't Jessie made the connection? How had she missed it? She'd just been so relieved that Dorinda had a man and would get her claws off Stan, and that

Jessie could leave the whole affair in that compartment box in her mind where she'd locked it.

'Christ, I'm sorry, Jessie. I swear I had no idea.' She'd barely heard Stan speaking over the roars in her head. She didn't want his apologies. She didn't want his words. She just wanted to be anywhere but there. That's when she'd realised that she had two choices – either rant, rave and lose her mind in front of the two people who had created this absolute carnage of a situation… or she could be Jessie McLean. She could hold her head up. And she could refuse to let them see just how deep this had cut her.

She'd chosen Jessie. And Jessie was the person who, unlike these two lying arses, cared about other people.

'Does Alyssa know about this?' she'd asked, directing that at Dorinda, who'd blinked, visibly surprised at Jessie's newly adopted composure and deathly calm.

'No.'

Jessie had nodded slowly, turned back to Stan. 'Then I suggest you get that test done pronto, because that poor lass deserves to know the truth. I think we all do.'

If he'd had words to say to that, he hadn't got them out, because that was when Kayleigh had come charging along the corridor.

'Gran, I've been looking for you everywhere! We need you inside. Cake time! Come on, Grandad, you too!'

That's how Jessie had ended up standing in front of everyone as they sang 'Happy Birthday', desperately trying to hold it together, and she'd managed it until she'd looked out at all those faces when she was giving her speech, and she'd fallen apart in front of every bugger she'd ever met in her entire life.

Hopefully, they'd all just put it down to the emotion of saying thank you and goodbye, but even now, sitting in the loo, her face was burning with embarrassment – for the outburst, and for the fact that she'd somehow missed this ticking timebomb that had been waiting to explode in their lives for all these years.

Alyssa. That lovely young lass. Jessie had known her all of her life and she was one of those kind, decent souls that did her best for everyone. She didn't deserve any of this. Especially after the news Kayleigh had shared about her losing the café. The poor love had already had a terrible blow and now her whole her world was going to be rocked again.

'Jessie, doll, are you in there?' Val's voice interrupted that thought and Jessie knew there was no point ignoring it, because Val wouldn't give up easily.

'I am, Val.'

'Right then. I've got my make-up bag here if you've got a face like a burst ball after all that weeping. Jeez, I haven't seen you sob like that since we watched *Steel Magnolias* and Julia Roberts was just a lass.'

'Thanks, Val. I'll be out in a minute.'

'Right, well, I'll just leave it here for you. Will I wait or do you want me to stand outside and divert all comers to the gents' loo next door?'

Despite feeling that her guts were being shredded, that made her smile. What would she do without her pals? And wasn't that the same thing she'd been thinking for weeks and months now?

'Aye, if you could create a diversion, I'd appreciate it. Just need a few minutes to gather myself.'

'I'm on it, doll,' was the last thing she heard before the door opened and closed again, and then there was silence, apart from – oh the irony – the sound of Moira and Loretta singing 'I Will Survive' pounding through the walls.

Puffing her cheeks out, she exhaled, then straightened up and left the cubicle. As Val had promised, the make-up bag was there, and Jessie took out a pressed powder, a blusher and a lipstick, doing what she could to fix her face. When she was finished, she stared at her reflection. Passable. Good enough. Almost normal. But there was something else... As she faced the woman staring back at her, she had the sudden thought that if that person was a friend, Jessie would be giving her good advice. It's your life. Live it how you want. Don't sacrifice your happiness for someone else's choices. So why wasn't she listening to herself?

Dabbing her lips together, she spotted a tiny bottle of Charlie perfume in Val's make-up bag and was immediately transported back to the eighties, when it had been her scent of choice. Twenty-year-old Jessie McLean would definitely have had something to say about everything that had happened today.

She gave it a quick squirt, breathed it in, then zipped it back in the bag, feeling a wave of strength and clarity that had been missing just a few minutes ago. This was her life. And she'd be damned if Stan, Dorinda, or anyone else was going to control it.

She marched outside, gave Val the bag and a kiss on the cheek. 'Thanks, ma love.'

Val took in the sight of her, assessing her wellbeing. 'Are you okay? Do you need me to do anything? Get you a drink? Bury a body?'

Jessie faked a smile and then surprised herself by realising that she meant it. There was something empowering about making decisions and taking action and that's exactly what she was about to do now. 'No, I'm fine. I just need to speak to Stan.'

He was standing further along at the end of the corridor, in the same place they'd spoken earlier, waiting for her. His face was now a wretched shade of grey and for a second her heart went out to him. She'd loved this man for over forty years – it was a habit she didn't know if she could break.

'Jessie, give me a chance to explain.'

She put her hand up to stop him. 'Stan, let me speak.' Her voice was surprisingly calm, but left no room for arguing or discussion. 'Let me tell you exactly what I'm going to do, and I don't want to hear a word of objection.'

Steadily, without emotion or hysterics, she spent the next five minutes telling him what was going to happen. Then she left him to find the other person that she needed to speak to right now.

She found her over at the bar table and reached for her hand.

'Georgie, come with me. You and I need to talk.'

30

GEORGIE

Georgie's first reaction when her mum came for her was to groan on the inside and kick herself for even thinking that Jessie would have let this go. Of course she wouldn't. Her mother was the maternal equivalent of a robot vacuum, constantly on the move, on an unassailable mission to pick up other people's messes. This was no different from the time that fifteen-year-old Georgie had her heart broken when she found out her boyfriend had asked out Linda Nesbit, who still, to this day, lived next door to Jessie. Linda's mum, Fi, had been in the salon getting her highlights done and had shared news of Linda's new suitor, unaware that he was already seeing Georgie. Jessie had remedied that straight away and both women had been enraged that their daughters were being played.

Georgie had wanted to hide away and die, but her mum had other plans. At 8 p.m. that night, when her traitorous ex and Linda, who was now in on the plan and happy to go along with it, had sat down in the cinema, Jessie, Georgie and Fi had gone in five minutes later and sat in front of them, then all four conspirators had giggled and crunched their popcorn all the way through *Sweet Home Alabama*. The young guy had fled that night, and the sight of Reese Witherspoon probably still gave him traumatic flashbacks.

Now, Georgie had the feeling she was about to face a similar level of ambush. Up on the makeshift stage, Moira and Loretta had fashioned two tambourines out of packets of crunchy pasta and entered their country era, so her mum went in front, cutting a path between the dancers, back to the space at the front door where she'd been stationed earlier. Mrs Dawson and her sister were still happily tapping their feet to the music while their fingers worked their magic on their needles.

'In the name of the holy jumpers, they brought their knitting?' Jessie spluttered, chuckling, before telling Georgie to, 'Wait right here and don't move.'

Georgie did exactly as commanded, already trying to pre-empt the conversation, and come up with excuses, arguments and explanations as to why she'd kept Ollie's job offer to herself and why she'd rejected it... even though the very thought of that still made her wince. That said, she knew she'd done the right thing. Definitely. Absolutely. It was just going to take a minute to stop feeling like it could turn out to be a huge regret.

Her mother, meanwhile, disappeared into the throng, giving Georgie the chance to have a quick scope of the street outside. A couple more inches of snow had fallen since she'd arrived and the streetlights were creating a stunning glow that made the whole scene look like the set of a Christmas movie. It was completely deserted too, so no sign of the Nesbit triplets. Hugo had almost given himself a heart attack chasing them earlier. Georgie just hoped that no one was planning on driving home from here tonight because there wasn't a car out there with four inflated tyres now. Apparently, it was their party trick and their mortified mother, Linda, had explained that they'd bought some gizmo off eBay that took the air right out of the valve, before despatching her husband to track them down and get the mini-rogues home. Linda was now recovering from the incident by boogying on the dance floor while belting out 'Man, I Feel Like a Woman'.

However, the Hemsworth-esque bloke who'd arrived in the big Range Rover might not recover from the triplet's tyre-deflating mischief quite as quickly. Georgie was beyond curious to know who he was. Alyssa's new boyfriend? If so, she'd kept that quiet. Georgie had no idea Alyssa was even seeing anyone.

Two minutes after she left, Jessie was marching back this way, carrying a tray with two cups of tea, two small glasses of sherry and a plate with two slabs of cake. She put it down on Mrs Dawson's table and was rewarded with beaming smiles from both sisters and a squeeze of the hand. 'Thanks, Jessie,' Mrs Dawson said, her voice croaky with the passage of the years. 'Best night out I've had in ages. I told Olive it would be worth missing *Coronation Street*.'

'Aye, she did,' Olive, sitting next to her, fingers going like fury, concurred.

'What was that?' Mrs Dawson asked, straining to hear her equally hard of hearing sister.

Now that her mum was satisfied that Mrs Dawson and Olive had been taken care of, she flipped her attention back and Georgie braced herself for impact.

'Georgie, I need to ask you something and I need you to be honest. And just so you know, your brother already caved and told me the truth, so there's no point lying to make me feel better.'

Georgie made a mental note to kill Grant later. He never could keep a secret from their mother.

'If there were no obstacles in the way of it, would you have wanted to take that job in America?'

'Oh Mum, there's no point in...' she began to argue, but Jessie stopped her immediately.

'Just a yes or a no, pet.'

That's when Georgie accepted that resistance was futile.

'Yes. But, Mum, it's done now and—'

Jessie stopped her again, cutting in with, 'And what were you planning to do after it? Come back to the salon or do something else?'

The question surprised her, mostly because it was one that she'd barely contemplated. She'd figured leaving the salon and coming back after six months wasn't a viable option, especially because there was also the possibility that the TV job could be extended or renewed for another season. She repeated all that to Jessie, who took it all in.

'So if there was a way that you could take that job—'

Now it was Georgie's turn to cut her mum off. 'Mum, no. Absolutely not. I've told you, I'm not letting you change your plans for me. No way. You're leaving tomorrow and that's it.'

Her mum shook her head. 'I'm not.'

Georgie felt sick. 'Mum, you are. I can't let you give that up for me. You've done enough.'

Her mum glanced over her shoulder, to check that no one was within earshot, and that the two lovely old dears next to them were still happy.

'Georgie, much as I love you, I'm not giving it up for you. The truth is, I never wanted to go. I've been dreading it since the moment I agreed to it.'

Wow. This was a shocker. Back in the salon this afternoon, when Cathy had asked her about Jessie's feelings on leaving, Georgie had assured her that her mother was happy about it. And even when her dad had hinted at Mum's reluctance earlier, Georgie hadn't believed him because her mum had acted like she was totally on board with the plans. First prize for faking enthusiasm goes to Jessie McLean.

'But what about Dad?'

Her mum frowned, and Georgie felt her heart sink. They'd had a fight. Had they split up? Was she going to be a thirty-eight-year-old woman navigating her parents' divorce? And who was getting her and Grant in the custody battle?

No, not possible. Her mum and dad loved each other.

Or was that something else her mum had been faking?

'Actually, your dad isn't going yet either. We've both decided that we're going to stay here a bit longer, at least until after Christmas. Or maybe spring.'

Now she knew that something was definitely amiss. Her dad had been so fed up earlier. Was this why? Had he realised he didn't want to go yet either?

'But why?'

The only answer to that was a cagey, 'It's a long story and he'll tell you all about it later, but right now I'm more interested in getting you sorted. So tell me, if you could take the job and still have a salon here to come back to if it didn't work out, what would you think of that?'

'I'd think I'd wish I knew that before I turned the job down because I would have given a different answer. But I still don't understand how that could work, Mum. You're going to have to explain it to me.'

Over the next ten minutes, Georgie's chin must have gone up and down a dozen times, as Jessie mapped out her plan. Every time Georgie had a handle on her reaction, another detail would be forthcoming, and she would reel to another emotion, travelling through surprise, outrage, shock, encouragement, reassurance, and finally...

'I think that's genius,' she blurted.

'Really?' her mum checked. 'I don't want to put you on the spot, Georgie, and I would have waited until tomorrow to discuss it, but I don't want you losing out if they have time to offer the job to someone else. Now or never, love. What do you think?'

What Georgie thought was that never in a million years would she have seen this coming. This morning she'd been resigned to life in Weirbridge. No, not resigned. That made it sound like she was being kept here in a siege-type situation. The reality was that she'd been comfortable here, and content that her whole life was mapped out in front of her. But that had changed now. It was as if the last week had opened a tiny window to the rest of the world and now that she'd started thinking about the possibilities, she wanted to reach out and explore them. Kayleigh wasn't at home and relying on her any more. She was very definitely single. If she could take a chance on a different life, while keeping the safety net of the salon here, wouldn't that be the best possible scenario? And how amazing would it be to travel? If *The Clansman* got commissioned for another series, she could travel round America in between shoots, with Kayleigh joining her for as much as the university holidays would allow. Or maybe come back to the UK and spend time with Grant in London. Oh, and maybe meet a bloke – one that she hadn't been married to and one that knew nothing at all about solar fricking panels – and have that one-night stand. It wasn't as if some incredible guy was ever going to find her in a hairdressing salon in Weirbridge – even though they did offer a 20 per cent discount on haircuts for men, ever since old Shug, the barber, had given in to his gout and retired.

'I think that I'd bloody love it, Mum. Are you sure though? Absolutely positive?'

Her mum threw her arms around her. 'Couldn't be more sure. Although, I'll have to return all those "going away" presents,' she said, nodding to the fully stocked gift table. 'But I'll worry about that later.'

Georgie counted at least ten gift bags containing bottles. 'It does look like there's a lot of wine there, but those are for your birthday too, so I'm sure no one would want them back. We could just have another party and invite everyone again.'

'Not your worst idea. But let's wait and make sure that job in America is still available, then we can celebrate. I'm just going to go and speak to Alyssa. You might want to make that phone call.' Mum squeezed her in another hug, then, in true Jessie style, checked on the elderly dears next to her before she left. 'Would you like another drink, ladies? Tea or sherry?'

'Well, I wouldn't say no to another sherry, Jessie,' Mrs Dawson croaked.

Olive was of the same opinion. 'I'll have one of those too, since you're offering.'

Their hearing seemed to dramatically improve when it came to the subject of a tipple.

Although, right now, Georgie could empathise because she could do with a stiff drink herself. Was she really going to do this? She mentally calculated the time difference again. It would be late afternoon in LA, so she wouldn't be calling at an inappropriate hour.

Her bag was still lying under the nearby table where she'd left it when she'd arrived, so she retrieved it and glanced around for a quiet spot to make the call, deciding that phoning back to beg for a second chance might not go down well if the sound of laughing, glasses clinking and Cher's 'Believe' were all going on in the background. Even the toilets weren't safe, because last time she was there, Val was on guard outside and redirecting everyone to the gents' because of a burst pipe or some other toilet emergency.

In the end, she saw there was only one thing for it, but a quick search for her jacket drew a blank, and she was woefully underdressed.

Time for improvisation.

'Mrs Dawson, can I borrow your knitting for a second?' she asked, raising the volume.

Mrs Dawson acted like this wasn't an unusual request in the slightest. 'Of course you can, dear,' she said, handing it over.

Leaving the knitting needles dangling from the bottom of about a thousand rows of cable knit, Georgie wrapped the scarf around her several times, and stepped outside, immediately regretting the decision as the freezing cold air blasted into her pores.

She wasn't particularly religious, but she sent up a silent prayer on the off chance that anyone was listening. *Please let the job still be available. Please let the job still be available.* Which quickly morphed to, *Please don't let me die of hypothermia before I find out if it's available.*

With hands that were trembling from the cold or the fear, she located the number in her recent call log and dialled it again.

It rang. And rang. And rang.

Until... 'Hi, this is Bonnie Katowski.'

'Miss Katowski, hello. This is Georgie Dern. We spoke earlier about the position working with Ollie Chiles on *The Clansman* set. You may have received a voicemail from me...'

'Yes, I did. I'm sorry you won't be joining us.'

'Well, that's the thing. I promise I'm not usually indecisive and a flip-flopping nightmare, but circumstances have changed at this end, and I'm now in a position to take the role. So I just wondered if it was still available?'

31

ALYSSA

Alyssa was sitting, staring straight ahead, wondering if she'd somehow entered some kind of parallel universe. Or maybe she was in one of those movies where it turns out you're living a false reality, in an artificial world, and there are actually secret cameras everywhere and millions of people at home, eating pizza while they watch you go about your life on their telly.

It was even more shocking because, until ten minutes ago, everything had been perfectly normal. If Lachlan Morden, former arch nemesis, sitting at her kitchen table, waiting for the AA to come out with a pump to reinflate his tyres could be called normal.

It had definitely paled into insignificance compared to what had happened next, when her mother had come into the kitchen with Stan McLean following behind her. That had immediately puzzled Alyssa. She'd only ever seen the man in passing, and now he was apparently hanging out with her mother? Her first thoughts had been that perhaps there was a problem with the party. Or that he wanted to make a request on Jessie's behalf. Had they run out of wine again?

Dorinda had immediately tossed Lachlan out. 'Can I have a moment with my daughter please?'

Lachlan had shot up and Alyssa could almost see him considering his options. He could go into the café and join the party. Or go freeze his bollocks off outside.

He'd decided on the latter option. 'I'll just wait outside at my car.'

Meanwhile, her mother had slipped into a seat at the table. 'Darling, I have something to share with you.'

How much champagne had her mother sunk? Not that this was a particularly unusual occurrence – Ginny used to joke that their mum listed her occupation as Wine Chugger on her passport application form.

She'd tuned back into what her mum was saying. 'The thing is, Stan and I...'

Stan and I? Alyssa had no idea that there was a *Stan and I*.

'...have something to discuss with you. Stan wanted to talk to you tomorrow, but I wasn't convinced he wouldn't bugger off to Tenerife and dodge the whole issue, so I'm insisting we tell you now.'

Definitely must be a complaint about the party, Alyssa had decided. Someone had said earlier that the ladies' toilet was out of commission, so maybe it was something to do with that, but her grandad had gone off to check and had assured her it was fine.

Her confusion had lasted even after Stan had sat down next to her mother and begun speaking. 'Alyssa, I'm so sorry about this. I still maintain that this isn't the right time or place...' He'd cast a glance at Dorinda, who'd smiled sweetly back at him. 'But since your mum was set on telling you tonight, and I feel that this is my responsibility too, I wanted to do it myself. You see... you see...'

Alyssa's stare had been going from her mum to Stan back to her mum to Stan. And the fact that he was taking forever to get to the point made it even more excruciating.

Drunk Dorinda had obviously felt the same because she'd suddenly lost patience, rolled her eyes and blurted, 'He might be your father.'

Of all the things Alyssa could have imagined coming out of her mother's mouth, that wasn't on the list.

'What? Is this a joke, because it's not funny.'

Stan had shaken his head wearily. 'It's definitely not a joke and definitely not funny. I'm in a state of shock myself about it all, so I can only imagine how it must feel to hear this and I'm so sorry.'

Alyssa hadn't even known how to process that, so she'd focused back on the eye of the storm. Leaning forward on her elbows, she'd glared at her mother. 'I think I'm going to need a bit more information here. I thought my dad was an ex-boyfriend who did a runner when I was a child?'

'Possibly,' her mother had admitted. 'But the reason he did a runner was because he found out... and by "found out" I mean I let it slip that when I began dating him I was still seeing Stan here. We were in love.'

'We weren't in love, Dorinda. There have been enough lies. Don't be adding any more.' Stan's words had been dipped in weariness, not anger. He'd turned back to Alyssa. 'But she's not lying about our affair. It was a brief fling, but it did happen.'

Maybe it had been the use of the word 'affair' that had dropped the bomb of realisation in her mind.

'Oh no,' she'd groaned. 'You were already married to...'

'Jessie.' A flash of embarrassment or pain or shame – Alyssa didn't know him well enough to judge – had crossed his face. 'Yes. I'm not proud of it. It was a long time ago and it was the only time that I was ever unfaithful.'

'He was crazy for me,' Dorinda had interjected, before giving him a touch of side-eye. 'Although not enough to leave his wife, despite having the option of a life with me.'

'Dorinda, enough!' His words were low but sharp, and they'd had the desired effect of shutting her mother up. 'I was never leaving Jessie and you knew that right from the start.'

Her mum had shrugged and Alyssa had known he was speaking the truth.

'Although, I'm not sure that matters now,' Stan had said, 'because that's all in the past. I did something terrible that I'll always be ashamed of, but all that I care about now is that I do the right thing for you and for my family. I'm so sorry, Alyssa. I wish we'd been given the opportunity to have this discussion long before now.'

Alyssa couldn't even respond to that.

She had no idea how long they'd sat in silence, maybe seconds, maybe minutes, because all she could do now, in this moment, was stare straight ahead. It felt surreal. Bizarre. Like an out-of-body experience. Bloody. Actual Fuck.

Finally, time and reality kicked in, and she found her voice.

'Stan, does Jessie know about... you and my mum?'

'To be honest, I wasn't aware that she did, but she told me tonight that she knew all about it at the time, and decided to overlook it for the sake of our children. They were only young at the time. Like me, she didn't know there was any possibility that you were my daughter though. We only found that out when your mother told us tonight.'

Alyssa couldn't even imagine how difficult that must have been for lovely Jessie. His comment made her mind pivot to another thought. *The sake of their children.* And that came with the newsflash that if Stan was her dad that would mean Georgie and Grant were her brother and sister. Her brain flicked up photos of them both and she automatically began trying to identify any similar features. They were both a few years older than her, but it wasn't out of the question. Ginny would have to lie down in a dark room if she heard that she wouldn't be the only sibling with presents under the tree at Christmas.

Actually... She asked Stan the question that had just occurred to her. 'What about Ginny? Could she be yours too?'

'No, like I said, it was a brief affair and we were long over by then. The point that I want to stress again, though, Alyssa, is that I had no idea there was even a possibility that you were my daughter. I don't get involved in village life and I didn't even know your mother was back here or had children until years later. I might have put two and two together if I had. I'm sorry. I know that makes me sound like the worst kind of person...'

'It doesn't make you sound great,' she conceded. But then, Georgie always talked about how lovely her dad was, so maybe she should give him the benefit of the doubt.

'I see that. But for what it's worth, now that I know it's a possibility, I'd like to take responsibility for what happens next. That's why I'm speaking to you now and why I didn't want you to hear about this without me here. You mother is suggesting we do one of those DNA tests.'

Her mum immediately became animated. 'We could apply to do it on that TV show that reunites families.'

'Mum, no! Oh God, I can't do this...' Alyssa put her head on the table in front of her, left it there until she had the strength and fortitude to lift it again. 'Okay, first, Stan, yes – I think we should do a DNA test. I don't know how that works or what we'd need to do, but I think it's important to find out for sure.'

He nodded his agreement to that plan, so Alyssa moved on.

'And, Mum, no, we are not doing it on the fricking telly. And just so you know, a heads-up about this at some point in the last twenty-seven years would have been tickety-bloody-boo.'

Dorinda's cherry red lips formed into a petulant pout. 'I was protecting you, darling.'

'From what? The only thing you were protecting me from is your past. Did you ever wonder how I would feel? Or what would be best for me? Or... Forget it. Of course you didn't. Why tell me now? Tonight? What were you thinking?'

'Well, he's about to swan off to the sun tomorrow and who knows if he'll ever come back. Why should he have this easy life and I'm still stuck here? I should be the one doing that. I deserve it, not him and Jessie!' The venom in her voice said so much more than her words and Alyssa understood it all. Same old story. Jealousy. Self-obsession. Bitterness. A chronic need for attention. Dorinda couldn't bear that someone else was going to be happy, when she was so fricking miserable with her own life. And, of course, her mum's vitriol and the nastiness always escalated when she was wasted. Alyssa and Ginny had watched her in drunken rants all their lives. That was the mother Alyssa had always known, so it shouldn't be a surprise. However, Alyssa was cut from a different cloth, one that cared about other people too.

She turned back to Stan. 'As I said, I'll do the DNA test, because I'd like to know for sure – but I'll only do it if it's okay with Jessie.'

'I'm right here, Alyssa,' said the woman who had just appeared in the doorway, the one who was standing there now with the most shocked and horrified expression.

Alyssa watched as Jessie's eyes threw daggers at her husband. 'Stan McLean, what are you doing here?'

Her mum answered for him. 'We've told her, discussed it like adults and they're going to do a DNA test.'

There was something in her mum's expression, a little triumphant sneer, almost smug, and Alyssa wanted to put her head back on the table. It was so damned obvious. The reality had been there right in front of her the whole time. The reason she'd sensed her mother and Jessie couldn't stand each other was because of this. Jessie knew about the affair. And her mother hated that she hadn't won Stan.

Whatever the undercurrents between them all, Jessie was now furious. 'In the name of all that is holy, why would you choose here and now, after all these years, to share that information?' she blazed to the two people on the other side of the table. 'You're a pair of clowns, you really are.'

As she approached the table, she focussed on Alyssa and her whole demeanour changed.

'Alyssa, I'm so sorry for all of this. Sorry too that I never realised, because if I had... well, you know we love you, whether we realised you were family or not.'

For the first time since the beginning of the conversation, Alyssa felt her bottom lip start to quiver. Stan's shock hadn't moved her. Her mother's attitude hadn't cracked her shell. But this? Jessie being kind and thoughtful and loving was about to make her dissolve into a puddle on her freshly mopped floors.

Alyssa managed to get out a strangled, 'Thank you.'

'I mean it, love. And crazy as it sounds, after everything you've just heard, none of that is the reason I came in here.'

A fear of what was about to come gripped Alyssa. What else could there fricking be?

'There will be plenty of time to discuss that when you're ready, but I know you had another bombshell today. Kayleigh told me what happened with your lease, and I think I might have a solution. I know there isn't another available shop in Weirbridge that would be big enough, but how would you feel about moving over to the salon?'

Glad to be pushing the newly raised question of her paternity out of her mind for a moment, Alyssa took a second to switch gears. As soon as she did, she could see the obvious flaw in this. 'But, Jessie, I know nothing about hair.'

'Let me start that again. How would you feel about moving the café over to the salon? I own that building. My mortgage on it was paid off when I retired last week so we could make your rent lower than you pay here and that would leave enough over for you to rent a flat. There's one going up above the nail salon next door so that might work for you.'

Nope, Alyssa still wasn't grasping this idea. 'But if you close the salon, what about Georgie?'

Jessie had an answer for that. 'The only thing we would ask is that we leave the back section for a small hairdressing room, so that we can still provide hair facilities for the elderly folks that don't want to leave the village. Either Georgie or...' She paused and Alyssa could see she was picking her words. '...Or another stylist will work there. Your café space might be a little bit smaller than here, but you'll have the extra trade of the salon customers, so hopefully that would balance out.'

'But Jessie what if it turns out that I'm not... Stan's daughter.' Had she just said that out loud? *Stan's daughter.*

Jessie shook her head. 'Alyssa, none of this has got anything to do with that. Whether you're his daughter or not, I'd have made you this offer. This is about a solution that suits us both.'

Both Alyssa's top and bottom lips were wobbling now as she tried to process that. In so many ways, it made sense. More footfall. The salon was gorgeous. The location and size were perfect. But then it came right in like a sledgehammer – the one, insurmountable thing that they'd overlooked.

'Jessie, I can't. It cost me thousands to kit this place out and I don't have the money to do it again.'

Now she could see that Jessie was the one who didn't understand. 'But you've got everything here already...'

'Yes, but I'd still need to fit a new kitchen. Build a new counter. Adapt the space. There would be construction. Plumbing. All that work is so expensive and it's money I don't have. But thank you. Truly. I'll figure out something else.'

If the room wasn't full of people, she'd have cried like a baby. For a second, there she'd got her hopes up and now they were dashed again.

The moment of emotional crisis was diverted when, at the doorway, Lachlan cleared his throat. 'I'm so sorry to interrupt you, but the AA have just arrived, and they need my car key in case they set off the alarm. I left it there on the table.'

He grabbed it, went back towards the door, then stopped, turned around.

'Look, I'm sorry, and please forgive me if I'm overstepping. But I just heard you saying you didn't have the funds to fit out a new café. I don't know if I mentioned earlier, but I'm a builder. And it turns out I have a couple of weeks to spare, and I wouldn't mind spending them here. So maybe I could stick around and help you with that?'

32

LACHLAN

Lachlan had no idea if anyone else had missed his flight due to inclement weather or their car being vandalised by what he'd now learned were twelve-year-old triplets, but he knew for certain that if they did, it was highly unlikely that, an hour later, they would be sitting in a café, with about one hundred strangers, watching two women standing on coffee tables singing the absolute wonders out of 'Caledonia' – with everyone in the room joining in, including two old ladies who were still doing their knitting.

That thought took his gaze to the woman who was sitting next to him at the corner table, because when he'd seen her outside earlier, after Alyssa's mum had kicked him out of the kitchen, the first thing that had struck him was that she was dancing in the snow on a freezing cold night. The second thing was that she had two knitting needles dangling from a pink woolly scarf around her neck.

'Are you okay?' he'd asked her warily, wondering how many beverages it must have taken for her to be twirling around in the middle of the street at 11 p.m.

She'd stopped as soon as his voice had snapped her out of whatever song was playing in her head.

'Yes! I'm fine. Great.'

Damn, she was bonkers. Or wasted. Either way, much as there was something endearing about the huge smile on her face and the mass of copper curls that blew out as she danced, he had tried desperately to come up with a way to avoid her. And failed. Especially as he'd just realised his plan to sit in the car was a non-starter because he'd left the damn key inside.

She'd continued to walk towards him. Bollocks. Situations like this made him deeply uncomfortable. Maybe there was a medical professional inside that could help.

'Sorry, you're probably thinking I've lost the plot.'

'No. Not at all.' He definitely was.

It was only when she'd reached him that he'd recognised her as the woman he'd spoken to when he first arrived. The one who'd told him where to find Alyssa.

'Only I just – and please go with me because this will be the first time I've ever said this out loud – I've just got off the phone to a TV producer-y person in Hollywood and accepted the absolutely most incredible, out-of-this-world, job of my dreams.'

She'd started twirling again. But at least by then he could see that it was pure joy as opposed to pure alcohol. And he was pretty sure he was grinning, so it must be contagious.

'Congratulations.'

'Thank you! Urgh, sorry, my manners. I'm Georgie. And you're the unfortunate bloke who just had his very flash car incapacitated by the evil genius of a bunch of kids who think letting down tyres is hilarious.'

'Apparently yes, that would be me. I'm Lachlan.'

'Pleased to meet you, Lachlan. How do you know Alyssa?'

He'd wondered if she knew the circumstances of his meeting with Alyssa, but she wasn't threatening him with the knitting needles, so he'd guessed not.

'She's... she's... It's a long story. I only met her today for the first time, but she seems really nice.'

Georgie had agreed with that conclusion. 'She's great. It's my mum's birthday, retirement and going away party tonight – we like to milk all the occasions – and Alyssa has made her feel really special.'

He'd asked the obvious question. 'Where's she going? Your mum, I mean.'

'Oh. Nowhere. It was supposed to be Tenerife, but she's changed her mind. It's a long story. Anyway, why are you out here? I hate to break it to you, but unless you've got a sledge in the boot...'

'I'm waiting for the AA to come blow up my tyres.'

She'd considered that answer. 'This might be a crazy idea, but have you thought about sitting inside where there's heat and food, so you don't die of frostbite before the AA get here? There's a table at the window right there.'

Even when she was making fun of him, she was amusing.

'Plus I need to give Mrs Dawson back her knitting needles before she calls out a search party to find me.'

So that was how they'd spent the next half-hour, chatting at a table by the window, watching for the AA until they arrived and sent him to retrieve his car key. When he'd come back out, he'd discovered the tyre situation was terminal.

The AA guy had been shaking his head. 'I've got three of them fixed, but they must have broken the valve on that one,' he gestured to the one remaining flat tyre, 'because I can't get it to reinflate. I can get your vehicle towed for you, but I don't know how long that'll take in this weather.'

At this point, Lachlan wouldn't have been surprised if a tornado had come down the street and created yet another obstacle to his travel plans. There had only been one way to go with it though, 'Yeah, if you can arrange a tow that would be great. I'll give you the address of the car hire place to drop it off.'

The AA guy wasn't done. 'And do you need a lift somewhere? All part of the service.'

Lachlan had glanced back inside, seen Georgie chatting to a bloke who looked uncannily like her, and factored in that he still needed to speak to Alyssa again about the offer he'd made when he'd gone back for his key. Had he really volunteered to stay here and help her with building work? Apparently so.

'No, it's fine. I'll work something out.' His flight was long gone, so his best plan was to get a taxi to the airport and get a room there. Or find a local hotel for tonight. He didn't want to disturb Margaux's date by crashing at her place.

Fast-forward half an hour and now that his feet had defrosted, and he'd abandoned his plans to drive, he was on his second beer and still sitting with the woman who'd been dancing in the snow, listening to the whole room singing 'Caledonia', before they all burst into a round of applause at the end.

'Grant, why is our mother climbing up there?' Georgie asked the man on the other side of her. He'd joined them ten minutes ago, and had already informed Lachlan that he was Georgie's brother, before asking his name, home location and enquiring as to whether he had a criminal record.

Lachlan followed Georgie's gaze, and watched as one of the women he'd seen in the kitchen took a microphone and tapped the top of it.

'Ladies and gentlemen. Some of you might have noticed that my earlier speech wasn't my finest moment...'

That got another cheer, and she took a bow.

'I might need therapy after this,' Grant whispered.

'So this time I promise to hold it together. At least until I've made a wee announcement to you all.'

Beside him, Lachlan could see Georgie's eyes begin to glisten and her smile get wider, and he had absolutely no idea what was going on.

'But first I need to thank you all for coming here, for being my customers, my friends and my neighbours. I know exactly how lucky I am to have you all.'

Another cheer and stamping of the feet caused the candles on the wall shelves and the fairy lights draped across the windows to flicker.

'As you all know, tonight was a party for my birthday, my retirement and a going away shindig because Stan and I were planning to leave for Tenerife tomorrow. Well, I just want to let you know there's been a change of plan on that one. We've decided that we don't want to leave right before Christmas, so we're going to stay a bit longer. In fact, if I get my way, it might be a lot longer, because I don't know what I'd do without you all.'

Lachlan saw her eyes go to the tall man who was watching her from the kitchen door, and he nodded at her, as if agreeing to that plan.

'So thank you all again. Thank you to Loretta and Moira for being incredible entertainers tonight. Thank you to Alyssa, Ginny and Hugo, for the most amazing spread and throwing such a brilliant party. Thanks to my pals, Val and Cathy, for putting up with me all day today, and for the last forty-odd years. Thank you to my Georgie and Grant, who will always be my whole heart.'

Lachlan saw Georgie make the heart symbol with her hands and beam at her mum.

'And thank you again to every one of you who came to celebrate with me. You're all bloody marvellous.'

This time, there was applause with the cheers, until the gentleman who'd chased the tyre deflators earlier took the microphone from her and helped her down. The lights were up now, and Lachlan saw on his phone screen that it was almost midnight. Home time for the partygoers. Hotel time for him.

However, before he could catch Alyssa for a quick conversation, Georgie's mum made a beeline for their table and pulled out a chair.

Georgie hugged her. 'Mum, you were amazing. How are you feeling?'

'Relieved. It's been some day. Your dad and I need to speak to you about a couple of family things, but they can wait until the morning.' Her focus swung to Lachlan, and he figured she was probably wondering who this stranger was at her party.

'Mum, this is Lachlan. He's—'

'A pal of Alyssa's,' Jessie finished for him. 'We almost met earlier in the kitchen. Good of you to offer to help Alyssa. Especially given the circumstances.'

The emphasis on her words told him that she knew he was part of the problem too, but she'd seemed to be overlooking that in the light of his offer to help.

Georgie had more news to share. 'His mum used to work here. In this café.'

'Really? What was her name?'

Lachlan took that one. 'Felicity. Her maiden name was McSlay.'

To his shock, Jessie responded by letting out a loud chuckle. 'Oh, hang on, son. Val! Val!'

A few yards away, the blonde woman he'd been dancing with earlier responded with, 'Christ on a bike, Jessie, I'm right here, not half a mile down the street.'

Jessie ignored the reprimand. 'Remember Felicity McSlay from over in Burnbank?'

'Red hair, tall lassie, only child, smart, did well at school, worked here on the weekends, couldn't ride a bike to save her life, married some loaded guy and went off to live in Glasgow.'

Georgie leaned towards him. 'She has an encyclopaedic memory. It's slightly terrifying.'

'So you don't know her then?' Jessie quipped to the blonde woman, both of them in on the joke.

Val shook her head. 'Never heard of her.' They were both chuckling now.

'Ach, well. I was just going to tell you this is her son.'

Val immediately took charge. 'Oh well, you come with me because there's a few people I'd like you to meet.'

That set off a whole round of introductions to everyone else in the room who would have known his mum, and to his surprise, Lachlan loved every single minute of it. More than loved it. He realised how much he'd missed this kind of interaction. Why had he allowed himself to shut out the world for so long?

By the time all the introductions were over, the room had almost cleared, so he went back over to sit with Georgie. As he reached the table, Grant went to speak to one of the singers, so that left them alone.

'So... Mr Range Rover With The Flat Tyres. My mum told me you'll be sticking around for a while and that you've offered to help Alyssa move this place across to our salon.'

He was impressed. How fast did news travel in this village? BBC News couldn't relay information this quickly.

'So now that you're stranded without transport, do you have a plan on how you're getting out of here tonight?'

'Taxi to a hotel. I'm just about to search for one online. I was waiting to speak to Alyssa, but I think she's probably busy enough now, so I'll come back in the morning to see her.'

Georgie thought about that for a moment. 'I have a couch that you're welcome to. I should tell you – because if I don't, my really embarrassing brother will – that I got a bit carried away with myself earlier, and thought I could embark on a wild spree of one-night stands, but the truth is, I don't have the courage for it. Or, you know, resistance to germs. I'd be too worried about where the one-night stands had been.'

He tried to keep a straight face. 'Good to know.'

'But I do have a very nice couch that folds out into a very comfy bed. It does mean that you can pop back in the morning to see Alyssa.'

'That's a very good point.'

She raised her glass. 'Sofa?'

He clinked it with his beer bottle. 'Sofa.'

Not long after, the café had been cleared, he'd let Alyssa know he'd pop back in the morning, and all the goodbyes had been said.

When they moved out into the street, Georgie linked arms with him as they made their way along the snow-covered road. That's when he looked around, took it all in. He couldn't help thinking that his mum would love this. And she would definitely approve of his decision to stay.

Because as his eyes locked again with the woman walking next to him, he decided there was a very definite possibility that he'd just found one very good thing at the end of the day.

EPILOGUE
SEVEN MONTHS LATER

Alyssa Canavan pressed the button on her brand-new coffee machine and watched as a perfect iced cappuccino poured into the glass mug on the silver drip tray. It had been her biggest new investment since the Once Upon A Time Café re-opened on the other side of the street from where it used to be. The refit of the salon had taken three weeks in total, but Lachlan Morden had been as good as his word and taken care of the labour and the construction costs. Apparently, the café offer had been ten grand over the asking price, and he was happy to donate his half of that – in advance of the sale being finalised – to the worthwhile cause of keeping the people of Weirbridge in teas, coffees and prawn toasties.

Of course, he wasn't the only one who'd helped with the work or the costs. Alyssa put the iced cappuccino down on the table that was occupied by one of her new regular customers.

'There you go, Stan.' The DNA test results had come in a few weeks after he'd provided his services as an electrician for the duration of the refit. Alyssa wasn't sure if she'd ever get used to calling him 'dad', but they'd both agreed she could stick with Stan until it felt right. Her mother had accepted Stan's paternal status pretty swiftly, but she'd been mortified that now that the truth was out, Stan hadn't taken the opportunity to ride off into the sunshine with her. Her delusion truly knew no bounds. All

Dorinda had succeeded in doing that night was embarrass herself and show her true colours and she'd suffered the consequences. Alyssa had come to terms with it and forgiven her mother for the sake of her family and her peace of mind, but the villagers hadn't. The rumours. The glances. The whispers everywhere she went. Dorinda loved attention, but not that kind. She'd never bothered to form friendships in the village, and now people actively boycotted her, after learning that not only had she kept such a secret from Alyssa, and then tried to weaponise it to wreck Jessie's marriage, but she'd showed absolutely no remorse for her actions. No one would give her the time of day after that. Dorinda hadn't given a toss about their judgements, but she did care that the locals would no longer even consider using her property services. Only a couple of months after the party, she'd packed her bags and moved to Benidorm, saying she wanted a fresh start where no one knew her. Last Alyssa had heard, she was working in a golf club bar there. Bit of a full circle moment.

Meanwhile, Stan and Jessie had covered the rest of the costs of the refit. Jessie had said it was only fair, because they owed her plenty of years of backdated child support.

In the meantime, Stan's daily visits and chats had become the favourite part of Alyssa's day. She was going to miss him when he went off to Tenerife next week.

She called back over to her favourite man, who was currently restocking the sausage roll shelf. 'Grandad, are you okay if I take a break and sit here with Stan for a few minutes?'

Hugo nodded. 'Of course, love.' He'd taken all the dramas remarkably well, and Alyssa knew that his friendships with Jessie and Val had helped him to get through it all. Her grandad would always love his daughter, but Alyssa sensed that there was a tiny bit of relief now that her mum was out of sight and no longer causing drama and turbulence in his life.

She was just about to sit with her d... *Stan*, when the door opened and Ginny charged in, bellowing, 'Emergency situation!'

'I've got this, Alyssa,' Grandad told her, before turning to his other granddaughter. 'And the emergency would be...?'

'Five caramel shortcakes, six ginger slices and three empire biscuits. I'm trying to bribe the film crew to give me more screen time.'

It had made absolutely no difference to their relationship that they now knew they were half-sisters with different fathers. Nor had her sister's dramatic flair subsided in any way since she had joined the coaching team at the Moira Chiles Academy of Drama and Music. What had changed, however, was that she'd developed high hopes of TV fame, as a documentary team had been filming at the Academy for months now, and the first episode was airing next week. There was going to be a watch party in the Academy's theatre, and their grandad had already booked out a whole row for their customers and his pals.

Alyssa was taking the night off, which was easier now that Kayleigh – *her niece* – was home from university for the summer. She was interning full time at her Aunt Helena's law firm, but keen to help out at the café a couple of nights a week for extra cash.

It was strange how everything had worked out. Every now and then, Alyssa caught herself wondering if she'd rather things had stayed the same. Still over at the old café. Still living in the flat above it. But the answer was currently getting out of the van that had just parked in front of the café window.

Casey Munn was one of the project managers over on the development of flats that were being built in the building that used to house the Once Upon A Time Café. He'd come to look at the property the week after Jason Morden had sold it, and fallen in love with Alyssa's empire biscuits. Last week, after four months of dating, he'd told her he'd fallen in love with her too. She was going to nip through to the salon later and Jessie was going to do her hair for their date tonight. She wanted to make a special effort so Casey would remember how she looked the first time she told him she loved him back.

* * *

Jessie McLean finished applying Cathy's violet rinse and moved her over to the mirrors so that she could get started on Val's blow-dry. Aye, she was still on her feet behind a hairdressing chair, but she didn't mind it in the least, because it was only two days a week. It was the best of both worlds. She'd kept the salon going for all her regulars in the village, and on the other three days a week, the chairs had been rented out on a one-year agreement to a couple of lovely lassies who were just starting out in their careers. All the younger ones went to them, and the feedback had been terrific. If Georgie ever came back, which was looking increasingly unlikely, then she could take Jessie's slot and she'd also have the income from the chair rentals and Alyssa's café rental, until she decided what she wanted to do with the salon. If she didn't come back, well, Jessie would retire one day, but she wasn't in any hurry. It wasn't like Stan was nagging her to go now.

Val must have read her mind.

'How are things going with Stan, Jessie?'

Her pals had been an incredible support over the last few months, and she couldn't imagine what she'd have done without them, because Lord knows it hadn't been easy. Burying Stan's affair for all those years had been one thing, but when it came out, it had forced them to take a long hard look at their marriage. It had been touch-and-go for a while, but they'd come out the other end of it all with a relationship that was different from before. There were no secrets now. No resentments. Just honesty and full disclosure on both sides. Luckily there had been a twenty-four-hour cooling-off period on the lease that he'd signed, so he'd cancelled that the morning after the party.

'You know, it was always you I loved Jessie. It was a mistake that I've been ashamed of since it happened,' he'd told her that night. She'd known that was true and he'd proved it every day since with his love, his loyalty and his determination to do right by his family, including Alyssa. She'd forgiven him for the affair a long time ago, but somehow this had all brought them even closer. In trying to wreck them, Dorinda Canavan had actually made them stronger. And for Jessie, that was a win that she'd take every moment of the rest of her and Stan's days together.

'They're going fine, Val,' Jessie answered honestly. 'He's off to Tenerife next week and I'll join him for a fortnight in August.' That was the new deal they'd struck. Stan would go over for a couple of months at a time, and Jessie would join him for a week or two in the middle. He got to play golf, and she enjoyed her time there... just as long as it didn't stretch out long enough for her to miss her pals. 'Hang on, my arse is buzzing.'

She groped into the back pocket of her trousers, and pulled out her phone, and saw that it was a FaceTime call from Georgie. She answered straight away, scanning the phone around the room so that Cathy and Val could give her a wave too. 'Hello, love! Is that you just landed?'

* * *

Georgie Dern grinned into the phone, while dodging other passengers as she left the baggage reclaim and pushed her gargantuan case out of the arrivals hall. 'It is, Mum. I'll be home soon, and I'll give you a shout as soon as I get there.'

Her mum was the second call Georgie had made since she'd landed. The first was to Kayleigh to make sure she remembered that she was supposed to go to her dad's house for the weekend. Kayleigh had started doing that more regularly now, especially since she'd got to know her dad's girlfriend, Monica, and they got on really well. So well, in fact, that Monica had asked her how she'd feel about getting a little brother or sister. Apparently, Monica hadn't broached the subject with Flynn yet, but she hoped that he'd be receptive to the idea. Georgie didn't have the heart to tell her. However, the fact that Kayleigh was open to the idea of a sibling was great news. Especially given the huge smile on the face of the man who was right there waiting for Georgie.

* * *

Lachlan Morden watched as his girlfriend of seven months came towards him and he scooped her up as soon as she reached him. The first time he saw her, she'd been dancing in the snow. Now they danced in his kitchen. In the park. On the beach.

Lachlan had slept on her couch that night of the party. The next morning, Grant had returned to London, and Kayleigh had gone to stay with her dad for a few days. Their departures had given Georgie and Lachlan the house to themselves and… well, it turned out Georgie's notion for a one-night stand had been a great idea after all. It had become a two-night stand. Then a three. Then a four. Then every night until she'd flown out to LA the following week. He'd stayed in Weirbridge to work day and night on the new café, then joined her in Colorado for New Year.

The sale of the old café building had gone through in time for Jason to get his money before his and Tanya's child had arrived. Lachlan had meant it when he'd told Tanya that he wished her well, but he had no idea how they were doing, and he was fine with that. That was a closed book. The past.

And the present?

For the rest of this year, it had involved a crapload of airmiles. He'd flown to America to see Georgie for a weekend in February. And March. And a month in April. And a week in May. And two weeks in June. He hadn't taken a holiday for three years, so he figured he owed himself some time off. Besides, he just worked longer hours at Dax's house on the weeks that he was in London. Turns out the footballer hadn't been transferred after all. He'd done two weeks in rehab, and then the club had advised him to adopt a wellbeing routine to keep him out of the casinos. Yoga was just one element of that. And there was definitely a romance budding with his new yoga teacher, one that Lachlan had recommended and flown down from Glasgow.

'Hello, you,' Georgie said, as he put her back on solid ground. He'd never been the gushy type. Or overly romantic or sentimental. But she brought something out in him that he just couldn't explain. Maybe that's why he was perfectly calm about the baby, even though they hadn't been together long. Contrary to what everyone thought, it had been planned. Or rather, hoped for. Lachlan had held his breath when he'd told her that he'd still like to have a child, especially when Georgie had admitted she'd had no intentions of ever adding to her family. But then she'd thrown her hands up, laughing, and pointed out that she was thirty-eight and if they were going to do it, they'd better get started. It had worked out perfectly. The baby would be born at the end of the next season of *The Clansman*, when she'd planned to be with him in London anyway. She loved it here, because she got to spend time with Grant too. This was her home. At least for now. They'd talked about moving back to Weirbridge when the baby was born, and to his surprise, he liked that idea. He wanted their child to have family. Connections. Bonds. So much love it would never feel alone.

And he knew his mum would have been delighted that they'd found that in the place that meant more to her than anywhere else.

'What are you thinking there, my very serious man?' Georgie teased him.

He took her case, his other hand slipping around her waist. 'I was thinking that I love you. Both of you.' He nodded to the bump under her jacket. 'And that for the rest of my life, I'm going to have two good things at the end of every day.'

* * *

MORE FROM SHARI LOW

Another book from Shari Low, *One More Day of Us*, is available to order now here:

https://mybook.to/OneMoreDayOfUsBackAd

A NOTE FROM SHARI...

Dear you,

Thank you for choosing One Snowy Day. I hope that you loved this tale of twenty-four drama-filled hours in the lives of Alyssa, Jessie, Georgie and Lachlan.

As with most of my books, this is a brand new, standalone story, and can be read completely on its own, but as you may know, some of my characters do like to pop up again and again in my world. In One Snowy Day, those characters included Val, Cathy, and Moira.

If you'd like to read other tales featuring the force of nature that is Val Murray, you'll find her in many of my titles including What Next?, One Day With You, and One Long Weekend.

It was a delight to bring back Cathy, the grandmother of the McLean family from One Christmas Eve, and Helena and Eve from that book are at Jessie's party too.

Prior to One Snowy Day, Moira was last seen retracing her younger days in One More Day of Us.

And one more familiar name in this book is her son Ollie, a global TV star who had an intriguing offer for Georgie. We first met Ollie in One Day and Forever, but the scandalous world of the original movie franchise that inspired his spin-off TV show called The Clansman, can be found in The

Rise, *The Catch* and *The Fall*, the gritty, glam Hollywood thrillers I wrote with my pal, TV presenter Ross King.

Speaking of the lovely Mr King, earlier this year he held a fundraiser in Los Angeles for those affected by the heartbreaking California fires, and during that event, Fiona Francois very kindly bid on an auction prize to name two of the characters in this novel. Fiona, thank you for your generosity, your kindness and for giving Margaux Mackay and Tanya Michaels their perfect monikers.

More thanks are due, as always, to the magnificent team at Boldwood Books – I feel incredibly lucky to work with this powerhouse of talent, creativity and care every day.

I'm also grateful for the book bloggers who give such stellar support to my new releases.

And of course, my eternal gratitude goes to you, the readers who have allowed me to do this job for more than two decades. I heart you all, beyond words.

If you'd like to hear all about what's coming next, please look me up on Facebook or Instagram, or sign up to my newsletter at www.sharilow.com.

Much love,

Shari x

ABOUT THE AUTHOR

Shari Low is the #1, million-copy bestselling author of over 30 novels, including *One Day With You* and *One Moment in Time* and a collection of parenthood memories called *Because Mummy Said So*. She lives near Glasgow.

Sign up to Shari Low's mailing list for news, competitions and updates on future books.

Visit Shari's website: www.sharilow.com

Follow Shari on social media:

- facebook.com/sharilowbooks
- x.com/sharilow
- instagram.com/sharilowbooks
- bookbub.com/authors/shari-low

ALSO BY SHARI LOW

My One Month Marriage

One Day In Summer

One Summer Sunrise

The Story of Our Secrets

One Last Day of Summer

One Day With You

One Moment in Time

One Christmas Eve

One Year After You

One Long Weekend

One Midnight With You

One Day and Forever

One More Day of Us

One Snowy Day

The Carly Cooper Series

What If?

What Now?

What Next?

The Hollywood Trilogy (with Ross King)

The Rise

The Catch

The Fall

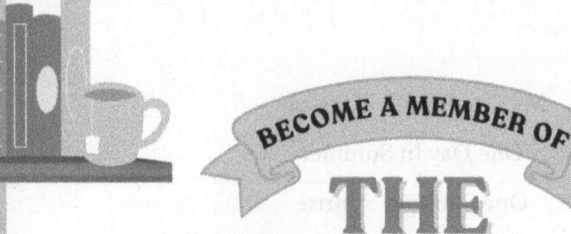

BECOME A MEMBER OF THE SHELF CARE CLUB

The home of Boldwood's book club reads.

Find uplifting reads, sunny escapes, cosy romances, family dramas and more!

Sign up to the newsletter
https://bit.ly/theshelfcareclub

Boldwood

Boldwood Books is an award-winning fiction publishing company seeking out the best stories from around the world.

Find out more at www.boldwoodbooks.com

Join our reader community for brilliant books, competitions and offers!

Follow us
@BoldwoodBooks
@TheBoldBookClub

Sign up to our weekly deals newsletter

https://bit.ly/BoldwoodBNewsletter